PRA...

Two strong, opposing forces run through *Run, River Currents* — one of rage, violence and shame, the other of grace and redemption… Set along the beautiful yet life-claiming Tobique River, Ginger Marcinkowski's novel is graced with narrative profluence and lyrical descriptions. It will leave you drenched, breathless, on your knees and gasping for air.
　—Sara Pritchard, author of *Crackpots* (a *New York Times* Notable Book of the Year) and *Help Wanted: Female* (2012–13)

There are important stories that must be told about children who are scarred, whose physical injuries and emotional damage are inflicted at the hands of those society has entrusted with their care. Bereft of kindness and wisdom from her own parents, Emily can only cling to her grandfather's kindly words: "You're not alone. God will never leave you." This is a tale of wrongdoing and the victimization of innocents, of forgiveness and redemption, that you won't be able to put down until the last line of the last page.
　—Gale Martin, author of *Grace Unexpected* (2012) and Indie Excellence finalist *Don Juan in Hankey, PA*

This family saga spans three generations of abuse, hoarded secrets, crippling guilt and, ultimately, a cleansing, cathartic redemption. Marcinkowski's great talent is for the breathtakingly perfect detail, the most exquisite turn of phrase. And she knows when to employ, with stunning impact, a single shocking action which will turn the tide of a character's life for good.
　—Lenore Hart, author of *The Raven's Bride* and Book of the Month Club selection *Becky: The Life and Loves of Becky Thatcher*

An amazing book…*Run, River Currents* is one young woman's heart-wrenching story of pain and abuse, rage and resentment… and her life-changing struggle to learn the power of unconditional love. A must-read.
　—Jim Jordan, filmmaker, award-winning celebrity & fashion photographer (*Elle, Marie Claire, Vogue*)

RUN, RIVER CURRENTS

Ginger Marcinkowski

Booktrope Editions
Seattle WA 2012

Copyright 2012 Ginger Marcinkowski

This work is licensed under a Creative Commons Attribution-Noncommercial-No Derivative Works 3.0 Unported License.

Attribution — **You must attribute the work in the manner** specified by the author or licensor (but not in any way that suggests that they endorse you or your use of the work).

Noncommercial — You may not use this work for commercial purposes.

No Derivative Works — You may not alter, transform, or build upon this work.

Inquiries about additional permissions should be directed to: info@booktrope.com

Cover Design by Greg Simanson

Edited by Lori Higham

Proofread by Thomas Dean

This is a work of fiction. Names, characters, places, brands, media, and incidents are either the product of the author's imagination or are used fictitiously. Any resemblance to similarly named places or to persons living or deceased is unintentional.

ISBN 978-1-935961-71-0

For further information regarding permissions, please contact info@booktrope.com.

Library of Congress Control Number: 2012913377

Dedication

To the glory of God

Acknowledgments

First and foremost, this book is dedicated to the glory of God. I am nothing without His grace.

Acknowledgments are difficult to write. The tone of gratefulness is never enough to convey what an author has in her heart for the people who have helped make her dream come true... so many kindnesses from so many people.

To begin with, the writing of this book would not have been possible without the encouragement, support, and guidance of my wonderful mentor: author Sara Pritchard. Your dedication as I flailed around trying to find my story and my voice was invaluable. The story you pulled out of me was a surprise to both of us. We worked through the pain together with tears and joy, and we shared many, many wonderful moments. I've made a lifetime friend to whom I will always be indebted, and I hope to make you proud to be my friend.

To Gale Martin, a talented writer and dear friend whose honesty and drive kicked me along this road more than once. The example of your work ethic and giving spirit drove me to completion, pushing me to places I didn't think I could go. You read and reread every word of this book, sometimes at the last minute, and never failed to make me feel like a winner. We are kindred spirits, and I am ever grateful to you, my dear friend and soul-sister.

To my publisher, Booktrope, who gave me the opportunity to publish this book, I thank you for the wonderful team you assigned to me and the honest way you deal with your authors. You have taken publishing to a whole new level, and for that I am indebted.

To my editor and book manager, Lori Higham. I prayed for someone to come along and really "get" my book. You did. With your gentle heart and wonderful enthusiasm, you pushed me in the gentlest way and helped me bring the real story forward. We are on a wonderful adventure. You are a partner and a true professional and a woman of so many, many talents. Few people could be as blessed as I feel having you by my side.

Many thanks to authors Kevin Oderman, whose wisdom gave me the foundation for this project; Mike Lennon, for the passion you instilled in me for the written word; Lenore Hart, whose instruction made me learn discipline; Beverly Donofrio, whose loving words brought me through a tough piece of this book when you didn't even know it; Jeff Talarigo, whose way with the English language showed me how stunning words could be; and finally, Kaylie Jones, with whom I shared "mother" stories, (yours, the upper class; mine, the Walmart version.) You showed me I could still laugh through the pain.

To my entire cohort of friends and instructors at Wilkes University, thank you for being the craziest and most talented group of writers I've ever met. To all of you I give my undying gratitude for changing my life.

I am grateful to all who supported me in various ways during the completion of the project, especially through the honest critiques that came from the special women of the Des Moines Writing Club. I couldn't have done it without you. Your truthful evaluations — from brutality when first presented with this book to praise when you reread it — was a Godsend. Thank you, Jeanne Glaser, Barbara Willey, Kathie Tenner, Sylvia Richards, Joyce Petro, and Susan Mahedy-Ridgway. I couldn't have made the book what it is without you.

Thank you also to my beta readers who provided the best feedback. An author can never express sufficient gratitude for your assistance.

To all of my brothers and sisters — Milton, Kent, Peg, Susan, Beth, Jeff, and Tanya — I offer my love and gratitude for your constant prayers and encouragement. You taught me how to forgive by your example. The good memories we share of Plaster Rock are still such a beautiful part of our lives.

To godly grandparents who, though now passed, continue to influence me with the warmth of their love and the example of their walk.

And finally, to Michael — the love of my life, the very reason I can live my dream of being able to write — thank you for always believing in me, even when I gave up on myself. I love you.

—Ginger Marcinkowski

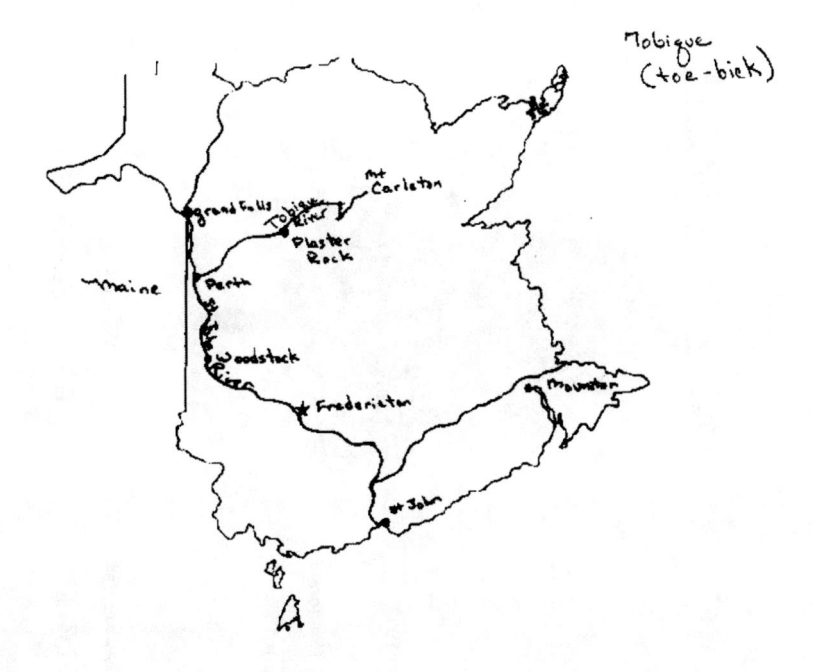

FAMILY TREE

John Polk
Father

Ellen Polk
Mother

Maureen Polk Douay
Daughter (Born 1932)

Carol Polk Timmons
Daughter (Born 1934)

Richard Douay
Father

Greta Saunders Douay
Mother

Denny Douay
Son (Born 1930)

Stephanie Douay Kendall
Daughter (Born 1948)

Emily Douay Evans
Daughter (Born 1950)

Darren Douay
Son (Born 1955)

Prologue

Run, River Currents took place during a quieter, gentler time. Long before 9/11, during the time of innocence, minors could cross international waters, even smuggle alcohol on the plane. And they often did so, unchallenged by authorities.

But this time of quietness was also a time of silent disease… a time of the abuse of children. Social services were not as readily available to assist in curbing the violence that took place in thousands of homes across Canada and the United States. It would be easy to judge the contents of this book by the rules that exist today. You might ask — how could a father abuse his own child, or a mother neglect her baby? Why didn't people see what was going on and report them?

When family members did try to intervene, they were referred to the police, who often did little more than stop by the home to ensure that the children seemed fine. But how could an abused child respond to an officer when her parents were standing guard, especially as she remembered the threats against her life if she were to ever tell what really happened?

In the setting of this book, the rules were different. Abused wives and children rarely fought back. They didn't know homes could be filled with unconditional love; they only knew what they personally experienced. What went on in their lives was normal to them.

Even today, there remains a sad imbalance in the laws and care for children. While some parents truly love their children and struggle with the increasing regulations and criticism that can sometimes prohibit them from properly disciplining and raising their children, other parents heartlessly abuse their own, believing they answer to no one… not even to God, to whom all children belong.

PART ONE

Chapter 1

Emily Douay Evans
March 19, 1977
11:35 p.m.
Saint John, New Brunswick

THE WINDSHIELD WIPERS BANGED AT THE DRIZZLE as Emily screeched into the driveway. She was grateful to be home, though the house now sat empty. The business trip had come at the right time. She'd been in Toronto for two weeks working on a new project for her lumber company, J. D. Irving. Her resource skills in forestry had caught the attention of the owner, who was impressed with Emily's knowledge of the safety and forest preservations needed to conduct the company's logging efforts around the Maritime Provinces. She'd been called to Toronto to attend a merger acquisition as a consultant and was promised a healthy raise when the merger went through. She'd been an asset during negotiations and had aptly challenged some of the most highly paid forest biometricians in the country, even though she had little more than a high school education. She wished she'd been able to thank her grandfather John — a logger — for the knowledge he'd imparted to her when she'd accompanied him into the woods as a child. But he was gone, just like everything she'd ever loved.

She'd come to realize that nothing good ever lasted. And she'd proved that the night before she'd left on her trip to Toronto, exploding again — on purpose this time — picking a fight with Aaron, spreading his clothes across the lawn like fertilizer. Nine years. Gone. Aaron had rightly blamed her for their separation.

"I can't take your jealousy," he'd said that night, his voice softer than she'd ever heard it. "You're always accusing me of something. I'm not doing this anymore. I'll always love you, and I'm truly sorry for failing you. I made my mistake. I thought you forgave me. I do love you, Emily, but you've got a problem I can't help you with. I'm not the man your father was... "

He'd tried to call several times later that night, leaving apologies on the recorder, but Emily was never much on forgiveness. Not after what she'd seen as a child. She had a twinge of regret, fooling him the way she had and then pushing him out. She'd just never give in to forgiveness. It was better that he be free of her. He needed a *real* wife, someone who could give him more than she was capable of. Someone whose personal baggage didn't taint every corner of their lives.

As she emerged from the car, the door of the silver Corvette slammed shut quicker than she'd expected, catching her suit. It jerked her backward, causing the three grocery bags she had clutched to her chest to scatter across the unmowed lawn. The rain beat harder, soaking the new red suit she'd bought just for the meeting. Silk, now surely ruined.

"Great, just great," Emily yelled at no one in particular, crushing the last piece of the wet paper bag in her hand and hurling it at the car. Storming to the side of the house, she pulled at the back door. The house was like every other one on the avenue: boxy, with a front stoop shaded by a beige awning. The boxes were painted varying shades of green; hers, a forest color. Comforting.

She unlocked the door and jerked a canvas sack from a hook near the refrigerator. It was too late for the umbrella, which hung across the room like yet another disappointment. The answering machine sat on the countertop nearby, its red eye blinking. Four messages.

Later, she thought, *I don't need this*. She stomped outside to collect the groceries from the lawn. They'd scattered and rolled and now lay hidden in and under every bush, puddle, and flowerbed in the tiny yard. She'd get her luggage later.

No longer looking like the leggy professional who'd firmly negotiated many needed concessions for her company, she paused in front of her bathroom mirror and planted her fists firmly on the sink. Her dirty-blonde hair hung like drenched mop strings around her face, the makeup running down her face as though a child had drooled on it. She squinted and stared at the face reflecting back at her. She'd never liked what she saw and turned away, quickly tugging off her wet clothes and tossing them on the bedroom chair where Aaron used to sit while she dressed. *He loved to admire me from there, and I loved him being there.* She shook the thought from her head and reached for her old pink robe, wrapping her small frame inside its warmth. She padded to the kitchen and eyed the scattered groceries. *He used to do this for me.*

Shoving the last of the food on the shelves in the pantry, she found a bottle of Chianti lodged behind a Barbour's peanut butter jar. She held the container in her right hand — deciding — then put it back on the shelf. She clicked on the television set but paid little attention as it blared. Poring over the mail, she tossed the ads and past-due bills in separate piles. Her eyes darted between the blinking machine and the pantry.

I'll just have one.

An hour later, she'd poured the last of the wine into the long-stemmed glass, her hand bobbing up and down as the final cherry droplet fell from the lip of the bottle to the waiting glass. The relentless flashing device beat its crimson eye at her through the dark wine, shooting a blood-red prism that reminded her of a heartbeat across the kitchen walls. Staggering to the counter, she punched at the machine with her finger.

"Em, honey, I've got to talk to—"

She banged at the delete button.

"We can't go on like this, Em—"

She struck the button once more.

"Emily, it's Aaron. Please call—"

Her finger pounded *delete* and poised to strike again.

"Your father died last night." Her Aunt Carol's voice was flat on the other end of the phone. "The funeral's Wednesday at 9:00 a.m. I got ahold of Stephanie and Darren. Aaron said you might still be in Toronto. We'll all be there, but I understand if you decide not to come. Call if you get this message. Love you."

Emily pulled the receiver from her ear and stared at it as though someone had glued it to her hand, then torn it away, blistering her fingers. It was Tuesday night. She pictured her siblings' faces when they got the news. Stephanie, her older sister, might manage a sad smile, but then again, she'd changed so much over the years that she might really cry. Darren would be crushed. He'd never been the target of their parents' selfishness. He loved the idea of their father as a hero, a concept he never released, even as he grew into a man.

She plunged the handset into its cradle and clutched the sides of the kitchen sink, her aunt's words slowly turning to bile. First her mother, now her father. Had they ever really known what they'd done to her? How they'd destroyed her?

Stumbling to the pantry, she pushed aside the baking soda and pulled out another bottle of wine. She let the cork squeal as she pulled it from the mouth of the bottle, fine red drops bursting as it popped from the container and fell to the floor. The smell of a smoky oak filled her nostrils as she lifted the opening to her face and guzzled a few swallows, not caring that her wine glass sat just inches away. *If I leave by 6:00 a.m., I'll make the three-and-a half-hour drive just in time to see them close his casket..*

Chapter 2

Emily Douay Evans
March 20, 1977
10:02 a.m.
Perth, New Brunswick, Canada

THE FUNERAL CROWD HAD THINNED, leaving twenty-seven-year-old Emily Evans standing in the dim silhouette of the carved archway, waiting her turn to bid her father good-bye. A few stragglers, hands clasped and pressed to their chests, ambled up the center aisle toward the vestibule. Voices were low, reverent. No one detected Emily's presence as she slid along the outside wall of the ornate Catholic church, stopping only when she heard the nearby voice of a thin woman in a black, veiled hat say, "Such a sad way to die." As a child, she'd never been allowed to sneak into a church this way. She had come through the front door, hand tightly clasped in her grandfather's, proud to be entering the house of the Lord. But that was before her life had unraveled. Before she quit believing.

Emily lingered in the shadows as the stranger clustered with the others in the foyer, the tiny figure stopping momentarily to share condolences with her father's widow.

Trudy, her father's second wife, was a dumpy German woman whose pudgy, worn face showed relief. She stood hunchbacked and silent, her only emotion an awkward smile as mourners patted her hands and hugged her neck. Her hands wound a white handkerchief, twisting the cloth into a pointed dagger.

Trudy's dress was not black and not the least bit appropriate for the occasion. It stretched tight across her middle and permitted her oversized breasts to pitch from the V-cut neckline. Its wild floral print was a vivid yellow, a color Emily knew her father hated. *An odd choice.*

She watched the few mourners file out the immense wooden door to their waiting cars, the voices booming, then softening. Letting out a restrained breath, Emily continued her way along the wall to the coffin, the release of air sending a small hiss from her lips. The wake was over. Her father's casket would be closed for the last time.

She arrived at the open container, dark pewter with polished brass handles and a cream-colored satin lining. Her father was laid out in a black pinstripe suit and a dark shirt with a hideous white tie that made him look like a television mobster. He couldn't be older than forty-seven. Emily wasn't sure, but she didn't care. She closed her eyes and remembered him in worn Levi's and a dirty white T-shirt with a front pocket that always housed a pack of Camels.

He'd been a master carpenter, a trade passed on to him by a generation of hardworking, hard-living Frenchmen, though by looking at the many half-finished projects in their own homes, you wouldn't have known it. He was Catholic, though he'd been baptized like a Pentecostal in the Tobique River at his wife's — Maureen's — insistence. Interesting that her mother would have insisted on something like that, Emily thought. Maureen had explained to Emily so many times how she'd run from the smothering confines of her own forced church marches as she grew up in the little town of Plaster Rock. "I never did that to you, Emily. Never forced you to church. Never forced anything on you. I gave you your freedom. You won't be able to understand what it was like to feel so trapped." And she related her story again.

~ ~ ~ ~ ~

The first time Maureen had sensed she was smothering was the day she descended the worn path behind the Anglican church to the Tobique River, hand in hand with her father, John. She was six. Her mother, Ellen, had promised to bring Carol, her four-year-old sister, to join them for a picnic at noon.

From the edge of the shoreline, Maureen felt the warmth of the sun on her skin as she pushed her face at the sky. Her father stood nearby, waist deep in the water, flicking the line of his bamboo pole across the fluttering river. Maureen watched her father, his arm bent, snap his wrist, propelling the invisible string up and away, where the brightly colored feather lure danced against the vivid blue of the sky. His green plaid shirt was rolled up to his elbows and tucked deep into his green rubber waders. He glanced at her between casts, his eyes flashing a quiet warning. She watched him flick the pole over and over, his patience with the empty, darting line more than she could handle. She'd been told to stay on land, but the draw of the minnows teasing the shore had her wading knee-deep before she knew it. She felt no danger here.

Remembering the story, Emily felt herself shrug. It was difficult to picture this woman, her mother, as an innocent child. She'd bet anything Maureen was manipulative even then.

"Maureen! John!" From the top of the hill, Maureen heard her mother's voice. High-pitched and ragged.

"She's going to drown! John!"

Ellen flew down the narrow path clutching Carol, the picnic basket tumbling, the food inside scattering like dice. John dropped his favorite pole, the water sucking at his legs as he frantically made his way toward his daughter. Maureen froze, unsure of what horrible thing she'd done. She loved the water, the way it flowed between her toes and tickled her legs, the coolness numbing her feet.

Ellen reached the shoreline, her hair wild, her scream a bloodcurdling shriek. John yanked his daughter from the water. Then he just stood there, silent, as Ellen chided like a pecking bird, clutching Maureen hard to her chest, her hold slowly choking the air from her daughter's lungs. Carol stood next to her mother, wailing at the sky. The whole ordeal had terrified Maureen; it was as though some horrible monster were lying in wait beneath the surface of the river. She was never allowed to go to the water again, though the desire to have such an adventure remained firmly within her, acting itself out in rebellion as she aged.

~ ~ ~ ~ ~

After hearing her mother's story yet again, Emily found it beyond her comprehension why Maureen had ever pushed Denny into a baptism. It didn't prove his faith. But then again, it was years after she'd left Plaster Rock that Maureen had insisted he be baptized, by then realizing that some of her own mistakes might have been avoided had she given in to faith instead of giving in to Denny.

Emily stared at the dead man. Her father had been good-looking, strong, angry, and an alcoholic. She was glad she didn't look a thing like him. She'd been told she had her grandfather's face — long and narrow, punctuated with a pointed nose, thick lips, and blonde hair that was thin as broom wisps.

"Emily?" The voice startled her. She whirled around to see her brother standing behind her.

"Darren! You scared me."

Darren's hair had the same glossy sheen as their father's, shiny like vinyl. It was clipped short but still had recognizable waves. The color was not dark like their father's but the wild radish red of their mother Maureen's. He was simply dressed in a navy blue suit and a bright tie, knotted perfectly over a starched white shirt. He was almost twenty-two now, five years her junior, and happier since the last time she'd seen him, two years ago now. He'd married a girl named Betsy and joined some church in British Columbia near his latest army base. His lean body appeared heavy; his shoulders sagged, though his smile was wide and inviting.

"I saw you come in and thought you might want some company. I'm surprised to see you here. I told Aunt Carol you were still in Toronto. How'd you know?"

Darren reached out to envelop his sister. She hugged him, longing to hang on, but pushed back when she recognized the scent of their father's Old Spice.

"I checked my calls when I got home. Aunt Carol had left a message. I got back last night too late to call." Emily never flinched about lying anymore. "I'm fine. Go on with Steph. I just need a few minutes with him. I'll join you and the family back at the house. Carol left me directions on the answering machine."

Darren nodded and turned to leave, but then he stopped and swung around to face her. "I forgave him, you know."

"I'm glad you could, Darren." The words stuck in her throat. "I hope you don't expect me to."

He nodded and turned to leave, his head slumping forward. Emily was grateful he'd escaped most of their father's rage. He'd grown into a good man from what little she'd seen of him lately.

With Darren's footsteps fading behind her, she shifted her attention back to the coffin. She studied her father's face. Lily white, powdered with cake makeup. Perfect circles of rouge lay high on his cheekbones, as though someone had used a small rubber ball dipped in raspberry Jell-O to make the marks. His lips were sewn into a hard smile and painted the purplish red of a turnip. She'd heard the others say how good he looked — so natural. *Natural*, she thought. *Yes, if he were a circus clown.* His dark, curly hair had been slicked straight back, revealing a receding hairline. Thin strands of gray were evident, lying like newly painted stripes on a blacktop road. It was obvious that it hadn't been cut in months.

Emily leaned in over him, twisting her neck to face him full on, stretching to breathe in any evidence of whiskey lingering on his breath. Instead, he smelled like brewer's yeast, as if in a final joke, the undertaker had poured a beer down his throat.

She wondered what it was like to be dead, if it was any different from the way she felt as she moved through her life... robotic motions void of feeling, good or bad, and trusting no one. She pictured her best friend, Dave Cook, floating like a blue bubble on the skin of the Tobique River, peaceful, silent before his rescuers tore at him; she was unsure if he would've preferred life in this chaotic world to the quiet darkness of his death. And her mother? Was she glad to be gone as well? Glad to be rid of the responsibility of her three children? Glad to have escaped the memory of this man's angry fists?

Emily's head fell forward, her eyes closing as she recalled the last time she'd faced this man. They'd had few words between them. He'd talked — mumbled, more or less — spitting out a tale she could hardly fathom. It was just an excuse, she believed, to explain why he'd done what he'd done to her. Why should she care? What had happened to him took place forty years ago. He could have chosen to get over that, or at least not repeat it. He could have changed it all, changed at least the outcome of *her* life.

That day he'd told her the story indifferently, in third person, as if he'd distanced himself from the memory. As if she should do the same. She remembered staring at him as he spat out the tale, her mouth open like a mayonnaise jar. He really believed that she would listen and forgive him, believe he'd changed. As if he'd done nothing to her. His story swirled in her mind.

~ ~ ~ ~ ~

The boy was bent over a tree stump that had been chopped into an altar-like table just behind the woodshed. His pants, too small for a boy of seven, were wrapped around his knees. Deer meat and chickens were processed on the bloody stump, the rancid smell still thick. His brutish father stood to the left of the boy, a long, thin, birch branch clamped in his right hand.

"I'll teach you to lie to me, boy," the deep voice bellowed. "Teach you, like my daddy taught me."

The first slap across the boy's buttocks jolted Denny upward.

"I didn't lie, Daddy."

"You're telling me Father Milliken did? What do you take me for? An idiot?"

The second strike was swifter, harder. Denny rolled to his side.

"The bottle was gone before I opened that drawer, Dad. I swear. Please, don't—"

The next strike hit the boy across his hip, snapping into his genitals and causing him to grasp his crotch, a low scream rising from his throat. A smile slit into the man's face. He raised the switch again and again, beating the boy until he fell from the log and collapsed on the ground, the thin red welts on his back swelling into blood trails.

"That'll teach you to lie to me again," the gruff voice said. He threw the branch to the ground, its red tip bouncing up against Denny's face. "Now get in the house and have your mother wash you up."

His mother pretended that Denny had gone and caught himself in some thicket near the woods, wiping his fresh wounds and scolding him for not having a shirt on. She pulled his face close to hers.

"Your father loves you, you know. He just gets a little mad at us now and then. I'll send him in later, and you can talk it out."

Denny dreaded those talks. His father would show up with black salve to rub on his wounds. "Heal you up in no time," his father would say, pushing Denny's face forward on the bed, pulling off his pants again. The pain of the rub was as bad as the beating, with his father's callused hands massaging the cuts over and over. Denny would close his eyes when his father reached his buttocks, the thick fingers separating his cheeks, the hand lingering near his opening. A familiar feeling of revulsion would descend on him, covering him like hot tar. He'd never get over the helplessness he felt or the anger that welled up inside him every time he saw his father's face.

"This won't hurt nothing at all," the old man said, his hands greased with the slippery salve. Denny heard the zipper of his old man's pants and pinched his eyes closed.

~ ~ ~ ~ ~

Standing over him, Emily stared down. His stories and his lies didn't matter anymore. He'd droned on and on... his father beat his mom, killed her, went to prison. He'd said Denny would never be a man, never make anything of himself. *That much was right*, Emily thought. Who cared about his story? Her mother's, either. The effects of their actions coursed through her like an electric current. Emily drew back, her face muscles relaxing. She let her left hand linger at the edge of the casket, sliding her fingers back and forth on the cool surface. Her right fist began to ball. Without looking around, she lifted her arm up and away from her body. She drew in a long, hard breath, her muscles trembling, and then lunged forward, punching hard into his face.

The force sent her father's head cracking to the left, his lower jaw separating from his skull as though they'd never been attached. His nose pushed upward, making him look like a pig. A trickle of clear fluid began to drip from it. *"You'll never be dead enough,"* Emily whispered. *"Never."*

Chapter 3

Emily Evans
March 20, 1977
10:20 a.m.
Perth, New Brunswick

BUCKLING HERSELF INSIDE THE CORVETTE, Emily pressed her head to the steering wheel, stole a deep breath, and popped the clutch. She spun out of the parking lot, sending angry chunks of gravel spewing across the churchyard. She pointed the car in the direction of her father's house. Darren, her twenty-nine-year-old sister Stephanie, her Aunt Carol, and assorted acquaintances would be there awaiting her arrival. She slammed her car to a halt at the stop sign, one she didn't remember being there, sending the contents of her open purse spewing across the floor mat.

She hadn't been north of Saint John since her grandfather had passed away in 1966, the year she turned sixteen. Little had changed. The Saint John River still swept lazily between the tiny towns of Perth and Andover, towns whose people, Emily recalled, were stone-faced and judgmental, so unlike her grandfather. She looked left toward the road that would take her to her father's house, then right toward the long, steel bridge that spanned the Saint John River. At the end of the bridge, she remembered, the road jolted left and disappeared around a deep bend that clutched the Tobique River all the way to Plaster Rock, her grandparents' home.

She cracked the window of the Corvette and stared at the horizon, running her long fingers over her stinging fist. For a moment, she let the cool wind whistle through the car and tug at her memories of spring in Plaster Rock. *I was always happy there.*

Spring often arrived in the northeastern part of Canada like clapping thunder. Its roar of wind set in motion the thaw of the cold, deep winter. Emily remembered how her grandfather, John, would take her ice skating on the frozen Tobique River, a tributary that flanked the banks of Plaster Rock, New Brunswick. The river pushed eastward beneath the frozen mass toward Maine, merging with the Saint John River in Perth. The Tobique, she remembered, creaked and groaned beneath her with the air's coming warmth as she'd glide over a small patch of cleared ice. The river, once quieted through the winter by the quick slap of cold that descended in early November, lay as solemn as a graveyard, its skin a thick membrane cloaking the waterway.

Even now, as she sat beside the banks of the Saint John River, she could see that the seasons were still embracing one another, winter dancing into spring, the lead changing day by day, the temperatures rising and falling as their tango whittled away the icy banks of the river. Small dark circles were finally signaling that winter's dance was done, popping like polka dots through the surface of the white blanket on the river, quietly bubbling as if to announce the pending thaw.

In Plaster Rock, the Tobique would continue to sway, snap, and then gurgle before the first of its crust would give way to the flutter beneath its icy plate. If the new season was gentle, the ice would melt, watering the fertile land and coaxing a strong crop of potatoes from the soil. If winter continued to dance in and out of spring, the river would break and heave its body into ice masses that tore at the frozen banks and raged downriver, taking with it the bridges and buildings that dared underestimate its power. The ensuing floods would then wash away precious soil and leave potato farmers lacking a good yield. Yet in the arms of the coming warmth, Emily knew they would merge and eventually find peace downriver. Lily of the valleys were already spreading like welcome mats along the banks of the warming shores. Ospreys waded in the tributaries, waving young fish like newly won trophies. Everywhere, winter's anger seemed to be giving way to spring's joy.

Emily pulled her purse from the floor, leaving the balance of its contents on the mat. For a moment, she stared ahead; then she suddenly tossed her bag on the passenger seat, revved the engine, and pointed the Corvette toward the only place of solace she'd ever known. She didn't want to be the woman she'd become. Angry. Bitter. Undone. She wanted instead to harbor the love she'd seen in her grandfather... but now, with all the mistakes she'd made, the hurts she'd endured, and the hatred she held inside, she wondered if she could ever make it happen. She shook her head. No — she'd never be like him.

On the outskirts of Perth, she wound along the river road, passing through the Tobique Narrows where the cement dam held back the water, allowing electricity to be generated up and down the river. Here at the Narrows, the Tobique spilled into the Saint John, the rushing flow capturing the spring floods, surging south toward Hartland, New Brunswick. There it tumbled beneath the longest wooden covered bridge in the world.

The Corvette pushed through the winding roads as though pulled by a cord of remembrance. Log cabins dotted the river's inlets, their makeshift ponds allowing the owners a picturesque view of the rambling water. Birch stands — bark glowing white, edges peeling back like the pages of a parchment book — flooded by. They generated memories that began to blend with Emily's tears. *Isn't this what I wanted? Both of them dead?*

Sixty miles away, Plaster Rock hovered over the Tobique River, the sweeping waterway that cut through the beauty of northeastern Canada like a sharp bread knife. A chill rushed through Emily as her eyes searched for something familiar. She felt like a child again, alone and anxious, searching her memory for an answer to the question of how her parents' hatred, now so deeply rooted in her, had all begun.

Chapter 4

Maureen Polk
August 1943
Plaster Rock, New Brunswick

SUNDAYS IN PLASTER ROCK were spent inside the walls of Freewill Baptist Church. Family activities were constrained to traipsing solemnly to church in the morning and then again Sunday night. Eleven-year-old Maureen and her nine-year-old sister, Carol, followed their parents, John and Ellen, and their Aunt Amy into the white, shingled building. They climbed the four wooden steps and passed into the small, simple sanctuary just as they had done Maureen's entire life.

Often stopping in the vestibule before entering the church, Maureen lingered with her parents. Someone always pointed out her father's name carved on the wooden plaque that honored the war veterans of the church. Her father had been in the Canadian Army, a fact that made her mother smile but aggravated Maureen, who blamed her father for staying in Plaster Rock when all the while they could've lived overseas and experienced the excitement of a new place. Maureen politely nodded at the compliments paid to her father, but inside she felt trapped by the familiarity of everything. She knew every pew, every ritual, every hymn, every story of every parishioner in the church. Nothing was new.

Within the sanctuary, twenty oak pews were arranged on either side of the hollow-sounding room, the sheen of the wood worn off from sliding rear ends. Pebbly-surfaced, opaque windows were jammed open, held with wooden sticks to let in passing breezes. Maureen sat near the window, slump-shouldered, hoping to hear the strain of someone's rumbling car float through.

She watched the parishioners plod into the sanctuary, murmuring like old men. At the front of the church, two wide steps led to a small stage that housed the dark cherry pulpit. It was surrounded by four ornate chairs with stiff wooden backs upholstered in red crushed velvet, as though awaiting a king's arrival. Two raised rows of white, wood planks held a makeshift perch that was used for the church choir, an assembly of five of the deacons' wives and two gangly-legged teenagers. A well-used piano was crowded into the corner of the stage behind one of the ornate chairs where Mrs. Belcamp pushed her wide body onto the aging bench and began pounding the keyboard, frightening the perching birds on the windowsills and scaring Maureen into an upright position. Her father moved to the pulpit to lead the congregation in an opening prayer, his voice low and mumbling.

Churchgoers never knew whether Reverend Park would be a featured guest pastor, but she scanned the room for his familiar bald head bobbing in the small crowd. She knew he must be in town because the aroma of freshly baked apple pie and mile-high bread rolls had seeped into every corner of their house that morning, a sure sign of company.

Later that day, her mother and Aunt Amy would skitter around the kitchen, heaping plates full of roasted chicken and mashed potatoes fit for a dignitary such as the Reverend. Park was a visiting pastor, young and excitable when it came to the preaching the Word of the Lord. When he traveled through the area, he often stayed with the Polks overnight after Sunday evening prayer meetings. His booming voice and fervent prayers put Maureen on edge, and the house filled with lively conversation, prayer, and the echo of gospel songs at his arrival.

"So you think, Reverend Park, that the invasion of Sicily was necessary?" John asked, his bread knife clinking on the butter dish.

"No one likes war, John," Reverend Park replied. "And I can't be the one to judge what the premier might be thinking."

"You'd think you were the politician, Reverend!" John laughed and scooped another heap of potatoes onto his plate.

Relegated to sleeping on the feather bed on the front porch while Reverend Park took over their room, Maureen longed to sneak away rather than listen to the young minister's windy lectures that stubbornly drifted in under the cracks of the bedroom door. She envisioned herself dancing with friends or swimming in the Tobique, though she knew her mother's fear of the water would never allow it.

"I want to be like Marjorie Reynolds, Carol," Maureen blurted. "All that gaiety. I just loved her at the movies!" She bolted upright from the bed and faced her sister, who was reading in the wicker rocker in the corner of the room, eyes rolling in disgust.

"Did you notice the dress in the final scene of *Holiday Inn*? The way it moved when she danced?"

"Shhhhh!" Carol said, jumping from the chair and racing to close the door to the living room. "Mother will kill us if she finds out we went to the movies with Daffney."

"I don't care. I don't see a thing wrong with the movies. Everybody goes but us." Maureen rose from the bed and swirled around. "Besides, I want to be in the movies, travel like the stars do. Go somewhere. Be somebody."

"You're such a dreamer, Maureen. Why can't you just be happy with what you have?" Carol said.

"I'm smothering here, Carol!" Maureen stopped twirling, her dress flattening against her legs. She folded her arms in front of her. "Can't you feel it, too?"

"No, Maureen. I'm perfectly content." Carol reopened her book and fell back into the rocker, closing the conversation as quickly as she had slapped shut her book.

Maureen spun toward the window, crossed her arms tightly against her chest, and stared down at the Tobique River. She was dying in Plaster Rock, drying up like some old apple hanging too long in the sun. She was sure of it. *And I'm not always going to be everybody's goody two-shoes, either.*

At fifteen, Maureen snatched a pack of Lucky Strike cigarettes from her best friend, Jenny Graves, grabbed her righteous little sister, Carol, and pushed her into their outhouse.

"Mum and Dad will kill us if they catch us," Carol said, her face white, eyes big as saucers.

"You big sissy," Maureen said. "They're not going to catch us. Live a little, will you, Carol? All we do is go to school and go to church. I'm sick of it. I need to try something new for a change. All the girls are doing it! It must be OK."

She pulled the cigarettes and a pack of matches from her jacket pocket and tapped the pack expertly into her hand, just the way Jenny had shown her. One white cigarette popped from the small opening. She tugged at it, pulling it from its holder, and drove it into her mouth. Cupping her hands around the thin stick of tobacco, she scratched a match across the wood of the door and watched the flame burst from its end. Carol's eyes were wide and wild as she watched her sister tap the flame to the cigarette, the tobacco end turning bright red as Maureen sucked at the stub. Maureen's body jerked, tobacco burning her throat as it filled her lungs. She gagged and then passed the cigarette to Carol, who shook her head rapidly back and forth.

"No. No. I don't want to!" Carol whispered, tears puddling down her face.

"Do it, or I'll say it was your idea!"

Carol took the cigarette and pulled it to her lips. She made a valiant attempt to suck on the thin white paper but began to gag immediately, the smoke rising and circling her face. Maureen grabbed the cigarette, the first of the ashes drifting to the outhouse floor.

"This is so easy. Why do you have to always be such a baby?" She felt lightheaded and sick to her stomach, something she'd never reveal to her sister. "This is fun!" Maureen pulled another long drag, watching the ash on the end of the cigarette lengthen again.

They heard the footsteps too late. The door of the privy flew open, and their Aunt Amy stood there with a willow switch in her hand.

"Are you two smoking in here?" Her eyes were narrow and angry. Evil eyes. She cracked the willow branch like a cowboy with a whip. Maureen dropped the lit cigarette into the outhouse hole. Carol stood shaking, open-mouthed.

"No!" Maureen muttered, the smoke curling up from her lips.

"Yes, Aunt Amy! Please don't tell. Please don't tell!" Carol cried, throwing herself into a heap at her aunt's feet.

"Promise me you won't ever do that again, or I'll have your father give you both a good strapping!"

They promised, but that first cigarette gave Maureen a taste of freedom that no revival ever had, a freedom she'd just recently begun to explore. She recognized her Aunt Amy's troubled look, the old woman's face scrunched in judgment as she tugged Maureen from the outhouse while Carol slumped herself out behind them.

"Young lady, you keep making these kinds of choices, and you'll end up alone in some town where nobody cares about you."

Her aunt's voice was sharp and cutting in a way she'd never heard before. *What does she know?* Maureen's stomach rolled with nausea. Her father had already caught her two months earlier in the barn with Brian Pelletier, the night before Brian ran off and joined the army. She'd embarrassed her whole family, angered her father, and smiled inside at the disappointment she saw in his face.

"Maureen, why?" Her father's face pleaded for an answer.

"I wanted to." Her voice was taunting.

"You are not to leave the house until I get a chance to talk to that young man." Redness crawled up John's neck, and the vein in the middle of his forehead pulsated.

"You can't stop me, Dad. I'm almost sixteen, and I'll do what I want."

John grabbed at his daughter's arm and tightened his grip.

"You'll do as I say, young lady."

"Or what, Dad?" Her eyes narrowed. "You'll break your promise to God and hit me? Maybe kill me?"

She knew he'd sworn to never let his anger rise again after he'd killed a man in a street brawl years earlier. She'd heard him pray for God's forgiveness and ask for help to never show his anger again after an act that was, in the end, deemed accidental.

Her father released her arm and dropped his head. She'd seen his tears but didn't care. She watched him walk away, slump-shouldered, as though she'd placed the weight of the world on his shoulders — although in fact it had been he and her mother who had tethered her, maddened her. *It's not MY fault. I did it because I've never been able to do anything the other girls do.*

She rubbed her arm where he'd grabbed her, sure she'd won this battle. Now she'd never tell them she'd gone off and married Brian earlier that day at the courthouse in Grand Falls, both lying about their ages. *Let them think what they want.* What she wanted was to be out of Plaster Rock, out of the smothering small town.

Brian was supposed to be gone only a few weeks, but the letter had come saying his orders had changed. Six months or more. As much as a year. He promised he'd send for her soon.

"I can't do this anymore, Carol," she told her sister two weeks later. "I need to get out of here. Church day and night. Why, even God said, 'Make a joyful noise,' but nobody around here has any fun! I can't take it. I'm going to that dance tonight no matter what they say."

Fourteen-year-old Carol huddled near the doorway.

"They'll just kill you, Maureen." Carol wove her hands one over the other. "Haven't you done enough?"

"I don't care. I can't wait one more minute." Maureen threw her husband's letter to the floor. She pushed the hangers in the closet back and forth across the rod, the sound of metal on metal piercing their ears. She pulled out the short red dress she'd borrowed from Jenny, slipped it over her head and down around her slender hips. "Besides, Brian won't mind at all. It's just a dance."

That night, Maureen heard the calling of field crickets as they blended with the rustling leaves of the crabapple tree. She lay restless in the feather bed on the back porch, fully clothed under the wrinkled sheets, while Carol dozed on the couch in the living room. The August warmth had driven the girls to the first floor, their parents to the root cellar.

Maureen pretended to be asleep when her father kissed her good night, slipping out a half hour later when she heard her mother's snore rise from the basement. The flashlight bobbed up and down as though on a spring as Maureen made her way down the gravel driveway that ran behind her house. She snuck through the Lincoln schoolyard and up the back sidewalk to the Legion hall. It was Saturday night, and the dance would be in full swing, the music already sailing out of the open windows and into the night. The sign for the Legion dance had been plastered all over town, and she'd heard that everyone would be there. Earlier that afternoon, she'd delivered a letter to the post office, promising her father she'd return promptly, but instead she'd ducked into the Squeeze Inn Cafe when through the window she saw two of her friends giggling in a corner booth. Tommy, the soda jerk, stood at the fountain wiping the counter off with a dirty towel and rolled his eyes when he heard their conversation.

"Do you think Denny Douay will be there?" Daffney asked, her brown ringlets popping like champagne corks around her head.

"Nobody really knows where he lives. I heard he was sleeping in old man Bain's chicken shed at Wapske Creek, so maybe he doesn't even know about the dance," Jenny replied, her hands jutting like logs from beneath her jacket. "Anyway, it's better that he doesn't show. That guy's trouble."

Denny Douay. His name gave Maureen goose bumps. She'd seen him at the Squeeze Inn a couple of times, cuddled in a corner with a girl whose dark brown hair tumbled down her back. Denny had been nudging the girl with his head, trying to steal a kiss before the owner caught him and threw him out for inappropriate behavior.

Maureen remembered the last time she'd seen him. Denny was wearing a worn black jacket and kept sweeping his dark hair off to one side with a push of his left hand. His body was long and muscular. Devilishly handsome. Standing near the door of the soda shop, he eyed everybody up and down as they came and went, staring as though he'd lost something and was sure the intruder had found it.

She'd heard he was eighteen but thought he seemed much older, more mature than the rest of the boys in town. He smoked, a habit no one else liked but Maureen found intriguing. Everyone said he was a bad egg, a thief, but Maureen thought no one had given him a chance after his father went to prison. How was he supposed to keep himself fed when he had no family? Even his only uncle hadn't taken him in. He'd walked by her one day earlier in the summer — she smelled sweet from a dab of perfume she'd tried on at Belcamp's store; he, like a freshly smoked cigarette. Today he pushed open the door of the Squeeze Inn to let her in.

"Thanks," she said, turning to look back at him.

"You're certainly welcome." Their eyes locked for just a moment before another girl shoved in behind Maureen and forced her inside. She was certain there was something in his eyes, something that begged at her.

By the time she reached the Legion, it was 9:30. She stood outside watching as people pushed through the door, some in, some out, the strains of "Twelfth Street Rag" beating the air. Her girlfriends were huddled along the wall near the band, their feet tapping and hips moving as they waved to her through the crowd. Another group of girls danced in a circle in the center of the floor, while couples bumped bodies into gyrating positions that seemed natural to the quickening jive. The room was foggy, as though someone had burned a roast or put out a fire. The curls of smoke wrapped the bodies of the attendees and drove a scorched odor across the room.

Suddenly, the tempo of the song changed, and Bing Crosby's "Be Careful, It's My Heart" began to play. Couples grasped hands and clutched each other close. A quick tap on Maureen's left shoulder had her spinning, the skirt of her red dress whirling around her legs. Denny stood behind her, his right hand extended. Daffney and Jenny remained silent, glaring at him.

"No," Jenny said, "she doesn't want to dance with the likes of you."

Maureen felt a burn rising, her face flushing. She reached for him, defying her friends with an intimidating smirk. He pulled her into his arms, his lips curled next to her ear, a mocking grin aimed at Jenny. Maureen loved the touch of his hands as they moved up and down her body. She felt herself melting as though her spine had given way. His breath was hot on her cheek, his promises weakening her.

"I'll give you a lifetime of dances, Maureen. Just be with me." Brian Pelletier, her husband of two months, slipped from her mind.

Chapter 5

Maureen
September 1947
Plaster Rock, New Brunswick

"I'M PREGNANT, DENNY," she'd said a month later.
"How do you know for sure, Maureen? Couldn't it be too soon?"
"A woman knows. What are we going to do? I can't tell my parents. They'll kill me."
"I want to marry you; you know that. It's just that—"
"Just what, Denny? You've *got* to marry me. You just have to!"
"I don't even have a job! How am I supposed to support us, let alone a baby?"
Maureen wrapped her arms around his neck and kissed him gently. "We can make it, Denny. We'll leave this place tonight. Get married. You're eighteen. You can join the army! Or we'll find jobs. You said you have family in Perth. I don't care what we have to do. We'll be together. A family." She leaned in against him and purred in his ear until everything seemed almost right again. Maureen had no idea that years earlier, one hard smack by Denny's father's callused hand had left Denny almost deaf in one ear. The army had turned him down.
Without Denny's knowledge, she'd already written to Brian and told him her father had forced her to get an annulment, warning him that he should stay away until things blew over. It was a lie, but after all, nobody else knew.
Two nights later, Denny and Maureen stood in front of a justice of the peace and swore their lives to each other. They moved into a tiny one-room apartment over Perth's only gas station. A month later, her parents came by with a few pieces of furniture and helped

the couple create a little corner for their coming grandchild. Ellen busied herself hanging curtains and placing rugs around the room while John helped his new son-in-law set up the crib they'd brought as a gift. The glances between her parents echoed their disapproval, but they worked steadily and quietly until the apartment felt more like a home.

After dinner, Maureen stood in the window of the small apartment, coiling her apron into a wad around her finger as she watched her parents' blue Chevrolet disappear along the river road. She held back the urge to call after them, to shout that she was making her own decisions now and that she'd done the right thing by marrying Denny. *Someone just had to believe in him, that's all.*

"Dad said he'd get you a job in the woods with him, Denny," Maureen said shortly after her parents had left. "You could go to work by next week, and we certainly need the money!"

"I'm working on something, Maureen," he charged back at her. "There's a few houses being built on the other side of town. They know my work. Besides, I can get my own job."

She looked away, uncertain about his angry reply. *A bad day*, she thought.

Stephanie was born seven months to the day after the Legion dance. Snow was piled up to the roof of the gas station. The midwife made her way up behind Denny as he re-shoveled each step of the staircase that ran alongside the old building. The wind howled and blew the snow into tiny tornados that blanketed their every step. Maureen's cries ignited the night and carried deep into the morning until their little girl was born.

"I can't believe she's so healthy for being premature," Maureen said, her eyes never meeting Denny's.

Premature. The midwife held Maureen's pleading eyes, her brows pinched into a question mark; then she busied herself with leaving. Maureen's lie burrowed itself into their lives.

Stephanie was beautiful, dark-haired, and independent like her father. Maureen allowed her little girl to curl her tiny fingers around her hand, pulling her child near enough to smell the sweet odor of the newborn. Denny curled up next to them, whispering that now, everything was perfect.

*   *   *

"Can't you get her to shut up?" Denny yelled one evening weeks later, grabbing at Maureen's arm. "I can't make a living or get us out of this hole if I can't get in a day's work because I'm tired! Do something with her!" He threw back the quilt and stormed into the bathroom, the slam of the door rattling the room.

In the shadows of that night, Maureen felt him slip from the bed. She rolled onto her side to watch him edge himself across the room to the crib. Stephanie's lungs were still filled with anger, her tiny mouth wide and birdlike as she belched guttural, high-pitched screams that tore at the shadows. Maureen's eyes were adjusting to the dark, her husband's silhouette etched in the dim light of the window. She watched him raise his arms, moving at a snail's pace as though he were thinking. She saw the outline of something puffed around his hands, swallowed by white, although she could not make out what it was. He turned to look back at her, then pushed it into the crib.

"Denny!" Maureen screamed, flinging the sheet to the floor, rushing to his side. "What are you doing?"

She pulled at him, finding a mysterious strength, her hands wildly punching the air, connecting when she could with his face, his arms, his body. He fell backward, covering his head with his forearms as she continued to beat at him. Denny slid down the wall, whimpering like a child; a sucked-in scream released and vomited back into the air. Maureen grabbed Stephanie from beneath the pillow and clutched her close to her chest.

"What were you doing, Denny? Were you trying to kill our baby?"

He acted surprised, defiant. "What?" He shook his head in disbelief. "You're crazy! I was just kissing her good night. What's wrong with you, Maureen?"

Pushing himself back up the wall, he seemed dazed at her attack. He shuffled back to bed, tugging the strewn bedding up around his face. Maureen stood over him, the uneasy feeling of her spontaneous and self-serving choices beginning to reveal itself in the stranger she had chosen to marry. *I know he wouldn't do this. I was probably just seeing things in the dark.*

* * *

A little over a year later, some nosy neighbor showed up on their doorstep announcing that Denny's father had died. Denny didn't even blink, slamming the door in the man's face as he was explaining that someone had stabbed Denny's father during dinner at the prison. Maureen watched Denny's skin jump with excitement, bumping up as though it had been massaged with steel wool. His pleasure pooled into an eerie smile. Maureen stood across the room, puzzled.

"Don't be silly about this. You've got to go to the funeral, Denny," Maureen chided two days later. "No matter what happened in the past, he's still your father."

"What do you know about my father, Maureen?" Denny screamed at her. "Just shut up and leave me alone! This is none of your business!"

She watched as he strode to the kitchen and pulled out a bottle of whiskey he'd hidden on the shelf over the refrigerator. He turned and stared coldly at her, then took a long swig of the copper liquid.

"Do you really need that right now, Denny?" she asked.

"Why are you nagging at me, Maureen? I've finally got something to celebrate, and you go and try to ruin it." His face flashed with anger as he grabbed his coat and slammed his way out of the apartment.

Chapter 6

Denny
August 1949
Perth, New Brunswick

THE DAY THEY BURIED RICHARD DOUAY, Maureen dressed Stephanie and went to the graveyard with the pastor. She guessed Denny's father wouldn't have any friends. Fewer than a half-dozen people circled the grave, counting the pastor. She didn't recognize any. Even Denny and his uncle hadn't showed. No one cried a tear. It was over in minutes. Only Denny understood why.

~ ~ ~ ~ ~

The farmhouse burned down with his mother in it when he was thirteen. He heard the fight, saw it through the window of the back porch. He watched his old man beating his mother until her frail frame dropped to the living room floor. His father stooped to shake her. Her face lapped to one side; a trickle of blood pooled on the wood floor next to her. His father stood and began pushing his big hands over his mouth, rubbing circles in his face, glancing from side to side in disbelief. Then he cocked his head and cupped his hands over his mouth.

"Denny?" he heard his father yell up the wooden stairs. "Denny? You here, boy?" Denny pushed himself tightly against the unpainted clapboard siding when he recognized the agitated twitch in his father's face. He knew what would follow if he heeded his father's voice. Denny edged himself backward, jumped from the porch, and ran past the neglected barn straight to the empty chicken pen. Once inside, he stood silent, breathless, one eye peering through a crack in the wood, waiting. The unmended hinges screeched a warning with the sound of the back door slamming. His father hastily made his way to the barn, then returned with a tin can that Denny knew contained kerosene. He couldn't look anymore, his stomach buckling him in two. He should've helped his mother, but instinctively he knew she was already dead.

A whooshing sound brought him upright in time to see the fire lick the side of the house. The old Ford truck emitted a deep rumble as it tore down the driveway, turning, not right toward town but left toward the border of the United States. Moments later, Denny stood paralyzed on the back steps of the burning building, listening to the hollow sound of the flames as they engulfed his home, his mother's body leaving a scent that would forever remind him of burning meat. His skin prickled at the thought of what he'd just witnessed. He had to get out.

The sweat cut into his skin. The branches smacked against him over and over as he stumbled through the woods. His lean body was that of a runner — too thin, long, and lanky — one that could take miles of punishment on open roads but was easily torn by the thickets of underbrush. With every glance back, he remembered his mother's face, tormented and distorted as his father inflicted each blow. Denny knew she was better off dead but was tortured at the thought of how he'd left her, her pretty face beaten beyond recognition, blood seeping into her long brown hair. *No time to mourn now. Just run.*

Seven months later, he faced his father for the last time. He'd been fearful of testifying to what he'd seen that night, knowing his father's rage. But the haunting memory of his mother's face and the smell of her burning flesh gave him the courage to sit in the witness stand and face his father's wrath.

"Guilty!" the judge cried, and at the slam of his wooden gavel, Denny's father was handcuffed. As the two burly officers struggled to drag his father from the courtroom, the big man turned to face his son.

"Make you feel like a man now, boy? You ain't never gonna be a man! You as weak as your mama was! You'll let some woman run right over you! You'll never be a man!" The wooden door closed behind him like the lid of a coffin, final, complete, leaving his father's words draping over him like a heavy wool blanket.

~ ~ ~ ~ ~

Denny made sure no one saw him crouched in the woods just beyond the gravesite, mumbling to himself as they lowered his father's casket into the ground. *I'm glad you're dead,* he whispered to himself. *I wish I would've done it years ago. Look what you've done to me.* His thoughts reverted to his tiny daughter, her mouth open like a squawking bird. Denny remembered standing over her a year earlier, a feather pillow clamped in his hands. *My father would've handled it that way, did handle it that way.* He remembered gasping for his own air, his father's thick hands clamped over his mouth and nose until he went limp in his father's arms. "That'll shut you up for a while!" Denny had heard his father's voice rumbling in his head as he'd closed his own eyes and pushed the pillow onto his daughter's screaming frame, her tiny legs flailing beneath his weight. *How had things gotten so out of hand?* He shuddered, shaking the memory from his mind. He could have never done that, *yet he knew that he had.*

The tiny funeral group dispersed, each nodding to the others as they strode away from the grave. From the woods, Denny watched Maureen as she turned back toward the casket, sadly shook her head, and climbed in the pastor's car, their daughter swinging in her arms.

He squatted to rest on the trunk of a log, drinking, and waited. The last of the sun's glow had disappeared beneath the forest's covering before Denny drove his vehicle to the back of the graveyard, pulled a shovel and a can of kerosene from the bed of the truck, and staggered to his father's grave. He dug for hours, the newly covered tomb not easily reopened, the smell of fresh soil mixing with whiskey. He reached the wooden box just before midnight, the firm taps of metal on wood signaling his find. He punched a hole in the wooden casket with the shovel blade, tearing at the wood until the light from his truck beams revealed the shadow of his father's body. He lit a candle and held it over his father's face, the wax dropping like tears onto the old man's forehead. Blowing it out, he hunched over the box and splashed the kerosene up and down the corpse. He paused for just a moment, then spit — hard. Climbing out of the grave, drunk and angry, he struck a match and watched the flames jump from the hole and swallow the man who had murdered his mother.

He didn't remember much more than stumbling back to his vehicle, feeling the truck's rumbling surge through his body, eyeing the rearview mirror as the flames beat the air. The next morning, Jim Winters, the local cop, tapped on the window of Denny's truck after finding it in a ditch, Denny sprawled across the front seat as if he were dead. Denny's head was spinning as Jim placed him in the back of the squad car.

"Someone set your daddy on fire last night," Jim said, as nonchalantly as if he'd just shared the weather report. "Right there in his own coffin. Dug him up and set him on fire."

"That so?"

"Yup. Think it might've been the Taylor brothers. They've been in a bit of trouble lately. Now they've gone and disappeared."

"Hummm," was all Denny could manage before he hurled his stomach onto the backseat.

Maureen was standing at the window when the squad car pulled up. From the street, Denny couldn't tell whether she was mad or not. Her red hair was all bunched up, her eyes almost pinched shut as she stared down at him. It didn't matter. All he cared about was a shower and a drink. She was waiting in the kitchen, practically attacking him as the door swung open.

"Get off me, Maureen!" he said, shrugging his arms in the air.

"Denny, I didn't know what happened to you! I was so scared." She flung her arms around him again, pulling him close. He pushed her, knocking her to the ground. It felt good, pushing her.

"Denny!" Maureen said picking herself up from the floor. "What did you do that for? I was just worried."

"Listen, Maureen," he said, moving toward her, "I don't need no woman questioning me, you hear?" He grabbed her arm, squeezing until she pulled away. "I'll do the questioning. I'm the boss in this family."

After that, Denny came home later and later every day, the stench of whiskey cloaking the room when he entered. A few weeks later, it amazed him when Maureen gathered courage and spoke up.

"We can't go on like this. We don't have enough money for the bills," she pleaded.

"Shut up, Maureen!" He stood toe-to-toe with her, his lips curling over his teeth.

"But—" The word was barely out of her mouth when his hand landed hard on her face for the first time, sending her reeling backward.

"It's about time you helped out, Maureen," he said, standing over his cowering wife.

"You're going to go to work at my uncle's restaurant. We'll see how you like slaving away all day."

The next morning, he was sober. "I'm so sorry, Maureen. I don't know what I was thinking." He rubbed his hand over his face and shook his head. "Forgive me, will you? I know things have been just a little tough. It really would help if you'd think about working, though. Will you?"

"I don't know how long I can help, Denny," Maureen said, her back turned toward her husband. "I'm pregnant again."

He felt his shoulders slump as though someone had climbed on his back.

"That's just great, Maureen," he said half-heartedly as he walked up behind her, wrapping his arms around her small frame. "It's not great timing, but we'll be OK."

A neighbor watched Stephanie on the afternoons Maureen worked at Douay's Restaurant. For a while, Denny was content to not be carrying the whole burden of their debt and quickly adapted to the extra income, moving them to a bigger apartment and then later to their first home on Richard Street. But the reality that Maureen seemed to be enjoying her work at the restaurant more than he'd anticipated made him wonder if he'd given up too much control of his wife to strangers.

Chapter 7

Emily
April 1950
Perth, New Brunswick

IT WAS EARLY APRIL WHEN JOHN AND ELLEN drove Carol to Perth to stay with Maureen until the new baby arrived. No one mentioned the bruises on Maureen's face and Stephanie's arms, though John had seen the tense exchanges between his daughter and her husband the few times Denny had come to Plaster Rock with his family.

"Is he hitting you, Maureen?" her father had asked.

"Why do you always think the worst, Dad?" she retorted, her face bristling with anger. "I'm just clumsy, that's all. He's a good man, and any bruises I have are my own fault."

John sucked in a deep breath, his shoulders heaving as he released it. He gathered Stephanie and Ellen and said good-bye without further questions, noting they'd be back a short time after the new baby was born. At least they'd have some time with Stephanie. Protect her. He stopped on the porch on their way out and righted a rocking chair that lay upended near the steps. He squatted to pull a few weeds from the unkempt flowerbed that reflected the mood inside. Maureen watched through the window, understanding his involuntary responses, knowing her father's way. She clenched her jaw as she saw his head drop to his chest, the hair on her neck rising.

"Why doesn't he just leave?" she spit out as she let the curtain slide back over the unwashed window. "What's he trying to prove? I don't need his prayers."

"Maureen," Carol said, "he's just worried about you."

"How do you stand it, Carol?" Maureen replied. "I know you've got to be glad to be here for a while. Away, I mean?"

"I like it at home," Carol said, reaching to touch her sister's bruised arm. "Mum and Dad love us, Maureen, and they just want to be sure you are happy."

"I'm just fine," Maureen said, pulling her arm away. "Why can't they see I'm happy?" She moved back to the window, pulled open the lace curtain, and stared at the car as it pulled out of the dirt driveway. "I'm just fine," she whispered.

Sixteen-year-old Carol had been with Maureen just over a week when the regular intervals of pain indicated that the day had come. The midwife arrived just after midnight. Maureen was doubled up, the sweat running down her face with each contraction, her fingers white as she clutched the bedsheets. A scream, long and loud, pierced the air. Carol dabbed at her sister's face with a cold rag and squeezed her hand for the next six hours as she writhed in pain. From the bottom of the stairs, Denny yelled angrily, "Are you ever gonna have that baby?" When the child arrived, it burst from Maureen's womb with an angry cry.

The smells of fresh-baked chicken and yeast rolls rose through the air as Carol prepared dinner a few nights later. Maureen was napping on the couch in the living room when Denny pressed through the back door, a grin crimping his face.

"I thought you were headed home today, Carol," he said with a slur.

"Uh — no — Mum and Dad will be here tomorrow, if that's OK with you," Carol said, wrapping her hands in a kitchen towel.

"Mmmmmm. Fine with me." He staggered toward her. "Where's she at?"

"She and the baby are sleeping. I told her I'd wake her for dinner." Carol moved away from him toward the stove and began stirring the chicken stew, an uneasiness creeping over the room. Denny stepped in behind her, forcing his body into Carol's and pinning her to the stove.

"So we've got a little time alone?" His breath was hot on her neck.

"Stop it!" Carol cried.

"Denny!" Maureen's voice was sharp.

Carol whirled around, knocking the spoon to the floor, her face reddening.

"Aw, Maureen," Denny slurred, "we're just having a little fun, weren't we, Carol?" A big grin crossed his face.

"Maureen — he — he—" Carol pushed away from him.

"I know—" Maureen said, motioning Carol toward her with a toss of her head. "He doesn't mean anything by it. Now, go on. We'll talk later." She passed the baby to Carol.

Carol looked at Denny, saw the muscles in his face tighten, and then glanced at her sister as she backed out of the room. Inside the bedroom, Carol clicked the lock shut and pushed a chair in front of the door. Even her sister's anguished cries did not bring her out.

They sat in silence at the breakfast table the next morning, Carol as though she'd just left the morgue.

"Honey, can I get you any more coffee?" Denny asked in a syrupy sweet voice. "Now that Carol's going home, maybe we can find a babysitter to help you out from time to time, dear."

The women glanced at each other, neither looking up when he spoke. Maureen's lips were cut and swollen. Her left eye had morphed into a ghastly lump the colors of a rainbow. Their baby lay silent, nursing from Maureen's cut-up breast.

When John and Ellen arrived with Stephanie, Denny met them at the front door. Carol was holding the new baby on the porch, her suitcase standing ready. Denny apologized for Maureen's sudden headache, glancing at Carol as he spoke, telegraphing what he'd do to Maureen if she said anything. Denny ordered Stephanie in the door and pulled his new daughter, Emily, from Ellen's arms, mumbling as the front door clicked his hurried good-bye. Maureen watched from the bedroom window, her eyes catching Carol's as they drove away. They wouldn't see each other again until harvest time.

Chapter 8

Maureen
September 1950
Perth, New Brunswick

IN VICTORIA COUNTY, ALL WORK CEASED in September when the potato crop was ripe for picking. Self-employed men scheduled their work around the potato crop; a good portion of the family's income was made during the three weeks of harvest. All able-bodied men and women stopped their year-round work to pick. Children were dismissed from school to aid the family with the yield. Rarely were babysitters needed. Maureen latched her baby to her body in a makeshift burlap bag sling, swinging Emily forward and back as she bowed in the cool air of the September morning. Carol picked beside her, the conversation light and easy. Denny eyed the women from three rows away.

"Are you all right?" Carol asked. "I've been worried sick about you since I left."

"I'm fine, Carol," Maureen said as she hugged her sister. "Really, that night was just a mistake. Denny had been drinking, and you know how men can be." Maureen pulled back from her sister and looked in Denny's direction. "He wanted me to tell you how sorry he was. It'll never happen again. He promised."

Maureen's voice was pleading. Carol thought her sister did look well. Maybe she'd just been there at a bad time. Marriages were like that.

"I just needed to know you were OK," Carol said. Maureen bobbed her head and held her sister's hand as they gathered the potatoes to the end of their row.

The foreman assigned each picker a length of row, known as a section, and staked the beginning and end of each strip. Every man, woman, and child had a section of varying length. They picked the row clean to the end of their stake and then moved the stake to the next row, where they bent and began again in the opposite direction.

The plows moved across the rich, dark soil, two steel discs discharging the potatoes from their earthy lairs, exposing the fruit and releasing the fragrance of rich, tilled soil. Large wooden barrels were placed at intervals between each of their rows. Maureen began at one end of her line, hunched over, a huge woven basket placed between her open legs. Searching the ground for the hidden crop, her hands sank deep into the black dirt, plucking the fruit and tossing it into the basket. Moving forward, she pitched the basket ahead, then leaped like a hopscotching frog, her child rocking between her breasts. When the container was full, she rose, placed the basket on her hip, staggered to the barrel, and dumped the heavy cargo into the waiting wooden cask.

The field dance went on all day, bobbing bodies rising and lowering, the thumping of rolling potatoes hitting wood, echoing across the fields. All workers were paid by the barrel, so they raced through the rows like marathon runners gathering medals at a finish line.

Breaks were rare. A whistle announced a quick stop for water. Another for a half-hour lunch, when men gathered to smoke cigarettes and women gossiped. Young children such as Stephanie acted like circus clowns, sometimes tipping barrels and jumping inside as other children rolled them around the fields.

Laughter broke the monotony of the tractor's hum. When the whistle signaled the end of the day, there was a slow rise of bodies from their bent positions. Men rubbed their backs and wiped their brows with dirty hands. A mother's call gathered children as though they were a brood of wandering ducks. During the harvest, no one remembered anything more than the ache of muscles, long days, and short nights in which sleep was as instantaneous as death. Maureen loved harvest time. It was the land that refreshed her, the toil of a day's work in the fresh air, not the cramped, greasy diner on Main Street she'd be returning to when the fields were cleared of the crop. Besides, Denny never hit her during harvest time.

Chapter 9

Maureen
May 1954
Perth, New Brunswick

THE DINER, DOUAY'S RESTAURANT, was named after Denny's family. His uncle, Roger Douay, had bought and refurbished it right after he returned from the invasion of Normandy during World War II. The restaurant flanked the Saint John River, but its builders had ignored the river's beauty, installing only one big window overlooking Main Street. It was the place where gossip began.

Jo Stafford's song "You Belong to Me" was playing on the radio the morning that Denny swaggered into the restaurant, the screeching hinges of the screen door announcing his arrival. He'd often stop into Douay's for a cup of coffee during supply runs, the smell of fresh cinnamon rolls and the chance to check on Maureen drawing him. A few locals called, "Hello, Denny." He bobbed his head in reply, never taking the time to start a conversation with people he didn't know or like. His face was worn and tanned, with deep ridges cutting like rivers around his mouth. He always seemed to be moving with a purpose.

Maureen was leaning deep into a conversation with a stranger at the end of the counter when she saw him. Denny's face tightened, and he quickened his stride. He grabbed her elbow and whispered in her ear between clenched teeth, his grip tightening on her arm. She pulled against him — hard. His hand dropped. She glanced around to see if anyone noticed, then followed him into the kitchen. Their voices were harsh and hushed behind the kitchen door. Patrons glanced back and forth at each other, shrugged their shoulders, and continued their conversations.

"How come every time I come in here, you're flirting with someone, huh?" Denny said, grabbing Maureen by her forearms. "You expect me to believe nothing's going on?"

"You're crazy, Denny," Maureen whispered as she tried to break away from his tightening grip. "I have to be nice to people. They tip me good."

"Maybe because they're paying for more than their meal." Denny jerked her close again. Maureen's arm flew loose and knocked a glass from the kitchen counter, sending crystal shards around the floor. Her husband's hands thrust at her neck, and her face reddened like a puffy balloon. She fought back, her arms thrashing as though she were a rag doll.

"Maureen? Everything all right in there?" a customer called.

Denny's face shot toward the door. His hold softened, allowing Maureen's gasping body to slump to the floor. Denny towered over her, the veins in his neck wild with pumping blood.

"Get in the other room," he hissed, his arm swinging to point her way out. He pushed his fingers through his slick hair. "I'm sorry," he said. "I don't know what got into me. It's just—" His voice faded, and he extended his hand to Maureen, who lay sobbing quietly on the aging linoleum.

"Maureen! More coffee!" the man yelled through the closed door. In another minute, she breezed out, her neck red from Denny's anger.

"You old coot," she said. "Get your own coffee." She flashed a fake smile and rubbed at her reddened neck. Denny emerged behind her and followed her to the coffeepot, poured himself a cup, and then swirled around to stare at the man Maureen had been talking to. The stranger was reading the paper, his hatless head close to the counter. Denny stretched to kiss Maureen good-bye. She twisted her face away. He slammed the cup down and stormed out, a puddle of hot liquid making its way to the edge of the counter and onto the floor. She grabbed a wet dishrag and swung around to wipe the liquid from the counter. Her eyes never followed Denny, instead focusing on the man at the end of the counter and then on a spot of apple pie that clung to the turquoise countertop, a spot she couldn't seem to rub away.

Chapter 10

Maureen
March 1955
Perth, New Brunswick

MAUREEN ANNOUNCED HER THIRD PREGNANCY the night Denny got a new job as foreman of a small subdivision being built on the edge of town. He'd been drinking less, content, it seemed, with the thaw of winter. His face hinted at a glimmer of joy when he heard the news. Seven-year-old Stephanie glanced cautiously back and forth at her mother and father, aware that this mood might change with one celebratory drink.

They ate dinner in peace for the first time in months. By the time Maureen tucked the girls in bed, their faces echoed the joy of the night. Moments later, Maureen slipped into the bedroom, expecting Denny's arms to envelop her with the love she'd not felt from him since the night the coming child was conceived.

But while he'd waited for her in the room, Denny's mood had changed. "How in the hell are we going to feed another mouth?!" he screamed, banging his fists on the dresser, sending shivers throughout the house.

The beating Maureen received that night was only the beginning. Three days later, her eyes still throbbed from beneath the somber swell of her face when her teenage babysitter, Samantha Bevins, confronted her.

"Your husband forced himself on me a few of months ago, Mrs. Douay," the girl said, her arms wrapped tightly across her chest. "I've got no money. Nowhere to go. I'm pregnant. You've got to help me," Samantha pleaded.

"Are you sure? I can't imagine him doing anything like that," Maureen said, well aware that he would. She'd heard the rumors about Denny's other women.

"I'll have to go to the police."

"No!" Maureen's reply was sharp. "We'll work something out." She wrung her hands one over the other, her eyes darting around the yard as if she were fearful that someone had heard this horrible confession.

"If word gets out," she whispered, talking to herself, "we'll be ruined." She ushered Samantha into the house, grazing past Emily as she played on the back porch. *Who will come to the restaurant to support such scandalous people? Denny's a carpenter. Who'll hire him or trust him ever again?*

For the rest of the afternoon, Maureen pretended that everything was fine, playing hide-and-seek with Emily, awaiting Denny's return from work. When he arrived, he brushed past Maureen with little more than a peck on her cheek and wound his way upstairs for a bath. Maureen forgot about Emily as she prepared to confront Denny with his sin.

He was in the bathtub. Stephanie was at the neighbor's house. Maureen had sent Samantha to gather the laundry from the clotheslines before the storm set in. She knocked and then pushed at the door before he could protest. From the partially opened door, she saw that he already had his eyes closed, his right hand draped out of the tub, clutching the silver thermos.

"Why, Denny?" She swallowed hard.

"What the hell are you babbling about?" He sat upright, the water rushing toward his hips.

"She's pregnant."

"What?"

Maureen didn't move.

"How did this happen?" he asked, dragging his hand to his face, rubbing at it over and over.

"How do you think it happened, Denny? Haven't you put us through enough?"

"Does anyone else know?" His face was white and hard.

"Not yet." Maureen turned and reached for a towel from the rack above the toilet.

"The girl doesn't have anywhere else to go." She held her arms close to her body and swung her head from side to side in disbelief.

As he stood, she looked over his muscled body in the mirror's reflection. She could feel her face crinkle with disgust.

"Look what you've done to us — to her." Her words were peppered with hatred.

"Shut up, Maureen. I'm trying to think." He wiped his hand over his face, then his head, the droplets of water trickling down his body, latching to the thick, dark hair on his legs.

"I told her she could stay here until the baby is born." Maureen turned toward the open door and stared past the hallway into the closet. Emily's eyes reflected back at her through the sliver of the opening in the closet door. She pulled her hand to her mouth to cover her words.

"You what?" He stepped from the bathtub and jerked the towel from Maureen's hand.

"What am I supposed to do, Denny? Throw her in the street? Let her tell everyone that the baby is yours?" Maureen faced him fully again, lowering her voice so that Emily couldn't hear, and then pushed him. "What were you thinking? I'm pregnant, and you can't keep your hands off the housekeeper for what, even three months?"

She raised her hand to strike him, but he grabbed her wrist and twisted her arm until she swung away. He pulled her arm up tight into her back and jerked her close, his voice just above a whisper in her ear. Maureen prayed Emily couldn't see them.

"You've been sick for three months. I've got needs, Maureen." Denny wrenched her arm upward again. She winced, the pain driving into her shoulders. He thrust her head at the open door. She felt something in her face give way like a rotting board, and she fell forward, part in, part out of the bathroom. The warm blood pooled near her face on the cold tile. She saw Emily, cupped in the shadow of the hall closet, her eyes pinched tight, her tiny fists balled at her mouth.

"You'll see to it that she stays inside and speaks to no one, or you'll both be sorry. Hear me?" Pulling Maureen by the hair, he dragged her back into the bathroom and slammed the door.

Maureen was half-conscious when she heard Samantha's approaching footsteps. Denny kneeled to cover Maureen's mouth, signaling silence with his index finger on his lips.

"Mrs. Douay? Are you all right?"

He pulled his hand from her face and stood up, swinging the bathroom door open and moving into the hall, only a towel wrapped at his waist. Maureen hunched on the floor behind him, arched like a heaving cat. She couldn't contain her vomit.

"Mrs. Douay is just fine, Samantha. Glad to have you staying with us a while. You two can sleep in your room." He smirked at the girl as he passed. Too close. Maureen remembered nothing more as the day spun into a dark tornado of helplessness. She awoke hours later in the tiny bedroom, Samantha standing over her with damp, bloody rags, a look of pity and fear stamped on her face.

"Thank God you're alive, Mrs. Douay." She dipped a clean cloth into a basin of cold water that sat on the oak dresser. "He's drunk again. I told Stephanie to stay at her friend's tonight. I found Emily in the hall closet. She fell limp as a rag doll when I tried to pull her out. She's terrified. I think she saw everything. I stayed with her until she fell asleep."

Maureen's swollen lips wouldn't part. *Poor Emily. At least he didn't find Stephanie tonight. He's never beaten Emily, but Stephanie?* Samantha forced a sip of water into Maureen's mouth, gagging her as it trickled down her throat.

"I'm going to the police this time, Mrs. Douay." Her voice was pleading. "We have to get help before he kills you."

A sharp pain drove through Maureen's head as she tried to shake it. She grabbed at Samantha's arm, squeezing as she mumbled through her broken jaw, "Nooooo!"

Samantha's tears fell like salt crystals, stinging Maureen's cuts, causing her to tug her arm away from the girl. *I'm sure things will get better. I'll apologize for angering him — explain that I'll keep Samantha hidden — work something out. People can't know. It's my fault, after all.*

Chapter 11

Emily
April 1955
Perth, New Brunswick

EMILY'S ONLY HAPPY CHILDHOOD MEMORY of her father was of how she'd danced on his feet the day she turned five. Denny waltzed into the kitchen with the news that Maureen was having a new baby, picking Emily up and swinging her around before he pulled her close. Emily loved the smell in the crook of his neck, a sweet smell she'd remember always. Old Spice. Stephanie bounced down the stairs, her face looking sour as though she'd bitten a lemon. Samantha, the babysitter, pushed her head from the upstairs bedroom and watched the spectacle unfold below, her forehead furrowed, the lines unbecoming at her young age.

"Put on that new Bill Haley record, Maureen!" Denny said, a smile covering his tanned face. "Come on, girls, we've got to celebrate!"

Maureen rushed across the room and placed *Rock Around the Clock* onto the record player, pausing to clap as Denny dropped Emily onto his shoes. Clasping her hands, he moved around the room, Emily's feet pushed tightly against her father's work boots. Years later, she would recall the warmth of his face as he beamed down at her. She remembered that moment specifically. It was locked in her mind, a snapshot of her father before he stopped loving her.

Emily was hiding in the upstairs hall closet playing hide-and-seek with her mother when her father arrived home that night. There was a flurry of footsteps as he passed by her and disappeared into the bathroom. She waited silently for her mother to find her, but her mother followed her father, forgetting the game. Emily pushed at the closet door. A soft glow shot through the closet. In the bathroom to her left, she heard the rising anger of her father's voice. She closed her eyes and pulled her fists to her face, afraid again. She heard a woman's cry and peeked between the cracks in the door to see her mother lying on the bathroom floor, blood trickling from her mouth. Emily's fear was mirrored in her mother's face. Maureen's eyes were pleading with Emily to be silent. Emily was afraid to cry, to move. Hours later, long after her father had slammed the door to his bedroom, Samantha found her in the closet, curled like a beaten dog.

The mood of the house changed. Maureen began to sleep with Samantha in the tiny room at the end of the hall. Stephanie was conspicuously absent, spending several nights at a girlfriend's house, two blocks away. Samantha warned Emily to stay out of her father's way. For a week, it felt as though someone had wrapped the house in a veil, the anger of her father darkening every corner of every room. Emily had no understanding of the silence that had settled on their lives. She was a child until the night her father stripped her innocence away.

Emily remembered first hearing the creak of the third step many days after the stillness cloaked the house. The door to her bedroom opened, a sliver of light outlining the frame of her father as he invaded the room. He paused, the bright red glow of his cigarette highlighting the circle of smoke that swirled up around his head. He tapped the cigarette butt onto the heel of his shoe and then shifted toward Emily's bed.

He kissed her on the cheek, his sun-peeled lips scraping across her skin. His breath was hot and smelled like diesel fuel. This was a game, she thought, clamping her eyes shut as she pretended to sleep. Her eyelids fluttered as she feigned slumber.

In a swift move, he clamped his callused hand over her mouth and warned her to be quiet. She began to kick, recognizing something ugly in the man whose shoes she'd danced on just a few months earlier. She wiggled free and cried out. He grabbed at her and covered her mouth, pushing her nightgown up and away from her body. His hands were strong; Emily's strength was no match for her father's. His hand roamed from her mouth, tracing a path down her small chest, landing between her legs.

His breathing accelerated. She felt a finger enter her, having no understanding that it would not be long before he hovered over her with his thick, heavy body and hurt her with something much bigger than his finger. When it was over, Denny lay beside her, panting like a winning horse.

He whispered, "Don't tell anyone, even your mother, or I'll kill you all. I love you." And then he scraped his lips across her cheek and was gone, leaving Emily to rub her aching crotch, pushing away her stinging tears. No one noticed her cloud of silence or the way she pulled at her panties as she sat at the kitchen table the next day. She'd forever be afraid of the dark, waiting for the next warning creak of the third step and the act that would follow whenever his shadow crossed her bedroom door.

Chapter 12

Maureen
June 1955
Perth, New Brunswick

CAROL AND HER HUSBAND, GEORGE, suggested to Maureen that Emily and Stephanie join them at the Hartland Baptist Bible Camp for the summer. Carol loved the children who surrounded them there; they made her forget her own barrenness.

"Come on, Maureen," Carol insisted. "The girls will be fine. I'm one of the chaperones. Besides, you look like you could use the rest before the baby comes."

Maureen paced back and forth on the cracked linoleum, understanding that Carol knew it wouldn't take much convincing. Her sister had seen the marks on Maureen's face, knew what Denny did. People around Plaster Rock were talking about Denny's violent temper and his liaisons with other women. It could just be rumors, Maureen had told her — after all, Denny had that reputation even before he and Maureen were married.

Maureen had told Carol she'd probably asked for it, nagging at Denny, taunting him by bringing a pretty young girl like Samantha into their lives just to help her with the children. She'd confessed she hadn't been an angel, either, flirting with men at the diner for extra tips. But she'd seen that it had shocked Carol when she told her about Denny's temper with Emily just a few weeks earlier.

"He never forgave me for not reminding him about his lunch," Maureen told Carol, reliving the event.

She'd gathered Emily and the metal lunch pail that morning, hurriedly pushing her daughter toward the door. Denny had taken the truck, and Samantha had already left to walk Stephanie to school. It was two months after Emily's fifth birthday. The spring air was heavy and moist. Maureen ordered Emily to walk close to her side, her tiny hand wrapped around the handle of the black, battered pail. They walked for what Maureen thought must have seemed like hours to the little girl, her daughter's legs pecking the oiled surface of the tar-laden road, the lunch pail banging her left side.

"We're almost there." Maureen told her. "Just one more corner."

The pounding of the hammer covered the sound of their approach. Thump. Thump. Thump. Thump. Maureen smelled the sweetness of freshly cut two-by-fours, heard the pull of the sharp-toothed saw against the clean, white lumber. She could see the roofers on the top of the house, bent over like pickers of cotton. Their flannel shirts were soaked with sweat, their mechanical moves ordered and meticulous.

One man was pulling at a black, sparkling shingle wedge, tossing it to another who banged it on the tar paper and quickly hammered the piece into place. In moments, he'd shifted his position, hopping to his right, where he extended his hand for the next piece. The dance continued until the full roof was covered with a new dark covering.

Maureen saw her husband, his back wet and muscled through his shirt, as he reached upward to bang at the porch overhang. The precision with which he hit every nail was measured and systematic. Even from behind, his anger was evident in the stiffness of how he worked. They were entering the long gravel driveway when Maureen heard her husband call to his men.

"Break, fellas!" Denny yelled, climbing up the ladder he'd positioned on the front porch.

The tools' hollow drop echoed to the unfinished roof as the men made their way from the top of the house to the shade trees near their parked pickup trucks. Denny kept pounding at the overhang.

"Denny!" one of the men had called, "break is for you, too, you know."

His hammer stopped in midair. Denny whirled around, a wild look etched deep in his tanned face. By now Maureen had reached the front lawn of the new house. Denny caught her movement from the corner of his eye, his face reddening. He dropped his hammer, the metal making an empty thump as it struck the porch floor. He looked left toward his coworkers as they broke into wide, mocking grins, picking their teeth with splinters of wood. He looked back at Maureen and strode toward her, the muscles in his face tight as though he were clenching his jaw. Maureen pulled the black lunch bucket from Emily's hand, holding it in front of her like a sacrifice, her other arm across her pregnant stomach. Denny latched his hand over her elbow and pulled her to the side of the half-built house, out of sight of the others.

"You trying to make me look like a fool?" he hissed between his teeth.

"I — I — just thought you'd forgotten it," Maureen had said.

His hand came fast and hard on Maureen's face. She gasped, dropped the lunch box, and drew her hand to cover the reddening flesh.

"*You* forgot it!" he said.

Her daughter's eyes widened just before she broke into wailing sobs. Denny pitched toward Emily, grabbing her by her shoulders and shaking her before Maureen could recover. Emily's neck snapped forward and back, over and over, like a rubber band. She fell limp in his hands and crumpled to the ground, her thick-strapped dress scrunching up around her tiny, sweating body.

"No. Denny. No!" Maureen screamed as she pushed him from the lifeless child.

Maureen stooped to the red clay driveway, gathering Emily into her arms. The scream had alerted the others, and they rounded the corner of the house, running. Denny whirled at them, standing in front of Maureen and Emily to shield them from the others' view.

"She fell, guys," Denny yelled at them, flicking his hand as though dismissing troops. "She'll be OK. Get back to work."

The men stared for a moment, shrugged their shoulders, and turned to leave, their lunch break cut short by the disruption.

"Get out of here, and don't ever come back to my job," Denny told Maureen, dipping his body toward the red dirt to retrieve his lunch pail.

As he rounded the corner of the rough-framed house, Maureen could hear his high-pitched whistle through the fog of her thumping head. She clutched their little girl, watching Denny until he disappeared.

"Emily, I know he loves us," she told her daughter. "He just gets a little mad now and then." As Maureen walked away, the suffocating feeling she'd felt in her youth moved over her again, that feeling she'd tried so hard to leave behind. Somehow, she'd never managed to escape it.

Chapter 13

Carol Polk Timmons
June 1955
Hartland, New Brunswick

TWO SUITCASES LEANED AGAINST the blue church bus a week later. Carol had been right. Maureen needed rest, with her third baby coming and all. Maybe now she'd have time to formulate a plan for the housekeeper's child, too. No one would blame Maureen — Carol was sure of that — but she was also sure the girl would have to move away from Perth. Such things weren't tolerated in small towns, especially if Samantha wouldn't say who the father was.

Carol begged Maureen to let Samantha know she'd take the baby. No one in Plaster Rock would guess where the child came from. She and George had made no secret that they were trying to adopt. In fact, Carol suggested that George wouldn't even have to know. They'd signed all the papers. The agency said that when and if a baby was available, only one of them would have to accept the child, just in case George was out of town. Carol would think of something, if Samantha would only consider it.

Carol hoped their parents hadn't heard the gossip. Maureen had been enough of a disappointment without their hearing about her caring for this unfortunate girl — as though she didn't have enough on her hands. Carol couldn't understand why Maureen was helping Samantha. Imagine living under the same roof with that girl. But maybe Denny didn't hit Maureen with the girl there. Whatever the case, Carol was happy to be leaving for the summer and glad to be taking the girls with her. At least they'd be away from that turmoil for a while.

The drive to Hartland was the biggest adventure the girls had ever had. Stephanie was unsure about the whole situation; at seven years old, she'd told Carol she was too big for the whole summer camp thing. She stood by her mother's car, her shoulders slumped in discontent. Carol approached to tell her that eight-year-old Jake Adams was going, and then she all but fainted with excitement.

"Well," Stephanie said slowly, trying to hide her pleasure, "I guess summer camp sounds better than being home, with Mom and Sam having babies and Dad drinking and mad all the time."

Such talk from a child. Carol glanced at her sister and then around the area to be sure the pastor hadn't heard their conversation.

"Stephanie, honey, please don't say those things in front of anyone. You don't want people to think poorly of your mother, do you?" Carol said.

The girl shrugged her shoulders and looked around as though she couldn't care less and then ran to board the bus, her cotton skirt billowing as she moved. Emily clung to her mother's bulbous frame, her hand under her own dress, pulling at her underwear.

"Are you OK, Emily?" Carol asked, touching the girl's chin and raising it to face her own. Emily's eyes appeared swollen and blue, as though she'd been stung by a bee. "Ladies don't do that," Carol said, pulling her niece's hand out from under the crinoline.

"She's just fine, Carol," Maureen snapped. "She fell last night. She's fine, aren't you, dear?"

Emily stared at her feet, pushing one over the other as she bobbed her head up and down. Anger surged through Carol's body, prickling her skin.

"Come on, Carol! Let's go!" George yelled from just yards away.

"Be good for Aunt Carol, and have fun at camp!"

Maureen shouted good-bye to Stephanie and then patted Emily on the head as though she were a dog someone insisted she touch. Carol thought Maureen seemed a bit too anxious to let her children go to camp, but then again, Carol knew her sister well enough to realize how stifling the life Maureen had chosen must be. *Two children and one on the way. A job. An abusive husband. Not quite what Maureen had in mind for herself when she'd left Plaster Rock.*

Emily walked stiffly beside her aunt, boarding the bus like a compliant soldier. She stood on the cracked black seat and stared blankly out the window at her stony-faced mother. Carol thought Emily seemed ready to cry, but the tears didn't come. She didn't recognize this child. Just months ago, Emily was as bright as a field of wildflowers. Now she stood as lifeless as a blown-out candle.

In moments, Maureen was gone, the Pontiac careening from the church parking lot as though a rocket were latched to it. Emily fell like a stone to the leather seat, looking forward, eyeing the arriving stream of children who were beginning to stomp noisily onto the bus.

Mr. Belcamp had volunteered to drive the old school bus. The vehicle was stuffed with small rucksacks and large boxes of food and supplies that tumbled from the bus when the door was edged open to accommodate more luggage. Several men and women of the church, designated camp counselors, snaked behind the bus in assorted vehicles. Carol rode two seats behind the girls, next to Mary Belcamp, the church's pianist.

The bus buzzed with excitement. Two or three children piled into each leather seat, their fingers wrapped over the bench in front of them. They bobbed and weaved back and forth as the bus hummed its way south.

Stephanie huddled near several of her summer church friends, eyeing Jake, who sat two seats ahead. Emily was pushed up next to the window, clutching a plastic Kewpie doll she'd received from a nurse a year earlier when her tonsils were removed. Six-year-old brat Dave Cook was planted next to her, poking his chubby finger at Emily's doll until Emily cried. Carol reached up and tapped him on the shoulder, eying him until he left Emily alone. She knew it wouldn't last long; he acted up in church, too. He was quite the pest, provoking other children time and again when he had the chance.

All of the counselors wondered if they'd done the right thing, allowing these little ones to be away from their parents for so long. But for so many, it seemed the time far from home might be the best option for the children. Dave's father beat him mercilessly, working him like a grown man. Carol had noted how the boy ran to the bus when his pale mother had walked him into town. He never once looked back as the bus pulled away. And Emily appeared puny and foreign, like an abandoned child with little knowledge of where she was going or why. Carol watched from behind as her niece hugged her doll and stared at the passing landscape, the telephone poles clicking by.

Emily turned again to the window. She was oddly quiet, her face pressed against the glass. She'd probably seen Denny hit Maureen. Carol stiffened at the fleeting thought that Denny might have hit this child, too — that her bruises were from his angry hands. But no — even he wouldn't hurt such a small child. His child. Would he? She put the thought away and returned to her conversation with Mary.

The bus screeched to a halt on the west side of the bridge, jolting several of the children from their seats. The Hartland Bible Camp awaited their arrival on the other side of the Saint John River.

"OK, kids!" Mr. Belcamp's voice was sharp as he yelled into the rearview mirror. The voices went silent. "Right now we're crossing the longest wooden covered bridge in the world. Before we cross, take a good look to your left." He wiggled his hairy finger out the window. "There — across the river — you can see camp."

A cluster of twelve tiny cabins perched in an offset circle near the edge of the river, the unshaven grass of summer high against the dark-beamed structures. A white clapboard tabernacle rested farther back and to the right of the cluster. The banks of the river were low, graded to the water, making it easy to wade in. Several people stood in the river, splashing water into the air as they raced along its edge. One reveler noticed the bright blue bus and began to wave frantically.

Hanging out of the open bus windows, the children waved and cheered. Mr. Belcamp beeped the horn, revved the engine, and edged into the darkening bridge. The bus went silent for just a moment before Emily began to cry. Carol lunged forward, but Stephanie had already rushed to her sister's side.

"It'll be all right," Stephanie said as Emily buried her face in her sister's lap.

"Beeeeep."

Emily jumped again, a tiny scream forging from her lungs. The boy, Dave Cook, reached across Stephanie's lap and touched Emily's arm.

"It'll be OK, Emily," the boy said, his cherub face squeezed into a serious gaze. "I'll be right here."

Stephanie faced him, shook her head at her sister, and moved back to her seat. A smile grazed Carol's face when she saw Dave take Emily's hand. The rumbling floorboards of the bridge sent a hollow echo through the tunnel.

The children giggled and yelled for Mr. Belcamp to beep the horn again and again until they burst from the other side of the bridge and jutted left down a dirt road and into camp. Dave pulled Emily from the seat and held her hand as they filed off the bus. Carol's heart was warmed by his gesture, and she understood for the first time that he was not such a bad child.

Laura Cogswell, the spinster daughter of a local pastor, was assigned to Cabin D, where Stephanie and Emily and an assorted group of giggling girls assembled. Carol had known Laura for years; they'd attended church together since they were schoolgirls.

Laura was a quiet woman with a gigantic smile that dwarfed her tiny face. Though she was only twenty-four, an ancient tint of gray laced in and out of the dull brown color of her hair. But when she smiled, her whole body seemed to ignite, launching a feeling of happiness through the room that drew the giggling girls to her. She was an odd young woman, having never married. Yet Carol recognized the joy in her as that which could be attained only through the grace of God.

At the girls' cabin were four steep steps that led to a porch housing an oak swing. When anyone swung, the whole porch, steps and all, moved with it. Inside the small log structure were twelve bunks. An ominous outhouse stood behind the cabin, a narrow path joining the two. Because they were sisters, Emily and Stephanie were allowed to share the same bunk set. Carol settled into the cabin that loomed just feet away from that of the girls. The view out her window allowed her to see into the cabin and onto Emily's bed. Across the circle, Carol could also see the opening of the cabin where Dave resided. She resolved to tuck both children in before the night fell.

As the call for lights-out arrived, Carol stole into the girls' cabin. Emily was awake, her eyes wide and round, her fingers grasping the blankets that she'd pulled up to her neck. Every noise, every creak, every voice outside the little cottage seemed to be a siren to her, even as her sister lay snoring above her. Carol assured Emily that she was safe, but she was troubled that Emily clung so tightly to her hand. She stayed beside Emily until she felt the rhythmic rise and fall of her niece's chest, returning then to her front porch and stopping to breathe in the freshness of summer's first night.

The sound of chirping crickets broke her silence when she saw Emily's tiny face appear in the cabin's window, backlit by an oil lamp that hung above her head. Carol heard a tapping noise and turned to see a candle flickering in the cabin across the lawn. Dave's cabin. The light moved from side to side, shining on a small face. Dave Cook. She looked back at Emily, who was waving at him. He returned the wave.

Carol moved from the steps toward Emily's cabin, and the light disappeared. She heard a child's footsteps patter across the wood floor as she pushed into the cabin. Her shadow caused Emily to suck in a breath and lie as silent as a possum beneath the quilt. Her stillness puzzled Carol. Somehow Emily had learned to feign sleep, feign deadness. She reached for the quilt. Emily recoiled and then grasped at Carol in terror. Carol scooped Emily's hair from her face, cupping her niece's chin in her hands. Emily's eyes fluttered beneath pinched lids.

"You're safe here, Emily," Carol said with a soft voice. "God lives here." The assurance in her aunt's voice seemed calming, and in moments Emily was fast asleep.

* * *

The crackle of the morning campfire sent the rising smell of boiling porridge throughout the grounds, and one by one, the children emerged from the cabins, hungry and anxious for the days ahead. Over the weeks, Emily began to laugh the way Carol had witnessed during the past summers when Maureen had brought the children to visit their grandparents in Plaster Rock. Stephanie became a great helper in the camp's kitchen, working alongside the older girls. Emily, too, had blossomed. Unlike some of the children, Emily rarely cried, and never for home, hovering close to Dave Cook and Miss Cogswell when she needed comforting.

At meals, when the group prayed, Emily began to close her eyes, folding her hands and moving her lips to mimic those around her. Carol understood that her niece had begun to believe that God loved her. She offered to let Emily have her first turn at prayer in the girls' cabin that night. The little girl's plea was spoken barely above a whisper.

"Dear God, bless Mommy and Samantha and that new baby, and don't let Daddy hurt us anymore."

Carol doubled over, sickened by her niece's words. Her eyes searched the area to make sure no one had heard this little girl's prayer, and she cursed Denny, though she knew that wasn't what God would have her do. *If this child were mine, no one would ever harm her. What is Maureen thinking, staying there with that man?*

It was the last night of camp when Reverend Park called for everyone to meet at the edge of the river. The sun hung on the edge of the sky, blood red, hovering over a black land where the trees were silhouetted against the horizon. He handed each man, woman, and child a tiny cup with a candle and instructed the elders to assist in lighting and then securing them to the tin cups.

As the sun set, he prayed: "Father, we ask that you receive and grant the wishes of these children as they seek your grace and your wisdom. Keep them safe as they depart from this place, and bless them always with your presence and love."

The adults lit the candles one by one and instructed the children on how to drip the wax into the bottom of the tin, secure the candle in the wax, and make a wish before walking to the river's edge. Then they would place the cup upright in the water and allow the cup and their wish to float away into God's ears.

The children obeyed, and one at a time, cup after cup was pushed into the river, carrying away the desire of each person. The river was bright, soon lighting the banks of the shoreline, each prayer bobbing up and down as it drifted downriver. Stephanie waded in beside Jake, her eyes batting at her newfound love, her lips puckered as though she had bitten a lemon. Her wish was obvious enough.

Emily and Dave were among the last to launch their cups, Miss Cogswell restraining Dave by his arm as he tried to rush to the water's edge. Pulling away from her, he unleashed his cup with ease, the tiny flame moving effortlessly toward the others. The aluminum cup caught a swirl of water and twirled like a firecracker. The crowd clapped with delight. Carol clasped Emily's hand and walked slowly toward the river.

When Carol and Maureen were children, their mother had terrified them into thinking they would drown should their feet ever touch water, and Carol tensed now at the cool contact of the river. But Emily bent and slapped at the wet surface. Exuberant. Excitedly, she pushed the cup too deep, and water filled the container, extinguishing the flame. Carol lit her own candle, made a wish, and allowed Emily to make a wish, too, and try again. The candle drifted off slowly, carrying both wishes: one that would never be answered and one that, just three months later, would be.

Chapter 14

Carol
August 1955
Perth, New Brunswick

ON AUGUST 24, 1955, AN UNCOMMON HUMIDITY descended on New Brunswick. Windows were jammed open with wooden wedges to allow whatever breeze nature might spit venture through. Maureen began a long and fitful labor. Samantha and Carol remained beside her, wiping her face with a damp cloth, their nightgowns clinging to their sweating bodies. Maureen's swollen form heaved as the contractions strengthened.

Seven-year-old Stephanie and five-year-old Emily stretched their small bodies across the foot of Samantha's bed, falling asleep just after dark. Carol carried them to their beds, running her hand over their foreheads as they snuggled beneath their sheets.

"I need a light!" Emily's tiny voice squeaked in despair. Carol smiled back at her insecurity and flicked on the nightlight.

At 11:00 p.m., Denny swallowed another slug of whiskey and climbed the stairs to his room, leaving Samantha and Carol to birth his third child. Samantha was a slight girl with dark hair like that of Carol and George.

"It's moving," Samantha said quietly. Carol reached to touch the girl's inflated middle, her eyes closed, wondering what the child inside of her must feel like. Its tiny form punched Carol's hand.

"What are you going to do when the child is born?" Carol asked. Samantha turned away, wiping tears with the palm of her hand, and said nothing.

Suddenly a cry from the next bedroom had Carol rushing from the room. "No, Daddy!" the little girl whimpered in her sleep, her hand cupped between her legs. Carol pulled Emily into her arms and held her until she went limp, not allowing herself to think that her niece's dream might be a horrid reality.

Darren was born just after midnight, a full moon lighting the autumn sky. Carol packed a Moses basket into the backseat of her car and returned to Plaster Rock with the newborn baby while Maureen recovered and awaited the September birth of Samantha's bastard child. The potato fields were ready for harvest, as developed as the child who would burst from the womb of the woman whose child Carol longed for.

Watching for the green Pontiac a month later, Carol pulled back the worn curtains from the window of her brown clapboard house. Her eyes searched the long gravel driveway, her face swollen from the nights of tears since Maureen's call, knowing her sister's impending arrival would sweep Darren from her arms. George went to town; he couldn't face the removal of this child from their lives. He couldn't forgive Maureen, though they'd known all along that this day would come. They'd hoped Maureen might linger longer before her arrival. Carol would miss the boy, the baby who had been hers for these weeks.

A neighbor had noticed the diapers flapping on the clothesline the day after Darren arrived.

"My land, Carol, you'd think you had a baby!"

"I'm watching my sister's child for a few weeks. She's had a bit harder time recovering with this one. Practice," Carol said, "for when we adopt a baby of our own. Could be any time now!"

The neighbor nodded and smiled. Carol cupped the laundry basket to her left hip and hurried inside, still feeling uneasy about questions relating to Maureen's family. It all seemed strange, their keeping a young girl in the house who would bear some unknown father's baby. She wondered if her own father guessed that she knew more about Maureen's home life than she was telling.

Maureen arrived an hour later, well dressed, though her outfit was familiar. They were such opposites — Carol with mousy brown hair and in a clean calico housedress that was old-fashioned and frayed. Maureen was taller than Carol, and a redhead. Her wild hair and bright smile commanded an audience.

Carol met Maureen at the door, her hands punched into the pockets of her pink, ruffled apron, viewing her sister in a new light. She'd hated Maureen sometimes, or at least envied her... the way she always looked so put together. Her selfishness. Her quiver of children. The way she bragged about living away from Plaster Rock. But that had been before Carol really knew Denny and what he put her sister through.

But the old feelings resurfaced as Carol moved to the makeshift crib to retrieve the little boy she'd come to know as her own. Her barren womb felt emptier still after weeks of nurturing this baby. Weeks of lullabies, diaper changes, and giggles. Now she would have him ripped from her arms and her heart by a woman who cared more for some young tramp than for her own child.

Carol cried and held Darren like a sacrifice toward her sister. A flicker of sympathy sliced across Maureen's face. She seemed to sense the depth of her sister's pain, and she pushed Darren back at Carol.

"Oh, go ahead and keep him," Maureen said, her eyes wide and mischievous. "I've got more of them at home."

Carol was at first startled and then laughed out loud, although she felt a small resentment at Maureen's flippant gesture. Her own heart ached for a baby to call her own.

"Oh, Maureen, that's crazy. This baby is yours."

Maureen cradled Darren in her arms, strode to the car, and placed him in the backseat of the Pontiac. Carol watched, puzzled, as her sister shifted to the other side of the vehicle, her feet crunching on the ground beneath her. Maureen reached into a woven basket that rested on the seat beside Darren. She pulled a wiggling form, wrapped in a blue blanket, from the basket and twisted around to face her sister.

"Here is *your* son," Maureen said, tilting her head lovingly as she handed the infant to her sister. Carol's eyes went wide with surprise.

"What do you mean?" Carol said, pinching her eyebrows.

"Samantha died giving birth." Maureen folded her arms close to her body and looked at the ground. "She had no family. We had a private funeral. Denny says he's got a friend who'll take care of the adoption. I can't take on another child, Carol. I — I knew you'd want him." She looked at Carol, her eyes hiding something.

"Where's the baby's father? Who is he?"

Silence.

"It's Denny."

Carol swallowed a short breath, looking down at the boy and then back at her sister. Their eyes locked. The muscles in her face tightened as she clenched her jaw. She pulled her lips into a terse smile.

"I'll say I just got a call from the adoption agency, Maureen. That's all anyone needs to know. I'll call Mum and Dad after George gets home. Don't come home for a while. I'll need some time to think about this, to work out this lie without you around." Carol turned to walk inside, her arms warm from her newly found child. Then she stopped and turned to face Maureen. "We'll call him Peter."

Chapter 15

Emily
December 1958
Plaster Rock, New Brunswick

IT WOULD BE THREE YEARS before Emily's mother would return to Plaster Rock, instead allowing Carol to pick up the children for their annual summer and holiday visits. She excused herself with white lies until Carol finally insisted it was time she come home for Christmas.

The drive from Perth to Plaster Rock took just over an hour, what seemed like forever to the children as they sat in the back of the car. Back then, whenever their mother drove into the village, she'd pause to point out familiar sights and places the children didn't care about. She'd inch past the Tobique River, Fraser's Mill, and their great-aunt's brown clapboard house. She'd slow down to point at the Catholic, Anglican, and Baptist churches, driving the whole way with her foot on the brake. It was as though she wanted her own youth to recoil and recapture her.

Something in her mother's eyes told Emily that her mother missed something here, some unspoken peace, the same kind of comfort that Emily had come to love about this place and her grandparents' home.

The Polks' house rested uphill, behind Aunt Amy's cottage, which stood as proud on Main Street as the old woman did in church. Up a short, steep trail just east of the outhouse was a footpath that connected the two homesites.

Emily and Stephanie giggled at their mother's remembrance of the old woman clamoring up the path as a thunderstorm approached, Aunt Amy's skirt hiked up to her thighs, her thick stockings rolled low around her ankles. Emily found great solace in the storms that crossed the water, beating the surface of the Tobique River with great drops of rain. She'd told her mother a thousand times that she loved the flash of the lightning as it cut the sky, the pounding thunder signaling the storm's approach.

"Then you'll never be Aunt Amy," Maureen had said, laughing.

Aunt Amy had always found the deep rumble terrifying and would scamper up the steep path to the Polks' house, push her way through the kitchen, climb the stairs to the girls' attic bedroom, and crawl under the bed until the weather blew by.

Emily hadn't heard her mother laugh in a long time. But now her face shined as she shared her memories, her lips curling and pushing lines deep into the familiar face Emily still found beautiful. She liked the way her mother's hands seemed to tell the stories even before her mouth opened, her long, pale fingers tensing, releasing, pointing, as though speaking to a crowd who couldn't hear.

They veered at the post office and circled up and around the street that passed Dave Cook's house. He was still Emily's best friend. He could usually be found chopping wood with his father in the front yard of their run-down cabin. Darren stood in Maureen's lap, his tiny arms pounding on the car horn while Emily screamed out the window, waving her arms at Dave.

Dave dropped his ax and chased the car the quarter-mile to the Polks' house, his father's angry voice becoming little more than an echo. Emily hung out of the back window, yelling "slowpoke," her face covered in an ear-to-ear grin. Her mother turned onto her grandparents' gravel pathway and slowed the car even more, inching along what her children believed was the longest driveway in the world. Stephanie and Emily were hanging over the front seat, ready to jump out even before Maureen rolled to a complete stop.

Their grandfather, John, rocked in an old oak chair next to an open window, the lace curtains flashing with the breeze. Emily knew he'd be holding a Bible on his lap, his shoulders stooped as he strained to read it, thick glasses perched on the end of his long, thin nose. She saw him push open the curtains when the car crackled on the stone driveway, his face lighting up. His deep voice echoed into the yard as he announced to their grandmother that the children had arrived. The smell of fresh-baked bread, newly removed from the cast-iron stove, wafted out the window and into the yard.

The girls burst from the car even as it continued to roll toward the house, exploding through the door and into their grandparents' arms. Emily's grandmother was wiping flour from her hands onto the red-and-white apron Emily got to wear when they visited every summer. Maureen walked sheepishly in behind them, Darren firmly clutched in her arms. Emily's grandparents rushed to her mother's side and tearfully welcomed her home.

Dave arrived huffing and puffing, throwing his skinny limbs around Emily. They hopped like Mexican jumping beans across the kitchen. Emily closed her eyes and allowed the smells and sounds to cover her. It was always a moment when she felt God move.

The Polks' house was small, with a glassed-in veranda that ran halfway around the structure. A white wrought-iron bed nestled on the porch, the cozy haven heaped with handmade quilts for the visiting children. The kitchen, smelling of Nestlé's dark chocolate and Fleischmann's yeast, was large and open. A white porcelain wood-burning stove heated the house during the cold Canadian winters and supplied a surface where fresh apple pies could be cooled in summer.

A small, mint-green alarm clock rested on the windowsill. On its face, a red-breasted robin moved its body up and down as it tugged at a fake worm lodged in the ground. A saying, "The early bird gets the worm," was inscribed on the face of the clock, the click-click of its movement a constant reminder of the safety here beneath the roof of her grandparents' home. And on top of an oak cupboard sat a button box that Emily's grandmother brought down when something needed mending or when the children wanted a story.

Three-year-old Darren sat cupped in his grandfather's arms on the floral sofa. Ten-year-old Stephanie and eight-year-old Emily gathered at their grandmother's feet in the living room, warming their hands at the fireplace, eagerly waiting as their grandmother's wrinkled hands pulled a button from the metal box. It was a tradition to share the stories held within the button box.

A yellowed pearl cut from the gown of her own wedding dress evoked a hearty laugh as Emily's grandmother recalled how their nervous grandfather had put his trousers on backward. Her twinkling eyes saddened as she fumbled with an olive green button.

The sullen mood spoke of long nights of tears and faith as she waited for word of her brother's fate in the war. She rocked back and forth as the stories unfolded, weaving the family's heritage, her emotions cresting and then crashing as each button added history to the family story. A navy blue button had been cut from the work pants their grandfather had worn at the logging camp, a red silk button from the dress her own great-grandmother had been buried in, a button from Maureen's favorite yellow chenille sweater, and a silver button from their Aunt Carol's graduation robe. Each button was pulled one at a time from the box, each containing a story of its own.

Emily noticed a look of desperation pass between her grandparents when a drab brown button dropped silently into her grandmother's hand. A flash of anger. No story surfaced, and the button was laid to one side and then later disposed of with a clink inside the iron stove top, the flame licking it into a golden ball.

"I've done all the praying I can do for that man, John," Emily heard her grandmother say as she slammed the tea kettle to the counter.

"Dear," Emily's grandfather's voice broke in, "we can't ever stop praying for him or the children. It's the greatest thing we can do." He pulled her into his arms and cradled her head on his shoulder before escorting her back to the living room.

Their grandmother talked deep into the night until all three of the children toppled at her feet. As their heads bobbed in sleepiness, John lifted and then deposited them one at a time on the feather bed that waited patiently on the porch. He rolled each of them into the center of the sagging mattress, watching them curl together like newborn kittens. Then he kneeled at the foot of the white iron bed and whispered his prayers into the night. Emily often heard him mumbling and figured he had a special line to God. She could tell by the way he spoke that this God knew him as a good friend, listened to him.

She'd squint her eyes, pretending to be asleep, admiring her grandfather's persistence. She wasn't sure God listened to most people's prayers. Certainly not hers. Maybe God listened to people who prayed down by the Tobique River, where Reverend Park blasted at the heavens with his deep voice as he baptized the lost. Or maybe deep in the Canadian forests where, at times, the woods were so silent that Emily was sure God could hear everything.

But in her own home, where the wind bounced the limbs of the apple tree against the tin roof of the old house and the rain struck a steady beat during every storm? Here, where life was mundane and real? Emily was sure God wasn't listening here.

Chapter 16

John
New Year's Day, 1959
Plaster Rock, New Brunswick

THE RITUAL OF EARLY MORNING when John rose to stoke the woodstove stirred Emily from her sleep. It was the last day of their Christmas visit. All three of the children had been lying in a heap on a sunken mattress that draped over the iron bed frame on the enclosed porch, piles of handmade quilts providing warmth. John lifted the heavy iron lid and poked the kindling wood into the stove, its casing crackling with the new flames.

The scratch of a match against the tea kettle always caught his granddaughter's ear. John wondered why the noise — the strike of a match, the smell of tobacco — seemed to make Emily so nervous.

He glanced through the window separating the living room and veranda and watched as Emily crawled from the bed. She twirled her thin blonde hair into a ponytail, tiny wisps escaping the rubber band and circling her head like a see-through crown. She pulled on her house robe, too small for her frame, tugged on the handmade slippers her grandmother had given her for Christmas, and padded to the kitchen.

John filled the white metal teapot and dropped it on the stove with a thunk. In minutes, the kettle whistled its high-pitched "good morning!" He was already dressed in drab blue work pants, brown leather boots, and a green flannel shirt. Logging was a tough job, but John was lucky; his trees were harvested from land he had staked out and rented years earlier. He'd told Emily that many of his friends were not so lucky, having to log from Fraser's land, which cut their profit by half.

"Grampy, can I come to the woods today?" Emily asked, her head cocked to one side as she reached for a cinnamon roll left over from yesterday's breakfast.

"I'm sorry," John said, kneeling before her and clasping her shoulders with his weathered hands. "I wish you could, Em, but you're heading home today."

He kissed her on the cheek and then wrapped her in his arms. John could feel the unwilling tears tracing their way down her face. She grasped the old man tightly around his neck and molded her frame to his.

"I just want to stay with you, Grampy. I don't want to go home," she said.

He clung to her for a moment, sensing her need, and then pushed her away and pulled her chin upward.

"Honey, don't be afraid. You're not alone. God will never leave you. He'll be there no matter what happens. I promise." John's face broke into a smile. He pulled a nickel from his pocket and pushed it into Emily's hand. He stood up, tucked his ears under the flaps of his plaid cap, and strode out the back door to the barn.

He moved into the yard, glancing back to see Emily pull back the white lace curtain and rub a small circle in the frosty pane to watch him. He hoped Emily would not recognize his heavy heart in the way his shoulders stooped as he moved. He could do nothing to protect his grandchildren from his daughter's stubborn ways. He'd already reported his suspicions about Denny to the police in Perth, but nothing had come of it.

His hands moved quickly as he harnessed his old Belgian horse, Grady. When he was finished, he dropped his head forward to his chest, his hands clasped. Prayer. Something he did every day whether he was sitting at the kitchen table, kneeling at the bottom of his grandchildren's bed, or working in the Canadian forests. He'd learned over the years that nothing settled his soul, his anger, the way prayer did. He hoped his grandchildren would learn to understand the peace of God's presence at an age much earlier than that of his own awakening, an awakening that had come at the cost of another man's life. He knew it puzzled Emily, the way he'd talk to someone he couldn't see, believing in something without ever being able to hold it in his hands. She'd told him she could never do that. In fact, she'd told him she didn't even believe in the things you could see and touch because everything would eventually disappoint you, hurt you. Even with his prodding, Emily never would explain why she felt that way. John's anger boiled in his chest, his eyes closing once more as he sought to let it go. So many secrets in his daughter's house.

John clucked his tongue as the reins popped up and down. Grady strained forward; John limped behind, the long lead lines grasped in his strong hands. The chains and hooks that tugged the logs to the loader cut designs in the snow. It would be nightfall before he'd return, and his grandchildren would be gone.

* * *

The woods were dark and moody, framed with white birch trees that stood like sentinels guarding the treasures of the forests. John had brought Emily with him many times. Remembering her delight the first time she'd gone with him, he clucked at Grady, the horse he'd trained for lumbering in the thick Canadian forests. They started the two-mile walk to the logging site, chains clinking out a rhythmic song as they moved through the well-worn grooves of the logging roads. The work of Fraser's Mill began deep in the dense forests of New Brunswick, where John and other independent workers contracted to harvest the trees from the woods and transport them to the mill for processing. John, like most of the men who worked there, walked hunched over, pained from the toil of the heavy work.

He was a lumberjack, a woodsman whose love for the forest was surpassed only by the passion he had for fly fishing in the Tobique River — both passions he'd passed on to Emily. She often commented at the strength of his grasp on the wooden handle of his scarred ax as he lifted it high over his head. He seemed to have a sixth sense for the depth he should cut on each side. And then his hardened hands would instinctively feel the gap narrow, and he would pull the ax to safety just before the first crack echoed the timber's death.

"Timberrrrrrr!" John's cry would boom a warning to prevent anyone from becoming a victim of the widow-maker; he'd motion for Emily to stay well behind the falling tree. To Emily, the tree seemed to reach for a lifeline, snagging neighboring branches with its outstretched arms as it careened toward the ground. The soil grunted as the tree seared the ground, rose slightly, then rested. Its blood smelled sweet.

From a distance, she'd watch as another lumberjack, the wood bucker, busied himself, chopping the surrendered limbs from the listless trunk, knot bumping and smoothing the long, alligator-skinned beam into an armless log that would fetch a week's salary.

John always watched the men who cut these trees and had learned the sounds, the feel, the surrender of the forest. He wanted Emily to learn to feel as lucky as he did when a tree was felled straight and true, not bucked from its stump toward an unwary newcomer. He loved how her eyes would widen as she observed the armless victim being stripped of any leftover protrusions, its head and feet flattened by a two-man saw. The rhythmic movements of strong bodies rocking forward and back and the silver knife, its teeth sounding a quiet snore, became hypnotic.

When the flat face of the corpse was readied, John, along with others, would stab the log with a hand-like clasp and chain the lead to a horse's leather harness. The Belgian would wait in silence, his face pushed deep into a burlap feed bag, the munching occupying his time until he was called to work.

When she was with him, it was Emily's job to hold Grady's lead steady until one of the men pulled the feed bag from the horse's face, tapping him lightly on the haunches as they walked away. The Belgian lifted his right foot, then left, then right, in quick succession, anticipating the pull ahead. His tongue pushed at the bit, the silver mouthpiece clanging in his jaws. He was ready to work, knowing the familiar process.

The horse would stagger forward, its chest biting into the leather yoke. His nostrils flared, and wisps of wet air spit from his mouth. His hooves sank into the forest floor, the moss and needles sliding, causing him to stumble and then catch his footing. The wood dislodged, jerking forward a foot at a time until the Belgian's gait was set in a rhythm of a slow trot, the dead soldier sliding over the green mossy floor behind him.

John would drop the reins, allowing the horse to set his own pace down the narrow path that ran between a stand of small elms too young to cut. And the horse would run until he was out of breath, exploding from the shadowed forest to the gravel road where the loading crew waited, Emily rushing behind him. The foreman always allowed Emily to water the horse, the sucking noise breaking the spell of the quiet morning. The team would load the harvested timber with a chain and pulley, lifting it high to hover over the truck and then lowering it so it would settle into a nook of the other logs that lay torn and silent on the hearse.

As the wood was stacked by several workmen, the driver would turn the horse and face him back toward the woodland opening from where he had come. A quick tap of leather on skin sent the horse trotting, Emily padding behind, and they were soon swallowed by the thickness of the forest once again.

The men worked until the faint sound of the mill's whistle blew, calling them to lunch. The smell of hot coffee, made fresh from a quickly built fire, rose into the air and mixed with the aromatic smell of the surrounding pines. John would call Emily to join him and the others as the men sat on stumps of felled trees and shared tobacco, cool tea, and fresh bread someone's wife or mother had baked. Some bowed their heads in prayer, seeking safety for the work that lay ahead.

John knew Emily loved to hear the crew share stories of fishing, hunting, and family — lies blown to proportions that even the tale teller didn't believe. They never spoke of the men lost to the anger of the timber, just the solace the day had given them thus far.

Their first day together in the woods had ticked by, John noting the excitement Emily had found in the woods, an excitement that surged when her grandfather praised her for her work. He'd wanted her to see his callused hands, hardened from the scaling of the bark. He needed her to learn the lesson of faith early, a lesson he'd learned too late when his own anger had allowed him to kill a man. He wanted her to know this faith, how it had settled over him like the sweet smell of the pine trees that surrounded them, bringing him a peace that truly passed understanding. And he saw in her face that she longed to believe what he shared about the love of God. Yet he knew she'd witnessed many people, probably including her own father and mother, be baptized in the Tobique River and lie about receiving the promised grace that never seemed to really take hold.

Chapter 17

Emily
July 1959
Plaster Rock, New Brunswick

IT WAS DIRTY WATER. Emily never understood how anyone could be washed clean in dirty water. Reverend Park was Plaster Rock's favorite visiting preacher. Her mother, Maureen, referred to him as Mr. Clean. He'd come to town to wash away the sins of the lost. Maureen said she was already found so she didn't need him, but Emily did.

The revival was a weeklong outdoor gathering of lost and saved souls, held along the banks of the Tobique River. Local church deacons helped to seat people on folding chairs under the makeshift tent and collected the special offering taken each night to help support Reverend Park's ministry.

Mr. Cook was a deacon. He was Dave Cook's father. More than once, Emily had seen the welts on Dave's back from the thick brown belt Mr. Cook wore. She guessed deacons had special rights to do wrong just because they helped Reverend Park.

Foley was another deacon, a muscled man with carrot-red hair like her mother's. Foley must have had those privileges, too. Emily had seen him with her mother. Caught them half-naked in her Grampy's barn, while Foley's pregnant wife mowed the lawn next door. Emily never told; Maureen would've beaten her half to death.

The revival service always started with a windy prayer. Emily squinted her eyes, never really closing them, to take it all in. Reverend Park was a big man with a head like a bowling ball perched on his shoulders just above a stiff white shirt. His tie choked the words out of him, and he cried a lot. He wore thick black glasses. Emily's grandmother said he could see the good in people even if they were bound for hell. Emily didn't think you needed glasses for that.

Mrs. Belcamp played the piano as though she were playing in a tavern. She bounced side to side as her hat popped on her head. Aunt Amy didn't seem to approve; she shot the piano player one of those looks that said Mrs. Belcamp was doomed to hell.

Reverend Park always began his sermons peacefully. He leaned on the portable pulpit, pulled a crumpled hankie from his back pocket, and rubbed the sweat from his smooth head. Emily sat up straight as an arrow and listened to every word old Reverend Park had to say. She wasn't going to hell if she could help it.

"You have no place to go without Jesus," he said, shaking his head back and forth. "No place but hell." Then, in one swift, unexpected move, he lifted his Bible and slammed it to the pulpit. "Eternal damnation!" he screamed, scaring Emily clean out of the pew. Great-aunt Amy shot her a look.

"You'll burn in hell forever!" His voice was wild as clapping thunder. The crowd squirmed in their seats, but Maureen never moved once. The local gossip, Daffney Rogers, got the fever and broke into a fit of jabbering. Daffney was surely going to hell. Emily dug her fingers into her legs, leaving welt marks she knew would follow her to the flames.

"Hallelujah!" a newcomer cried, sending shivers up Emily's spine. People around her began talking loudly over Reverend Park's trembling voice in a language Emily didn't understand. Katie Turner, unwed mother of four, blurted out, "Thank you, Jesus," and then fell to the floor. Deacon Greene, possible father to at least one of Katie's children, rushed to her side with smelling salts, leaving his own wife open-mouthed in the row behind him. Several in the crowd bobbed their heads. Everyone's arms were flailing, and lots of people were crying. Emily shot her hands to the sky, waving them like a tambourine, and Aunt Amy shot her the look again.

People staggered and prayed their way to the makeshift altar while Mrs. Belcamp played a vaudeville rendition of "Just a Closer Walk with Thee." Reverend Park laid his log-like hands on each of the bowed heads and declared them "saved." Emily wanted to be saved, too — cleaned of what her father had done to her — but she didn't move, instead glancing between her mother and her old aunt.

From the back of the tent came Emily's father, his hands rubbing one over the other, looking at her mother and then all squinty-eyed at her grandmother. He was stone sober. Her grandfather limped slowly next to him. They crowded between Mr. Belcamp and Foley, Emily's father slumping his head like he'd lost his spine. The men eyed each other, and then Foley winked at Denny, as though he understood that Denny was only there because Maureen had nagged him into coming that day, the last day of the summer revival. She'd heard her father say that women had a way of holding out until their men gave in, though she had no idea what he meant.

Reverend Park gathered the dirty and the lost, including Denny, and marched them from the billowing tents, down to the river to be cleaned and saved. Everyone wore their best clothes under white choir robes and lined up like birch trees along the banks of the Tobique before Reverend Park summoned them into the murky water.

The rest of the townspeople dotted the hillside to watch the spectacle. Especially the Catholics. Emily's grandfather said the Catholics never understood why people would want to ruin perfectly good clothes when a light sprinkling indoors and a couple of Hail Marys could do the job. But even a few Catholics, like Emily's father, got baptized in the Tobique to satisfy someone.

Reverend Park waded to his waist, his white robe billowing around him like a forest mushroom. One by one, he called the offenders from the shore. With a mighty push, he wrestled the sinner under the water and shouted, "Dead to sin: Risen with Christ," as he pulled the gasping reprobate back up through the sucking surface. The forgiven emerged and congregated beside him like a growing mushroom cluster.

Emily watched seventeen people be saved that day. Saved and cleaned. Mr. Cook, Katie Turner, Daffney Rogers, Mr. Green, and Foley took the plunge again. After Denny was baptized, he stumbled back to shore without looking at Maureen. Emily was glad to see they all wanted to be clean. She just never understood how it worked; the water in the Tobique was dirty.

Emily doubted most were sincere, anyway, but the day seemed to represent hope for a few. And Emily's mother would later swear it was the remembrance of that day and of the many lies Denny told her that had given her the courage to finally leave him.

Chapter 18

Maureen
April 1960
Perth, New Brunswick

THE DAY WAS GRAY and rainy, as though an umbrella had opened and covered the sun. Maureen stood at the sink staring out the window, the dishrag swirling over a coffee mug as she watched the darkening sky. She hated rain, hated that an early downpour was a sign of a coming storm in their house. Late April. The daffodils had pushed their yellow heads from the unraked soil, announcing their arrival just days ago. On this day, they seemed stooped and sullen, depressed by the somber drizzle. Denny had been gone for several hours, trying to catch a partial day's work before the sky opened its faucet.

"Emily? I need some help setting the table." Maureen cupped her hands around her wide mouth, her voice carrying up the stairs.

"Be right there, Ma." Her ten-year-old daughter bounced down the staircase, her thin, blonde ponytail swinging wildly back and forth. Twelve-year-old Stephanie followed, half-pulling, half-yanking the arm of her brother. Emily seemed so slender next to her older sister, thin like a birch tree, pale, blonde. Five-year-old Darren followed the girls everywhere, his curly red hair flaming around his milky-white skull. He was a quiet little man, older than his years; he seemed content to follow his sisters anywhere they'd go.

"Will you put Darren down for a nap after lunch, Steph?" Maureen asked, wiping her hands on a kitchen towel.

"Sure, Ma." Stephanie pulled a stack of plates from the cupboard and dropped them on the metal dinette with a bang.

"Just two, dear." She eyed Emily as the girl moved quietly to the other side of the kitchen and stared blankly out the window, her hand pressed against the pane as though she were locked in a prison. "Your father and I are going to have lunch alone. We need to talk. You kids can eat in the bedroom."

Maureen walked to the window and ruffled the stringy blonde hair on Emily's head and then loaded the dishes with steaming turkey sandwiches, covering them in dark gravy.

"Now go on. I'll come up for the dishes later."

The girls balanced plates on small, metal TV trays and paraded toward the stairs. Emily said nothing but waited until her brother was two steps behind Stephanie and then poked her leg between his, knocking him to the floor, sending his metal cup flying. Darren howled and rubbed his mouth, a small trickle of blood racing down his chin.

"What happened?" Maureen asked, although she'd witnessed everything. Emily's behavior had begun to worry her; it was as though something ugly was boiling beneath her daughter's skin.

"He — he just tripped, Ma," Emily said, turning her head toward Stephanie and then back to face her mother, her eyes wide and innocent.

"There, there, buddy." Maureen pulled Darren into her arms, tugging a crumpled hankie from the pocket of her waitress uniform and dabbing at her son's lip. "It'll be fine. Just a tiny cut. You go on upstairs and take a nap, OK?"

She pushed Darren back, patted his shoulder, and sent him scurrying behind Stephanie.

"Emily, come here a minute." Maureen's face pursed.

The girl spun around and walked slowly toward her mother, her eyes resting on the floor.

"Are you OK?" she asked, draping her hands over her daughter's shoulders. "Is something wrong?"

Emily shook her head side to side, not looking up or saying a word. Maureen pulled her daughter into her arms, holding her tightly until she felt Emily pushing away.

"I — I've got to help Steph," Emily said, turning away. She quickly made her way up the stairs.

Maureen watched her daughter dart away, an unsettled feeling clutching her stomach. She'd wanted this day to be different from the others. Happy. Peaceful. But the gloom outside had settled inside as well.

The sound of the driveway spitting gravel into the air sent a shiver up Maureen's spine. The truck door slammed a hard, hollow thud. Same angry sound. Denny was a man of habits. Bad habits. He pushed into the kitchen from the front porch, the door swinging and then slamming behind him.

"I'm sorry about the weather today," Maureen said, as if she could've somehow changed it. She rubbed her hands over her hips at a furious pace. "I know you wanted to get that job finished."

Denny tossed his lunch box at the table, the container sliding across the dinette, slapping to a stop when it hit the metal lip that encircled the edge. He set his thermos on the table, screwed off the red cap, took a long drink, and then slammed it to the counter in a sharp move that made Maureen jump.

"Damn. Every time I get to a point where I can make some money — it rains." His voice was cigarette raspy and irritated.

"Denny, just relax," Maureen said, her face averting his. She felt his angry eyes boring through her. "I've made us a good, hot lunch. The girls are upstairs. They'll watch Darren when he wakes from his nap."

At that moment, Emily burst through the door. The tray she was carrying was piled high with dishes. She stopped abruptly upon seeing her father and then looked toward the floor.

"Put the dishes in the sink, dear, and I'll get to them when I get home," her mother told her. Emily carefully stacked the dishes in the sink and turned to go.

She passed her father slowly, never looking at him. He reached for her, tugging her to him by her arm. "She's such a skinny little thing," he said, rubbing his hand across his daughter's shoulder, "a very pretty little thing." A shiver rose through Maureen as she watched him stare at Emily with a look she'd seen before, a look that said love had changed to lust. Emily pulled from him and shrunk into Maureen as though her father's touch had burned her. Maureen was sickened by the uneasy thought of what she was accusing him of in her mind. Emily had always been Daddy's little girl, more so than Stephanie had ever been. *He'd never touch her.*

"Do you have to go to work tonight, Ma?" Emily asked, her face begging at her mother.

"I'll try and get home early, Emily. I promise."

Denny swigged from his thermos and slammed it to the table. Emily and Maureen jumped.

"How do you think we feed you, Emily?" His voice rose, rumbling and raspy. "You spoiled little brat!" He began to rise. Maureen pushed Emily toward the living room door and stood between her daughter and Denny.

"Stay in your room, Emily," Maureen said, turning to kiss her daughter on the top of her head. "Now go!"

Denny gave Emily an angry look as she disappeared, and then he dropped again to his seat, mumbling to himself.

Pulling a white apron from behind the kitchen door, Maureen tied it around her blue uniform. Reaching for the oven, she removed the meal and then busied herself with slicing the fresh bread, the aroma a pleasing blend of yeast and oats. She pretended everything was normal, though she'd long known it was not. Her stomach fluttered with a sick feeling about the way Emily was acting. *This is silly, Maureen. He'd never hurt his own daughter that way.*

"Tina called in sick, so you being home early will help me out today, Denny. Besides, we need to talk."

She kept her back to him, her eyes closed, awaiting his reaction. Then she continued. She pulled in a deep breath and straightened her shoulders before readying herself to face him.

"About last night," she hesitated.

"I don't want any of your damn food," Denny snorted, ignoring her. He snatched the silver thermos and the newspaper and thrust himself through the living room door, dropping on the worn, green sofa. "And what about last night?" he yelled at the opening, never seeing Maureen enter the room.

Her face was pinched with anger, the bruises from last night's beating flashing back at her in the reflection of the living room mirror.

"I want out, Denny!" She backed toward the kitchen, just out of his reach. "I can't take what you're doing to us anymore."

He put the paper down slowly, narrowing his eyes, his lips parting in a half-smile. "What in the hell are you going to do without me?" he said, and then he laughed and pulled the newspaper to his face again.

"I'll manage." She clenched her teeth as she spat the words. "We can't go on like this. We're going to talk more about this when I get home." She swept the keys from the counter, stood in the doorway, and jiggled them at Denny. "I'm taking the truck. The Pontiac's still in the garage."

The sound of the newspaper crushing in his hands had her spinning.

"What in the hell am I supposed to do if I need cigarettes?"

"I can't believe—" she said.

"Get out!" he screamed. "Get out before I kill you right now!" Denny gulped a long drink from the thermos, never taking his eyes from her, and then threw the empty container across the room.

Sometimes his anger frightened her, usually because his fists followed. But he hadn't been drinking enough yet that morning, which made it easy to defy him. Maureen cocked her head and wondered what she'd ever seen in him. His face was much too angular to be really handsome. His hair was longer than a man's should be. Though a smile hadn't crossed his face in years, she swore at one time he'd owned one. She'd been attracted to him, hadn't she? The thought spun in her head. Or had she been so ready to escape Plaster Rock — that smothering small town — that she would've left with anyone?

She threw the keys to the floor, grabbed her umbrella, and pulled at the kitchen door. Her uniform caught on a nail in the doorframe — one Denny had been promising to fix for months. She gawked at the tear, glared back at him, and pushed into the downpour.

Chapter 19

Emily
April 1960
Perth, New Brunswick

 STEPHANIE AND EMILY HEARD THE FIGHT from the top of the stairs. They'd become used to the angry words their parents slung into the night. Emily thought it was probably her fault; she'd interrupted them with the dishes, trying to make up for hurting Darren. She didn't know why she'd tripped him. She just wanted to hurt something, someone, the way her father had hurt her.

 The slam of the door as her mother left sent a shiver through her. She watched as Stephanie quickly tossed schoolbooks into a blue book bag and then raced down the stairs, Emily falling in behind.

 "Dad, a friend's going to help me with a school project. I'll be staying overnight, OK?"

 Their father waved his hand to dismiss her, not turning to say good-bye. Emily moved to the front door, standing to one side as Stephanie gathered a jacket from the hall closet. She paused to stare into Emily's face and then looked around to see their father take a long, slow drink from the silver thermos. She grabbed her book bag and pulled at the door.

 "Steph, please, don't leave me with him. Please!" Emily begged, her hands tugging at her sister's arm.

 "Stop it," Stephanie said, pulling her arm away, the purple welt below her right eye still visible. "I've got to go." Stephanie slipped through the opening and then turned to look at her sister. "It'll be OK, Em. He doesn't hit you." The door closed with a gentle click, leaving the house sounding hollow as a tomb.

 "Get me that brown bottle from under the sink," Denny yelled over his shoulder. Emily stiffened, looking left and right, hoping he hadn't seen her standing there.

"Now, dammit!"

She jolted to retrieve the jug, pushing it at her father with caution as though it were a grenade.

"Now, get upstairs."

Emily didn't have to be told twice. She'd developed a way of slithering out of his sight, remaining unnoticed for as long as she could, until alcohol and urges lured him up the stairs. Her acquired habit of slipping into a self-induced coma when his shadow crossed her bed never stopped him. Emily had taken to sleeping under her bed when her mother went to work. The darkness frightened her, its cloak little protection from what came from nights like this. But she preferred the dark to her father's probing hands and liquored breath as he lay panting on top of her. For now, he was silent.

The day had turned to night, the darkness creeping in like a preying cat. It was 9:30, and her brother had fallen into a heap in the corner of his bed. Emily pulled open the bedroom door and gazed down the stairs at her drunken father. The black-and-white TV blared *The Adventures of Ozzie and Harriet*. She crept down the stairs, scooting on her behind so that no sound would wake him. She slipped into the kitchen and pulled open the seldom-used door to the basement. Inching down the steps, she fled to a corner beneath the basement steps that she'd discovered just days ago.

"Emily?" his slurred voice called just minutes into her hiding. "Emily — where are you?"

She heard his feet above her, shuffling across the floor as if held by weights. Her eyes shot upward.

His movements were coarse, deliberate. The third step moaned as he staggered up the staircase, to her room, she supposed. She prayed Darren wouldn't wake. She cocked her ear upward to listen for her brother's cry. Holding her breath, she waited for the sound of his unstable pitch back down the staircase.

"Emily! You little witch." His voice was gravelly, muffled. "I know you're here somewhere. Get in here — now!"

She pictured him drooling from the side of his mouth, by now the whiskey accentuating his awkward movements. She could already feel his hot breath when she closed her eyes, smelled the liquor. Her father stumbled through the house above her, searching, angry, swearing. She didn't move. Instead, she clamped her eyes tightly and waited. She tried praying. She tried it every time her father appeared in the shadows, but she knew that no matter what her grandfather had said, Jesus wouldn't help her. He was just another carpenter, a carpenter like her father.

The footsteps above her stopped at the opening of the basement door. She heard the distinct creak of the knob as it turned, the hinges squealing their warning. The door opened, and a wave of light flashed onto the steps, sending dust particles shimmering through the basement like tiny crystals. The weight of his foot on the first step was startling, its sound cutting through her like thin metal wire.

"Emily?" The voice was low and jagged. "Daddy won't hurt you, girl."

The prick of terror sent goose bumps racing up and down her body. He continued to creep downward into the dark, his movements intentional. She saw his shoes through the slats of the steps, his hand clutching the railing unsteadily. He'd never ventured down the stairs before.

"This will go easier if you come out, girl." Emily imagined his face, creased with the look that echoed his thoughts. She did not draw another breath, holding onto the hope that he would not find her in this dank-smelling corner of the basement. His foot hit the bottom step. She saw a sliver of his head through the staircase opening, turning left, then right. He swung around to face her, his eyes squeezing in her direction, as if he now knew she was hunched in the bend of the basement. Her chest pumped slowly, as though someone were crushing her lungs. She knew that in a moment, she'd be his prey again.

Chapter 20

Maureen
April 1960
Perth, New Brunswick

MAUREEN ENTERED THE HOUSE just before midnight, squeezing quietly into the kitchen through the back door. The house was eerily silent. She took off her coat and hung it on the coatrack near the pantry, then edged her way toward the living room. The door to the basement was ajar, a thin stream of light beaming into the kitchen. She heard a faint sound like the cry of a cat coming from the opening and widened the door to listen. She hoped the children weren't harboring another stray. Her feet tapped down the steps, stopping midway to listen. The sound stopped. She glanced over the railing, a puzzled look etching her face. She shook her head and started back up the steps.

"Mom?" Emily cried.

"Emily? What are you doing down here?" Maureen crouched on the steps and stared into the gray corner of the basement through the slats of the steps. One dim lightbulb hung like a dead man just above her daughter's head. Bile rose in her throat as her eyes adjusted to the scene of her daughter standing in the corner naked, shaking, clutching her clothes to her chest, staring empty-eyed at her mother through the step opening. Denny lay passed out, partially unclothed in a heap of dank rags by Emily's side. Maureen cupped her hand to her mouth to keep from vomiting. Fifteen minutes later, Maureen loaded her three children into Denny's truck and drove toward Plaster Rock.

"Emily hasn't been well, Dad," Maureen said, tugging at her fingers as though she were trying to remove gloves. "Summer vacation starts next week anyway, so I thought you wouldn't mind if they came early. I have to work tomorrow, so tonight's the only time I had to get the kids here."

John eyed his daughter's face, familiar with her lies. Ellen was already carrying Darren toward the feather bed on the porch.

"Are you OK?" He touched his daughter's arm. Maureen recoiled, winding her arms around herself to hide her latest bruises.

"I'm fine, Dad." Her gaze followed the widening crack in the old linoleum. "Denny and I—" She paused. "We're having some issues. I — I don't know what's going to happen… " Her voice drifted off.

"We're here, Maureen. Just ask. You know you can always come home."

Maureen looked up and saw the pained look in her father's eyes. *He doesn't deserve this. My problems.*

"I'm not coming back here, Dad!" Her voice strengthened. "Not ever."

She gave him a quick hug and then followed her mother onto the porch. All of the children were huddled in the deep hollow of the bed. Her hand brushed back Emily's fine hair, causing Emily to cry out and recoil.

"It's going to be OK, Em," she said as her face closed in to kiss her daughter good-bye. "I promise."

"I'll be back to pick them up in September, Dad," she said, climbing into the car.

"And I'll be praying for you." She heard his whispered words as she backed from the driveway, the morning sun inching its way into the sky.

Just downhill from her parents' home, she found herself drawn to the worn path behind the Anglican church. She stumbled down the path, pushing the overgrown tree branches from her face until she reached the water's edge. The Tobique had offered little solace to her as a child, but the light shimmering across the flowing water that morning seemed to soothe her rambling thoughts. Though she'd always denied it, there was something special about this place. She couldn't put her finger on it. Maybe it was the way the river controlled the land, its swells and currents cutting traces into the banks that longed to hold the river captive. There was little she had control over in her life anymore. Running from Plaster Rock hadn't eased her longing to be free; it had only put her in a deeper rut, adding more responsibilities to her life than she'd ever wanted.

Maureen kicked at the red dirt, knocked a stone loose, and stooped to pick it up. It rolled in her fist for a moment, the crimson soil leaving a blood-like stain on the palm of her hand. Like the stains in the hands of the man her father had so long spoken about. She pulled back her arm and lobbed the stone high into the air, its splash breaking the silence — breaking the peaceful feeling that had shattered the moment Denny's face broke into her thoughts.

Chapter 21

Emily
August 1960
Plaster Rock, New Brunswick

    THE TENSE EXCHANGES BETWEEN EMILY'S PARENTS the few times her father had come to Plaster Rock with his family had rocked her grandfather. John had spoken to Denny, encouraging him to give his life to Christ, even stood beside him the day Maureen begged Denny to wade into the Tobique to be baptized. But the river frightened Denny the same way the river frightened Emily, and it did little to change him.

    Emily had always feared the Tobique. It swallowed boys whole, spitting them downriver. She saw the proof herself the day she was baptized. Poor old Reverend Park had the kids lined up like soldiers parading off to war. It was hotter than hell; at least that was what her mother had said. But Maureen didn't know that much about hell. Not like Emily did.

    Her grandmother tugged the seersucker dress on Emily, the one with the little red rose on the front. It used to have a zipper pull, but her grandmother took it off when snot-nosed Ronnie Dowd pulled it down one day, exposing Emily's chest for the whole Sunday school class to see. She'd never wanted to wear it again, but her grandmother said it was proper for the baptism.

    Ten-year-old Emily stood knee-deep in the river, waiting her turn. Reverend Park grasped the neck and forehead of the girl next to Emily. He yelled scriptures at the shoreline as those listening considered their heaven-or-hell-bound options. With the strength of a weightlifter, he pushed the unsuspecting sinner under, as though the river would suck her to a watery salvation. Just as fast, he jerked her up — gasping — to the surface, the girl shaking her head like a newly bathed dog. The crowd wailed, rocking back and forth as the shoreline choir sang "Amazing Grace." The river had given life yet again.

The Tobique River snaked through New Brunswick, entering and leaving in silence most days. The logs rode it, bumping and bobbing off obstacles, rocks, shorelines, and occasionally a sunken canoe. On rare days when the heat index made fathers swear and mothers' dresses cling, the river promised relief. But the Tobique was no place for kids. Its appetite for the children of Plaster Rock seemed insatiable.

The entry to the river was downhill from the Anglican church and opposite Fraser's Mill. The Tobique ran in a valley between the two — not steep, but enough to make the descent to the river a challenge. The red clay trail had been carved by the bare feet of the parishioners who filed down the narrow path to be baptized. The river was crowded that summer with the mined beech, spruce, and fir timber, the colors as mixed as a box of crayons.

People couldn't swim on Fraser's side of the river because of the log chute. The logs slid down the half-moon channel at irregular intervals, the timber launching from the slide and hovering just above the moving water for a heartbeat before they dropped like a stone. The river seized each log, twisting and turning it as though the water were wrestling an alligator. The log would eventually surrender, turning its flat head downstream.

The logs floated aimlessly, tapping other intrusions as the river tugged them downward. They pushed east beneath the wooden trestle bridge, where at least one troublemaker double-dared another to leap between the floating targets.

Emily's best friend, Dave Cook, was the instigator. Maureen was not fond of the boy; she thought he was a poor example of a rule-follower for Emily to be mingling with. But her grandfather, John, had witnessed Dave's kindness and chalked up Dave's reputation to rumor.

Dave sat behind Emily in Sunday school, always next to Ronnie Dowd — two evil boys, in Aunt Amy's estimation. Dave pulled Emily's hair and tossed spitballs until Aunt Amy turned around and gave him the stink eye. He was always the source of the unusual smells in church. He had choked up Reverend Park more than one time, causing the Reverend to cover his mouth with the white hankie he carried in his coat pocket while he gasped for fresh air. The church women would fan their faces frantically, everyone turning to look at Dave, who would sit with his hands folded like some wayward angel.

The day of Emily's baptism was oven hot, a day when children baked in their homes until mothers ran them outside to escape their heat-induced whines. Eleven-year-old Dave Cook was one of four boys who had skipped the revival, tagging along with older boys to swim in the river. Emily was sure Aunt Amy would catch them; she knew everything, saw everything.

Emily longed to join the boys. Dave had told her he'd already eyed the log gap from shore earlier that day. It offered forbidden refreshment, much more so than the swift dunking Maureen had chosen for Emily. Halfway across the river, the rushing water had heaved logs into the air, pushing them high and solidly latching the timber into makeshift diving platforms. Emily stood at the top of the path to the river, watching the carefree boys until Reverend Park called her name.

Kent Green, Dave, Ronnie, and Ronnie's cousin Rene Tibideaux stood on the riverbank, each daring the other to begin the run to the logjam.

"You go!" Dave charged.

"No, you go," Rene yelled back.

"What are you, chicken? Bawk! Bawk! Chicken!" Ronnie taunted.

The jeers continued, with Rene pulling at Ronnie's arm until Ronnie lunged forward and fell face-first into the red dirt. Ronnie grabbed at Kent's leg, jerking away from Rene's grasp. Finally, Dave, dashing from all of them, steadied his foot on the lead log and, feeling no movement, began to run. He crossed to the second log, a thin white birch, with little effort; its bark was peeled back, exposing a slippery beige skin. He hopped to another log and then another, his confidence growing. He was several logs out on a steady one when he turned to face the skeptics behind him.

"Chicken!" he clucked.

"Keep going, Dave!" Emily yelled from the top of the hill, her voice carrying down over the water as though she had a megaphone.

The boys flung their shoes into the air, and the race was on. They flitted log to log, mimicking Dave's route. Dave took off again, his arms gyrating like a windmill when he hit the sinker.

"Emily?" Reverend Park's thundering voice called her to the baptism pool. She swung around and ran toward him, losing sight of the boys in the water.

She figured it was about the time the logs had dislodged and separated, wide jaws bent on swallowing, that Reverend Park had pushed her head underneath the water. Going under, she pinched her nose, scared of swallowing any of the river and getting worms like her gram had warned her about. She didn't want worms. Karen Belcamp had worms one time. Karen's mother told the principal that she could see them under Karen's skin, puffed up and making tunnels on her arms. Emily clamped her mouth shut but kept her eyes open. The Reverend sucked her up through the water, and it was over.

Ronnie was the first boy they heard. "Help! Help!" He burst through the small grove of scrub trees that separated the baptism pool from the logjam. His flash of red hair was weaving wild across his pale head. Gasping, he choked out the news — the other three boys had dropped into the river when the spruce rolled beneath their feet, hurling them into the Tobique. The gap in the timber had opened, allowing the river to swallow them whole. And Ronnie, the lone, lagging runner, had watched horrified as the floating logs closed over them and sealed the boys beneath the surface of the river.

Foley ran toward the revival tent, pulling his Buck knife from his back pocket as he huffed his way uphill, stopping only when he arrived at the fluttering white tent. He thrust his knife into the thick rope, tearing back and forth until the rope snapped, releasing the tent that fell as though it were a deflating balloon. All other able-bodied men ran toward the river.

Rene and Kent could be seen clinging to the top of a spruce log that had settled just under the water. Everyone watched the men spread on the logs like ants, dividing their routes and then converging near the boys. The first man to reach them dropped onto the log as though he were riding a bronco. The boys thrashed at the rolling log, its bark tearing at their flesh, mixing blood with the silt of the river. Their panicked moves bucked the rescuer upward, allowing him to toss the rope close enough for the boys to grasp. Letting go of the log, the boys sank, the timber closing above them.

"Pull!" the rescuer shouted. Others joined the man, each feverishly pulling at the thick cord. All of a sudden, two heads bobbed to the surface, flailing in the few inches that would have sealed them under the water for good. Reverend Park was on his knees praying. Emily was on the shore with other onlookers who were clutching their open-mouthed faces. Dave was nowhere to be seen. Snatched by the river, she supposed, to a watery death.

A couple of hours later, Dave popped like a cork from under two logs that had worked themselves free from the jam. His body looked like a rubber raft, blue and still. Some of the men had waded downriver for the cargo they knew would come.

Mr. and Mrs. Cook had been summoned by the screams. They were bent over, tearing feverishly at the water, searching for any sign of their son. Neighbors surrounded them, trying to offer comfort, and the Cooks stood and seized each other, wailing and letting out low moans.

Two neighbors saw Dave pop. Emily had never seen a dead body, so she stayed near the edge of the water, her feet half-in, half-out of the river, red clay swirling up between her stubby toes. Two men gathered a rope and waded out to catch him, lassoing him as though he were a wandering calf. The water was swift. They struggled to pull Dave close enough to grasp him. One man dove on top of him so he wouldn't slip by. The pressure of the man's weight caused a huge burst of air to eject from the boy's body.

They dragged him to shore, mud mingling with ropes and rescuers. Dave's mother fell across her son in wrenching sobs. Her husband stood behind her, his hands trembling on her shoulders, his face putrid white, cold. Emily stood helplessly to one side, anxious to know how Dave must have felt. Wet and puffy. Dead and lost. Empty and void of any emotion. Like Emily.

It was mid-July. In northeastern Canada, it rarely hit eighty degrees, even in midsummer. The ripe smell of sweat trickling down the skinny arms of her brother suggested that the heat that day was a New Brunswick record.

Slippery logs and double dares were a deadly combination, but in Plaster Rock, the running of the logs was the same rite of passage as the running of the bulls in Pamplona. Everyone ran them at one time or another. Parents warned of the consequences, but no one listened. The Tobique River played its part by offering what it had: life or death. Both Dave and Emily knew that. Remembering the night her mother had pulled her from the dank corner of the basement, she wished the Tobique had taken her instead.

Chapter 22

Emily
September 1960
Perth, New Brunswick

THE GREEN LEAVES OF SUMMER had bloomed into bright colors of gold and yellow before Maureen returned to Plaster Rock for the children. Although school was just days away, the children had shown no interest in going home. Emily's skin was tan, her hair bleached by the sun from her daily chore of picking blueberries in the field behind her grandfather's house. Previous summers had offered a welcome respite from the gloom that covered the house on Richard Street, but this time the loss of her best friend in the Tobique clouded Emily's days.

"I told you that river was no place for children," she'd heard her grandmother say just days after Dave had been lowered into the ground behind the Catholic church, the only graveyard in town. But something in Emily still drew her to stand at the top of the path that wound its way down to the Tobique's shore. For weeks after Dave was buried, she found herself wandering there to gaze at the water, its current undisturbed by the damage it had done. She made her way down the worn path to the edge of the river. Even though standing at the edge of the river was threatening, she felt safer here than she did in her own home, as though this place were a shield against all things bad in her life. But even the river had let her down, swallowing Dave only to spit him up dead downstream. Everything had changed, and yet nothing had changed. Logs still heaved toward the sky, creating pools of water that tempted unwary children. Reverend Park still held the last baptism of the summer at the riverside the month after Dave was lowered into the ground.

And she was certain that the things that went on in her house on Richard Street would not change, either.

Preparing for their departure, John prayed with his grandchildren in the kitchen as Ellen folded newly baked cinnamon rolls in wax paper, packing them inside a wicker basket for the children's ride home. They followed Maureen into the yard as she loaded her children's suitcases into the green Pontiac. John pressed money into his daughter's hand and hugged her close as he bid them good-bye. The drive was silent for miles until Maureen finally spoke.

"I needed a little time alone, kids," Maureen said, her eyes never veering from the road, hands firmly gripping the steering wheel, "to sort things out." She explained the changes that had happened over the summer. Maureen glanced toward Stephanie, who sat slouched on the front seat, and then in the rearview mirror at Emily. "Your father won't be living with us anymore."

Five-year-old Darren began to cry. Stephanie turned to look at her mother.

"Really?" she said, her voice rising an octave, her eyebrows moving upward and pushing a gleeful look into her forehead.

"You are to tell no one, do you understand? I can't deal with Mum and Dad nagging at me right now."

Stephanie nodded her head, a tiny smile slipping across her face. Maureen glanced in the rearview mirror. "I'll need you girls to help with Darren. I've taken on more hours at the restaurant, but I've got it all worked out. We'll be fine."

Emily stared at the mirror as her mother's nervous eyes connected with her own.

"And I've got a special dinner planned to celebrate your homecoming!"

Emily turned back toward the window and stared at the landscape as it ticked by. A smile crossed her lips, then quickly disappeared. Gone or not, she'd always see his face, smell him as he arched over her in the dark. It just didn't matter anymore. Nothing did.

Maureen made a festive dinner that night — pot roast with the fresh green beans she'd picked from her father's garden. Every corner of the house smelled like brown gravy. Emily watched her mother work all afternoon restyling a dress with rhinestone buttons and black lace. She pulled her flaming red hair into a tight bun at the nape of her neck, secured it with a white pearl comb, and dabbed perfume behind her ears and then behind Emily's, something Emily knew her mother thought was too extravagant for most occasions.

She'd made a fuss about the girls dressing up for dinner and had bought them new ribbons for their hair. Emily sullenly arranged the flowers she'd picked from the neighbor's garden in the glass milk container while Stephanie set the table. Darren stood on a kitchen chair and licked the spoon of the chocolate cake Maureen prepared, his face a pallet of brown. Even to Emily, the air in the house seemed lighter, as though the veil of gloom had been torn away. At 7:00, Maureen put Darren to bed while the girls cleaned up the kitchen, the dishes clinking a rhythmic tune. It was 8:15 when an awkward jiggle of the handle on the back door broke through the evening chatter, stiffening each of them.

"Get up to your room," Maureen ordered, the look on her face telegraphing fear.

The girls raced to the top of the steps and flopped to the hallway floor, lying on their stomachs to watch the argument they knew would unfold. Emily's throat tightened as she waited for the first glimpse of her father, her heart thumping in her chest. Nothing had changed.

Maureen stood in the kitchen watching the handle twitch left, then right. They could hear his voice rising in anger. They could see a look of determination cross their mother's face, a look that telegraphed it was she who had changed.

"Open the door, Maureen. I know you're there."

Denny's voice was slurred and angry. Maureen walked toward the opening, one foot in front of the other, her face convincing the girls that this would be no ordinary fight. Midstep, Maureen stopped, turned back to the sink, and fumbled through the cupboard beneath it, retrieving something Emily couldn't see. Emily heard a clunk as the object was dropped on the counter.

Pressing her dress down with her hands, Maureen reached for the door, pulling it open with one swift move. Their father crashed inside. Emily drew in a breath and touched Stephanie's arm.

"You no-good who—" their father stuttered, then struggled to his knees.

"Come on, Denny," Maureen said, attempting to pull him to his feet. "Be decent just this once, can we? The kids are home. We've been having a good night for a change. You promised to stay away."

The next sound was the strike of her father's heavy hand connecting with her mother's face. The blow sent Maureen reeling into the refrigerator.

"This is *my* house—" Denny was fully upright now, fury hardening his face, "— and if anyone leaves, it'll be you."

He lunged at Maureen, his hands cupped as if to choke her. She grabbed at the object she'd laid on the counter. The sound was quick and hollow. The girls heard a crash.

"Nooooo!" Stephanie screamed, jumped to her feet, and dashed down the stairs toward the kitchen. Emily was behind her, her feet pounding the wooden steps. Stephanie stopped in the doorway, her eyes saucers of fear. Emily pushed past her and looked toward the kitchen table.

Denny was lying on the floor, face down, his arms outstretched over his head and pointed toward their mother's feet. He began to vomit. A lump had formed on his head and was bleeding. Maureen stood braced against the counter, a bloody hammer clutched in her right hand. Her mouth was open, her chest heaving up and down as though someone had stolen the air.

"Get Darren. We've got to get out." She turned to look at the girls, her eyes empty, her voice a barely audible whisper. "I can't do this anymore. I can't."

She grabbed at Emily, pulling her arm with her thin fingers, dragging her upstairs to gather what they could. Terrified, Emily's skin bristled. She knew her father would kill all of them if they didn't escape for good this time. Stephanie wrapped Darren in a blanket and carried him outside.

"Stay in the car," Maureen said, her face signaling urgency. "If I don't come out in a minute, get to the neighbors and call the police." She left the driver's side open and ran back to the house. In seconds, she emerged, running, Denny's wallet clutched in her left hand. He'd started to recover, staggering behind her as she ran from the front door. Emily saw his hand holding the spot on his head where her mother had hit him.

Maureen jerked the car into gear, the tires throwing loose gravel on the driveway, sending the rear end of the car careening back and forth, and tossing the children around like loose change. In the rearview mirror, Emily watched as her father dropped onto the front porch, first to his knees and then to his face. Leaves of red and gold fluttered from the trees, covering his listless form as though he were some crazy snow globe. Slamming on the brakes, Maureen spun her head to look at him out the back window of the Pontiac. She turned forward, grasping hard on the steering wheel, and then took a long, deep breath and jammed her foot on the gas.

Emily wondered if her father would die on the porch in his own blood and vomit; the icy vision in her head froze a smile on her face. She stared out the window as they drove away, her hands folded neatly in her lap, and prayed that she'd never see him again. The house on Richard Street faded behind her like a bad dream.

Chapter 23

Maureen
September 1960
Saint John, New Brunswick

MAUREEN'S BODY SHOOK the full distance from Perth to Saint John, twitching and heaving as the car lunged back and forth across the yellow line, the road disappearing as she fought to see through the tears.

"Where are we going, Ma?" Stephanie asked, her face etched with worry.

Maureen wiped her nose onto her forearm and swallowed a deep breath.

"I've got a friend in Saint John," she said. "Her name is Irma. She comes into the restaurant now and then when she's up here visiting her sister. She told me to call if I ever needed a place to stay."

Irma Brady had recognized the lies surrounding the bruises Maureen sported. Irma had recently divorced a man who'd left marks on her body similar to Maureen's.

They reached the outskirts of Perth just before 9:00. She called Irma from a phone booth at the Sunoco station. She'd get to Carol later.

"Irma?" Her voice trembled as she whispered into the pay phone.

"Maureen? Are you OK?" Irma said.

"I — I need a place. Just for a few days."

"I've got plenty of room," Irma said. "The kids can bunk together. It'll take you a couple of hours to get to Saint John."

"I don't care how long it takes. I just need to get out of here. I'm filing for divorce on Monday."

"You know he'll try to fight this in court, don't you? He'll try and make you look like a bad mother. He'll fight for the kids just to hurt you."

"No, Irma. I've got proof this time. He'll never get the kids. I'll need some help, though."

"I'll wait up for you. I've got the name of a good lawyer. It'll be OK."

Maureen let the phone line click before hanging up the receiver. She turned toward the car, staring at the three wondering faces of her children. *What am I doing? I don't have money. I can't ask my parents for anything more. I couldn't stand to go back there to hear them say, "I told you so."*

Yanking at the folding door of the phone booth, she saw the frightened looks in her children's eyes, echoing her mistakes.

Why have my parents always been right? Why didn't I listen to them? If I had, none of this would've ever happened, and I wouldn't be so trapped.

She clamped her hand over the silver car handle, took another deep breath, and pulled it open, sliding across the red leather seat as though nothing had happened.

"We're moving to Saint John," Maureen said. "My friend Irma says there are lots of jobs and money to be made there. Maybe we'll find a pot of gold!"

In the rearview mirror, she watched Emily cover Darren as he huddled next to her, smoothing the blanket across his lap. *It's all my fault for being a coward. I recognized the signs. I just couldn't believe he'd do this to his own daughter.* Emily looked so old. Too mature for her age. She stared blankly at her mother in the rearview mirror. Maureen saw in her daughter's face that Emily knew there'd be no rainbow or pot of gold in Saint John.

Chapter 24

Emily
November 1960
Grand Falls, New Brunswick

MAUREEN DRESSED EMILY AS THOUGH she were headed for church, pulling a hand-me-down dress over her daughter's head and pushing the black-and-white saddle shoes that Emily hated on her feet. Too big. Lots of girls at school had new, shiny patent leather shoes. But Emily didn't remember ever owning anything more than those ugly saddle shoes. She and Stephanie shared shoes as though they were sharecroppers, even though Emily's grandfather had said Denny made a decent living as a carpenter. A carpenter. Like Jesus. Emily decided that Jesus couldn't be as nice as everyone had said.

It was the middle of the week. Maureen's face was stern. She told Emily they'd be driving from Saint John to Grand Falls, the county seat.

"Why aren't they coming, Ma?" Emily asked, pointing to her siblings. Maureen's face was red and puffy. Stephanie looked away. Darren played with a metal Tonka truck on the coffee table.

"The judge wants to ask you some questions," she said wringing her hands in her skirt. "Stephanie's already spoken to the attorney."

"Did I do something wrong?" A lump rose in Emily's throat as she felt the room close in around her.

"No, dear. It's — it's about your father."

Emily's mouth clamped shut like an old bank vault. Head down, she stood limp as her mother tussled to get the pink crinoline over Emily's head. She closed her eyes and blinked back tears.

Two months had passed since they had run from him. Emily thought he was dead, wished he were dead. No word had been mentioned of him since they'd run away. Now she would have to tell a judge. Everyone would blame her. They'd never be able to move back to Perth again because she'd told.

An attorney arrived to drive them to Grand Falls, although Emily wouldn't be able to recall the ride at all. The attorney and her mother talked all the way, whispering about how they thought the court hearing would go.

"We should be able to get full custody with her testimony," the attorney said, his head tilting in Emily's direction. "And alimony for at least ten years."

Her mother took little notice of Emily in the back of the car. They whispered again. From time to time, Maureen spun her head around, her neck craning. Emily could feel her mother's eyes even while she stared out the window at nothing in particular.

The sound of the big, wide door to the courtroom drove goose bumps through the young girl. Maureen was greeted by a man she seemed familiar with. He pointed to a row of chairs behind him, and he instructed Emily to sit there. The adults whispered — he, shaking his head from side to side, and Maureen, dabbing at her eyes with a tissue.

Around the room, Emily stared at a few people who talked in low voices. Two women shook their heads in that "tut-tut" way. A police officer clutched a notebook. A tall man with two big shoes that punched from under his pants like paddles stood near the judge. Emily wondered how he could walk with feet so big.

The sharp bang of the judge's gavel scared Emily so much she almost wet her pants. She jammed a hand between her legs, her dress and crinoline swallowing her arm whole. She wondered why her mother was making her come here. Her feet never touched the ground as she sat waiting on the wooden pew, so like the pew of her grandparents' church where Aunt Amy would shoot her the stink eye and then push her face at Emily, her false teeth jutting from her mouth. Emily kicked her feet back and forth like wind chimes, waiting her turn and watching her mother nestle into the attorney's neck with quiet conversations.

"Next witness," a balding man in a black robe called. His voice echoed in the nearly empty chamber.

Maureen was on the witness stand telling everyone in the courtroom their business. Aunt Carol had always said that families should keep their business to themselves. Secrets, she called them. Emily continued to swing her feet back and forth, unwilling to look her mother in the face because she knew her mother would shoot her the stink eye, just like Aunt Amy did.

Emily felt ashamed as her mother confessed her father's sins. It just wasn't done. Emily had never told anybody anything, even when she'd heard the next-door neighbors gossiping about her parents.

"I can see why he beats her," they'd said. "All those kids, and she's never home. He's got his reasons."

Maureen rose from the wooden chair, stepped away from the judge's desk, and turned to Emily.

"Come on, Emily. The judge has a few questions to ask. Tell him what you told me. That's all."

She sat glued to her seat.

"Emily!" Maureen's voice was sharp.

Emily stood, her head cast to the wooden floor, knowing every eye was on her. She walked slowly to her mother's side, where Maureen took her hand and walked her to the rigid chair next to the judge's large desk.

The man with the big feet pushed a black Bible toward her. "Place your hand on the Bible and swear to tell the whole truth and nothing but the truth, so help you God."

Emily looked at her mother, who nodded her head and placed Emily's hand on the Bible.

"Sit down. Tell him what you told me," Maureen said with insistence. Her eyes beaded on her daughter.

"Ma, I don't want to." Emily's voice cracked, and tears welled on her small face. She was ten, but the burden of her confession made her feel like an old woman.

"You have to," her mother said through her teeth. "You have to."

The judge's deep voice softened.

"Emily, it's OK. Just tell me. Did your father ever touch you down there?" He leaned toward her, pointing at her skirt. She looked away.

"Ye — Yes." Emily pushed out the words with a tiny breath.

"I can't understand you," the judge said. She turned her face toward him, her hands and body shaking.

"Yes."

"Where did he touch you?" His voice was gentle, and in his eyes, Emily saw kindness.

"Right here," she continued, rubbing her hand under the crinoline between her legs.

"Did he do anything else?" he asked.

Shame covered her. Everyone would know. Her eyes searched for a place to run, but her mother was there, watching. *She promised not to tell. He'd kill them all.* Emily lowered her head, her hands ripping at the string that had made its way free from the hem of the hand-me-down dress.

"He — he put his fingers there, and then he laid on me and hurt me."

The tears burned down her face and then dropped to her lap. Her body began to shudder. She could feel her mother's piercing eyes. She hoped that her mother would come to her, comfort her, and take her out of this place. Instead, just as she had done when Emily's father had hurt her, Maureen looked the other way, mumbling into the attorney's ear as though she were satisfied. When the judge said Emily could step down, she ran to her mother, begging to be held.

"You did great; now go sit down," Maureen said, pointing at the pew behind her, dismissing her daughter. *Her mother couldn't be trusted ever again.*

"Bring him in," the judge called to the bailiff.

The loud wooden doors opened, and Denny entered with another man at his side. Maureen didn't turn to look at him, though Denny did not take his eyes from her until someone pointed to Emily, sitting stoically on the bench behind her. Emily wondered if her father had come to tell her that he hadn't meant to hurt her, that he was sorry. His stare locked on his daughter. His eyes narrowed, the warning they contained enough to make Emily sink low into her seat. She couldn't look away from him. She knew his fury, his strength. Even if he was there to tell her he was sorry, she'd never believe him now.

For two more hours, Emily sat terrified, clutching her dress around her legs. Neighbors told of having seen horrible bruises on her mother's body as they nursed her after beatings their father had given her. Kindly Dr. Allen spoke of the many times Maureen had brought the children to him in the dark of night, their bodies bruised and battered from Denny's drunken stupors. It was when Denny's attorney began to speak that Emily realized the pain was not yet over.

"That's her, Your Honor," the pumpkin-shaped witness cried out, her finger directed at Emily's mother. "She's been after my husband for years, every time he went into that restaurant. Why, if it hadn't been for Bailey Adams catching them together down along the river... " Her voice trailed off.

"We were just walking!" Maureen screamed as she jumped to her feet.

"Sit down!" the judge bellowed, banging his gavel on the wide desk. A rumble moved through the room. The woman wiped her eyes with the embroidered handkerchief she clasped in her right hand.

"He had his reasons for beating that one." She nodded her head in Maureen's direction matter-of-factly.

The attorney dismissed the woman and then slapped a large white paper on the judge's desk.

"Your Honor, you will see that this is a marriage certificate obtained from the Superior Court in Saint John." He waved the folded paper in the air. Maureen wiggled in her chair, her hands balling into fists.

"This will show, Your Honor, that just before she turned sixteen, Mrs. Douay married a certain Brian Pelletier a day before he joined the service and that there is no record of a divorce from this man before she married my client a few weeks later."

He raised his left eyebrow, his mouth curling into a snide grin. Emily could see her mother's eyes narrow as she turned to face Denny.

"And furthermore, Your Honor, Mr. Douay believes that the three children he has raised, fed, and loved as his own — may not all be—" the attorney paused, lowering his voice and raising his hands incredulously "— his children!"

Gasps were heard from the left side of the room, where the two plump women who had been tittering nervously now clutched each other as though they had witnessed a murder.

The attorney continued, "Mrs. Douay knew she was pregnant by this other man when she tricked Mr. Douay into marrying her. He found out just a few months ago when he accidentally overheard a phone conversation between Mrs. Douay's sister, Carol Timmons, and Mrs. Douay, two nights before she beat him with a hammer and stole the children from his life."

Maureen's face whitened to ash as she turned to face her daughter. Emily dropped further into the wooden bench, her mouth open in disbelief. She pinched one hand with the other, over and over, until they reddened and bled. The attorney continued the attack.

"Mr. Douay believes that his wife has had numerous affairs during their marriage and that at least one of the other two children may not be his, either." Across the room, Denny smirked at Maureen. Her eyes flared hatred.

"That's a lie—" Maureen's voice erupted as she jumped to her feet.

The attorney pressed on.

"He does believe, however, that the child Mrs. Douay arranged for her sister, Carol, to adopt was his — a boy whose mother was the Douays' babysitter and who died in childbirth in their home," the attorney paused and turned to face Maureen, "aided by Mrs. Douay."

The attorney clutched at Maureen's arm, his face tight with fury, and pulled her back into her seat. She jerked her arm away and faced Denny, her eyes deadly cold. Emily clasped her hand over her mouth and stared at her mother in disbelief. A picture flashed in Emily's mind. She couldn't have been more than five years old, but she suddenly remembered the scene as though it were yesterday.

~ ~ ~ ~ ~

She'd watched the moon swim a curved path on the wall of her bedroom. She heard a muffled sob coming from the bathroom in the house on Richard Street. She'd climbed from her bed, dragging her blue blanket behind her, and followed the cries.

"Aaaaaahhh!" the howl echoed through the hallway.

She stopped short of the bathroom, seeing movement through

the sliver of space between the wall and the open door. A young woman thrashed in the bathtub, her face distorted in pain. Samantha. Her mother was standing over the bathtub wiping the girl's face with a worn washcloth, a tendril of her red hair flashing across her face. Her father was sitting on the toilet swigging something from a brown bottle, cursing.

The girl clutched the sides of the bathtub, breathing in tiny spurts of air, sweating hard. Her dark hair was plastered to her forehead, her eyes streaming with tears.

Emily jumped as her mother yelled, "Push! Just one more."

The young woman in the tub pinched her lips together, rocked forward, and pushed until pocks of blood rose to her skin's surface and burst.

"Whhhaaaaa!" The sound of a baby's cry rose into the night.

Her mother swaddled the child and placed it on the tile floor. A deep, ugly cry came from the girl, and then suddenly the room went silent. She saw her mother's face turn white. Her mother dropped to her knees and placed her right hand on Samantha's neck. Maureen turned to look at her husband and then began to sob.

Her crying scared Emily, and she, too, burst into tears. Her father turned and saw Emily standing in the doorway, his lips parted and angry.

"Get back to bed before I give you a good spanking!" he yelled.

Emily ran and climbed into her bed, leaving the door open, awaiting the force of his hand. Stephanie's bedroom door was closed. Baby Darren was still at Aunt Carol's. Emily heard the muffled sobs of her mother, saw her father carry a blanket-wrapped body down the stairs and into the night. The house went silent, except for the faint cry of a baby.

~ ~ ~ ~ ~

"You monster," Maureen said, rising from her chair again. "You sick, cold monster. Look what you've done to your kids — again!" Her eyes beaded on his smirking face. "I hate you, Denny. You think you've won, but Emily told the truth about what you did to her. You'll never see these kids again."

Emily watched her father's smirk disappear, his downturned lips hanging on his face like a deflated balloon. She tugged repeatedly at her straight blonde hair, so unlike Stephanie's thick, curly, brown locks and olive complexion, or Darren's flaming red mop, his skin as thin and pale as onions. *Was Darren her real brother? Or Stephanie her sister? Did she belong to anyone?*

Fifteen minutes later, the gavel swung for the last time, banging Emily's father out of their life. Her secret had been laid out for the whole town to see, her mother's shame evident in Emily's own face. Maureen was visibly upset as they left the courtroom. She clutched her daughter's hand in a vise grip. Emily turned to stare back at her father. His face was cupped in his hands, and she couldn't tell whether he was crying or relieved. He looked up, caught her eyes. Emily clamped her teeth together, causing the muscles in her face to flinch. She still wished him dead. She turned back to her mother, who tugged her toward the side door. Emily caught a glimpse of a familiar, hunched-over figure as it slipped from the back of the room, and her heart crumbled beneath her jacket. *Grampy.*

PART TWO

Chapter 25

Emily
November 1960
Saint John, New Brunswick

THE ARRIVAL AT 156 DOUGLAS AVENUE came at the end of a three-hour drive from the Grand Falls courthouse to an apartment in Saint John. Irma Brady's cramped, reconfigured tenement was a haven from the abusive life they'd left at the house on Richard Street. Maureen found a job waitressing at a diner on Post Street and applied to rent the worn-looking house when she saw a balding man pounding a "For Rent" sign into the ground.

"This should be easy enough," she'd said to Irma as she smoothed her calico dress across her stomach and marched across the lawn to the portly man. Maureen's first date with the new landlord, a Mr. Cain Winters, cemented the deal. The gold band on his left hand meant nothing to either of them. They both had needs, Emily heard her mother tell Irma.

The house they rented from Cain was built around 1904 in what was known as the Trinity Royal District of Saint John. The two-story Victorian mansion had fallen into the hands of Cain Winters in 1956 after the previous owner hanged herself from the rafters in the attic. Since that time, some four years earlier, renters had come and gone quickly, citing the house as haunted.

The neighbors shared with Maureen that the original tenant had been a striking woman, her long hair often braided into a snake that coiled down her back. The night she'd hanged herself, she'd prepared herself for bed, donning a long, white nightgown and plaiting her hair, while her husband, Martin, sipped brandy in the den. It was said that she stood in front of the bathroom mirror and cut her red braid, placing it in a long narrow box with a note directed to her husband. She had known of his affair all along.

No one heard the groan of the attic steps as she climbed to her death. She placed the box with the note and braid at the foot of the chair on which she stood. She wrapped a thick rope around her neck, stepped up, and then jumped. Her husband found her swinging like a rag doll an hour later.

Renters swore that the woman roamed the house, making stairs squeak, doors open and close, and faucets turn on and off. Emily's mother thought it was all hogwash. This was a free ride for her. Cain would fix the house the way she liked it, and as long as they "dated," there'd be no exchange of money.

The house had seen better days. The oak floors were covered in worn floral carpet. The wallpaper was original, the pattern dull and faded as though curtains had always been drawn open, the sunlight beating the pattern off the walls. The building sat on a little knoll fifteen steps above the passing sidewalk and was wrapped with a wide porch that hugged the sizable structure. Views of the harbor along the Bay of Fundy allowed Emily to watch the ships sail out to sea, wishing every moment she might sail away with one of them.

The front door was solid oak with an etched glass pane of curlicues and roses, swinging inward to an ample foyer. An oak fireplace, dark with age, sat to the right, unlit, its mantle carved with pomegranates and tiny birds. A wooden staircase behind the door jutted upward to the second floor, its stairs creaking and groaning beneath newcomers' legs, as if pained by their intrusion.

Four bedrooms and one bathroom were upstairs. Maureen and Stephanie chose the two rooms whose large bay windows faced the front of the house. The other two bedrooms were connected by an adjoining closet that hid a secret set of stairs exiting upward into the attic.

Emily's room was on one side of the staircase, five-year-old Darren's on the other. The bathroom stood across the hallway next to the forward staircase. A short doorway with a burnished door handle huddled between the steps, and the lock housed a gray skeleton key that allowed entry to a second set of steps that led upward, again, to the attic.

"No need to go up there," Cain insisted as he showed them around. "I just use it for storage." He winked at Emily, his ever-smooth scalp and beer belly making her stomach curl.

The house felt uneasy to her, as though something were always ready to happen. Like Richard Street. She couldn't put her finger on it and never told her mother, but she didn't feel quite right about being alone there. After school she'd often make her way to the wharf in the Port of Saint John and linger there rather than wait alone in the house for someone to return.

The Port of Saint John bustled with activity as workers busied themselves with the renovation of the Long Wharf Terminal. People stood watching workmen fling thick ropes dockside from the deck of the giant vessels as they loaded and unloaded transported goods. Onlookers lined the wharfs as if they were orphans awaiting adoption, their curiosity overtaking common sense, and Emily saw one poor soul get flung off the pier by a wayward cable. Workers had scrambled to pull the man from the chilly water, tossing a white rubber ring at his frame while he continued to thrash, bobbing like a broken cork in the bay. The workers on the deck of the ship tittered and yelled as the poor man was hoisted, unharmed, back to the pier.

"Good thing it's high tide, buddy, or you'd find yourself up to your neck in mud!" a wharf man yelled, shaking his fat index finger at the sputtering fool.

The city was famous for its tides, the highest in the world. The clash of the waters generated a reversal of the city's waterfall twice each day, as the south-facing bay received the rush of the ocean's incoming tide. The waters collided, one lapping over the other in the narrow mouth of the bay's opening, and in a natural phenomenon, the conflict reversed the flow of the falls.

The bay was quick and full of bustling vessels bound for open water, their decks and hulls filled with massive containers of durable imports and exports. Small motor craft darted in and out, stopping for fuel, food, and merriment at the private marinas that lined the rim of the bay. Outfitters promised canoe trips, fishing trips, and sightseeing journeys to tourists who had heard of this uncrowded and watery vacation spot.

Emily strolled down the gently sloping hill to Long Wharf. The air smelled of warm salt and fishy tides. She sniffed the air like the harp seals in the bay, taking in the salty vapor and sharp smell of fish. The eerie screams of the gulls and the lick of the water lapping against the boats made her feel ancient, as though she'd stood here before. The day was warm, and her mother was at work. Darren was at a babysitter's, and Stephanie often stopped at a girlfriend's house before returning home. Taking her time, Emily walked the long distance to the water's edge of the bay to watch the ships arrive and depart, wishing one day she could make her way to another place across the ocean, stowed away in one of the great hulls, or find her way back up the Tobique River to Plaster Rock in one of the many canoes she'd heard navigated the waters of the Saint John. The rich city had become a refuge from their father, but it also represented Emily's loneliness, the separation from the people she loved the most — her grandparents.

Saint John was a mine of men for her mother, even though Maureen had hooked Mr. Cain. Most of Maureen's new men would parade themselves in and out of the children's lives before Emily ever really got to know them. Yet she tried. Her mother would fawn over each of them, sitting on their laps and hugging their necks until she chased Emily to her room. She never understood her mother's angry looks. She only wanted someone to love her. Someone other than her father. Or Cain.

* * *

Three months after they'd moved into the old house, the doorbell rang. Cain stood there, a half-cocked grin sliced up the side of his mouth. His eyebrows were wiry and wiggled as he spoke. Emily stepped back, uneasy in his presence, unsure of what he was doing there when he knew her mother was working.

"Came by to wait for your mother," he said, pushing his big body through the door before Emily could protest. His pants were cinched high above his protruding belly; his pant legs hovered inches above his unpolished shoes.

"She won't be here until at least nine," she said, backing her way to the steps.

"I got nothing better to do." Cain first let his eyes rove around the room and then hung them on her.

"Where are your brother and sister?"

"Steph should be here any minute. Darren's across the street," Emily said, her foot already planted two steps upward, regretting that she'd not stayed away from the house as she usually did. "I'm doing homework."

She pushed up the stairs, her feet clicking on the oak steps. Out of the corner of her eye, she caught him watching her, listening to her footsteps on the floor above him. Her instincts knew him, knew what he was thinking.

She closed her bedroom door and locked it, putting the skeleton key in her pocket, and then listened. A long slow creak, one she knew well, gripped her in fear. She pulled off her shoes and backed toward her closet, never taking her eyes off the door. The doorknob moved, first to the right, then to the left. Emily slipped into the closet and had put her foot on the first step to the attic when she heard a key fumbling in the lock. *Darned old houses.* She knew he'd found another key in the bathroom door across the hallway. She moved up the stairs one step at a time, her legs spread to the outside of the risers so the stair's noises would not give her away. She heard the door to her room swing open and imagined Cain's eyes sweeping the room.

"Emily?" His voice was muffled, but she knew what he wanted. "I'm not going to hurt you. You can trust me. Come on out."

She reached the attic and crawled on her hands and knees to one side so that he might not see her if he looked up the steps. Emily heard him searching below, items tumbling from her bed, the door to her closet finally swinging open. She wrapped her arms around her knees and pushed her face into them. She could see him through a crack in the floor as he stepped inside, first looking through the closet, then up the stairs. She held her breath.

"Emily?"

Silence.

She heard the heaviness of him on the first step. She pushed back, making a small sliding noise. In an instant, his steps came two at a time. Emily clawed her way to her feet, her arms swinging wildly at the dark as she tried to make her way to the other staircase and escape to the hallway below.

Cain was at the top of the closet steps by the time Emily had found the railing downward. She glanced back. A sliver of light from the attic vent beamed like a scar on his face, illuminating his leer as he rushed toward her. It was the look of her father's face.

Emily's feet quickened down the stairs — his, too, just behind her. She clamped her hand around the brass doorknob and pushed her body into the exit. Cain's feet were already tapping downward. The door was locked.

Why me? Why is it always me? She yanked the handle. It wiggled but did not give way. She felt him stop behind her, the silence signaling his victory. The smell of Aqua Velva hung in the air, a pungent musk that reminded her of the old cellar.

"Where are you going, Emily?" he whispered from the darkness above her.

Emily swung around, running her hand over the wall to her right. The light switch caught in her finger, and she snapped it on. Cain recoiled from the surprise illumination of the bulb above him; his eyes twitched and pinched together.

"Get away from me, Cain," she said. "I'll tell everyone if you touch me, I swear."

"Now, girl," he said, moving one step closer, his breathing slowing down. "You got nothing to tell. No one will believe your momma's boyfriend would do anything to the children he's so good to, now would they?"

He pushed downward, forcing Emily to the bottom step. Her back was to the door. He reached for her, grabbing her from behind, and jerked her face to his waist. Static made her hair fly around his hand as though he had electrocuted her with his touch. He pulled her up two steps and then forced his open mouth over hers. She wiggled her head just enough to catch his lower lip between her teeth and bit down — hard. He pulled back, yanked his hand to his bleeding mouth. Their eyes locked, her determined look piercing him. He punched her hard, crumpling her small body into the step just below them.

"Anybody home?" Stephanie's voice sounded muffled.

Cain's head jerked from Emily's face to the door below him. Emily screamed until her lungs held no more air. Cain punched her from above, struggling to silence her. A quick tapping on the oak steps, and then a voice came through the door.

"Are you OK?" Stephanie was hysterical as she tugged on the door handle. "I'll get the police."

Emily heard her sister's footsteps as she retreated for help. Cain tore up the stairs, across the attic, and down the back steps into the night.

* * *

"I'm sure you're confused, Emily," her mother said after arriving home. "Steph heard you scream when you fell. She didn't hear anyone else with you. The police said Cain was home when it happened." She rubbed her hand across her daughter's bruised forehead. "He's been so good to us. He'd never do something like that. It's probably just the bump on your head. I told you not to go up there."

Emily turned away, pulling herself to the other side of her bed. *She will not believe me, and I cannot trust her to protect me. She sees what's happening. She's always seen.* Maureen's face tightened as she tugged the blanket over Emily and walked to the bedroom door.

"You should be grateful to Cain, young lady. He cares about all of us. I'm just glad he understands what you went through with your father. I don't know what I'd do without him right now. Just go to sleep. I'll check in on you when I get home."

Maureen switched off the light and, with it, Emily's final bit of trust, leaving the girl cold and empty, her heart sagging, unsure if she'd ever be safe again. Her mother neither believed her nor stayed to comfort her. But then it *was* Friday night, and her mother had made it very clear that she had a date.

Chapter 26

Emily
October 1963
Saint John, New Brunswick

THEY OFTEN GATHERED IN THE BATHROOM for the weekly ritual of watching their mother prepare for a date, having survived three years away from their father. Stephanie perched on the rim of the claw-foot tub holding makeup while Darren and Emily shared the toilet seat, Darren's legs dangling like wind chimes. Eight-year-old Darren pinched and poked at Emily until Stephanie declared, "Enough!"

Maureen's routine was so precise that they knew in exactly what order to pass the tools. Makeup. Check. Rouge. Check. Eyebrow pencil. Check. Mascara. Check. Lipstick. Check. It was as precise as a surgical procedure; each of them was responsible for specific tools.

She slathered carroty-colored makeup on her lily-white skin, pulling the cream-based colorant to the edge of her face as though it were a cliff. It stopped there quite abruptly, leaving her looking as though she had glued on a mask. Her neck remained a pale marble pillar.

Tipping her head to one side, she clamped on cheap, dangling earrings that reflected enough light to clear any suspicion that her odd-colored face did not belong on her white neck. She needn't have done that; anyone who knew her was aware that she'd be entertaining enough to keep their attention focused on something other than her orange face or her careening eyebrows that took flight from the center of her face.

"Are these things on straight?" Maureen asked, taking special care to force her face at Emily.

"Yes, Ma," Emily retorted, smirking but never looking full into her mother's face.

Maureen whirled, her brow line furrowed and tense.

"You shouldn't laugh, young lady. This will be you someday."

The doorbell rang. Emily watched her mother pump her hair one more time while eyeing her figure in the glass of the bathroom window. *I hope this guy has some money on him tonight. Otherwise, what will Ma do for our lunch money on Monday?* Emily watched her mother sashay down the staircase, her skirt making a swishing sound as her hips swaggered back and forth, then out of sight.

With Maureen gone, Stephanie and Emily returned to the bathroom and circled the sink, ordering Darren to the toilet seat. Emily and Stephanie dipped their fingers in their mother's makeup jar and took turns slathering the tan cream over each other's faces, leaving orange finger marks on everything they touched. Darren threw his hands into the air, giggling and begging for Emily to paint his face as well. By the time they were finished, they looked like a half case of oranges.

Fifteen-year-old Stephanie primped and dabbed perfume on, then changed her clothes at least three times before settling on a bright red sweater that hugged her small breasts and a pair of blue jeans she had borrowed from a friend.

"Where are you going?" Emily asked her sister, winding her long, stringy hair between her thumb and forefinger.

"Ma's probably out all night," Stephanie said, rolling her dark hair into a mature-looking bun at the nape of her neck as she eyed herself in the mirror. "I'm going to a dance at school."

"She's gonna kill you if she finds out," Emily said, the skin prickling on her arms, bumps rising and flashing across her body. Stephanie twirled and stared Emily straight in the eye.

"Then she's not gonna find out, is she?"

"I — I guess not," Emily said, lowering her face toward the pink tiled floor.

"Don't worry, I'll be home before she comes in—" Stephanie put her hand under her sister's chin and raised her head "—and I'll call you, OK?"

Emily roamed the house all night, as she did on most nights when she was left with Darren. She tried on her mother's flashy clothes, walked in her mother's high heels, and rummaged through the dresser drawers, waiting for the phone call that never came.

She hated being alone. It seemed that her mother had all but forgotten she even had children since the divorce. Maureen left for work just before Emily got home from school, then disappeared most weekend nights with various men. She never bothered to ask where Emily had been or who she was with. She never asked if they'd eaten or had their schoolwork done. She seemed to stop caring at all.

Though Stephanie was supposed to be responsible for her siblings, even she had changed. Leaving for school each morning, her plaid skirt and knee-highs covered most of her legs. But Emily had seen her at Bernie's Drug Store after school, skirt hiked way up, buttons on her white shirt undone, showing off the slightest peek of her bra. A couple of skinny boys huddled near her sister, all smiles, while Stephanie puffed on a cigarette, flirting shamelessly. Three months later, Emily caught her sister stark-naked in the shadows of the garage, some boy bucking on top of her. Emily never told, pushing that secret deep inside with the other awful memories she carried around.

With Stephanie at the dance, Emily settled Darren in his bed, reading him his favorite book until he fell asleep. She brushed his hair to one side before she touched her lips to his forehead and then slipped from his room. For the balance of the evening, she roamed around the house, sipping on a glass of Dr. Pepper. The floors of the old house creaked under her as she moved from room to room. She caught her image in the bathroom mirror. A pale, unrecognizable thirteen-year-old girl reflected back at her. A car passed, its lights moving silhouettes through the room. A likeness of her father's shadow reeled across her. She stood clamped in the moment, rotating her face back and forth in the mirror and trying to push away the image of fear that seemed forever lodged there. She whirled around and ran to the window, pulling back the curtain, staring to the street below. Her eyes searched the darkness, trying to determine whether the shadow might really have been his. For fifteen long minutes she stood — shaking, terrified — her hands clasped on either side of the window. Her breath came in short gasps, releasing with an angry push. Her muscles kept a quick rhythm with her pounding heart. When her crying subsided, she slumped to the cold marble floor, wrapped her arms around her legs, pulling into herself, as she'd done when her father was finished with her.

And then she settled in her mind that she would not give in to that fear of him ever again.

Chapter 27

Emily
November 1963
Saint John, New Brunswick

THE SEASON HAD BEEN UNKIND, the wind cold, the snow blustery. Her mother scoured herself for another weekend escapade and called for Emily to bring a fresh slip from the dresser drawer.

As a young girl, Emily often watched her mother dress from the hallway, peeking through the half-opened bedroom as though she were watching someone she'd never known. She'd mimic her mother as she'd brush her own hair, throwing her head back and flashing her small hands through her blonde hair, pushing it upward and swirling it into a bun at the nape of her neck with a broken-toothed comb. Then she'd pretend to scrub her face, rubbing up and down and around with an invisible washcloth, as her mother did, pretending to throw it to the floor when she was done. Maureen was the cleanest woman Emily had ever known. Uncannily clean. Antiseptic. The walls of their house looked worn from her scrubbing. The kitchen, painted tangerine, needed repainting often because Maureen scrubbed it to melon.

Emily tugged open the well-organized drawer and retrieved the long, silky garment from beneath a harvest of pointy bras. She glanced around and then pulled a bra from the dresser. She moved to the mirror and held the bra over her own small breasts, cocking her head to one side and wondering why her mother even wore a bra; the small protrusions from her chest didn't warrant one.

Maureen was 5'8" and carried her 160 pounds well on her large frame. She had a quick wit and a sharp tongue, something Emily had grown to recognize in herself, too. Her mother's hair flamed like a torch — red, intriguing. Her breasts were small but well-disguised with the cheap, sparkling jewelry and interesting animal-print tops she wore. Her mother could light up a room when she walked in, but she'd become opinionated, a big drinker, and a shameless flirt after they'd left her father.

Returning the bra to the dresser, Emily pulled the slip from the drawer and caught a glimpse of a colorful book. Her hand was drawn to it. A woman was on the cover sitting with her legs crossed on a tall barstool, her elbows planted on the countertop. A martini was clasped in one hand, a cigarette in the other. Her face carried a wide smile. *Sex for One*, the title announced. Emily's eyes widened; her mouth fell open.

"Emily?" Her mother's shrill voice startled her, and she dropped the book, frantically covering it with lingerie. Running through the hallway, Emily slid to a halt in her stocking feet and then pushed the slip through the crack in the bathroom door.

"What took you so long?" her mother asked.

"I, uh, was, uh—"

"My date is waiting," Maureen said, taking no note of Emily's shaking hands or her answer. Her mother slipped the white silk over her head and down her body and then added her straight black dress.

Over the years, her mother's waistline had slowly disappeared, something her mother explained away as water bloat. "I'll just take a water pill, and it'll be gone in a day or two," she'd laugh, patting her stomach. But Emily knew it was liquor. It was a smell she'd never forget, a smell lodged in her senses. The smell of her father.

A deep voice boomed from the entryway below as Maureen made her grand entrance down the staircase.

"Wow, Maureen! You look like a real winner!"

But Emily knew the losers were the same every week — her kids.

With her mother gone, Emily slipped away from her siblings and tiptoed to her mother's dresser, removing the *Sex for One* book. Her face flushed with shame as she hugged the book to her chest. A voice seemed to tug at her — convince her — that she was doing something very wrong. She glanced back into the hallway, her head cocked, listening for her siblings in the room below. Feeling safe, she rushed to her mother's closet and allowed her eyes to skim the pages, a sliver of light shooting through the crack of the half-closed door.

At school, her teachers remarked that they were amazed at Emily's ability to read and understand material so quickly. But reading was Emily's escape. In her books, she found she could believe that fathers really loved their children and that mothers were always aware of their children's pain. In books, she became a girl who didn't see everyone around her with cynical eyes, and at times she believed she was almost good enough for someone to love.

But here she was again, unworthy, reading her mother's trashy book, barely able to contain her disgust. Her eyes grew as big as saucers with each turning page. When she could no longer contain herself, she hid the book under her shirt and raced down the back stairs to the kitchen.

"What?" Stephanie asked, cupping her swelling stomach with her right hand.

Emily was breathless and shaking.

"Steph, I have to talk with you — now!"

Stephanie scraped a grilled cheese sandwich out of the blackened skillet and balanced it on the end of a metal spatula, eventually depositing it in front of Darren.

"Did you get a letter from Dad?" Darren queried, pressing his hopeful eyes upward.

"You idiot," Emily said. "He's never going to write to us. He doesn't even pay alimony. Ma says he doesn't want anything to do with any of us, and that's fine by me."

Darren turned and slumped at his food. Emily widened her eyes and pointed her head to the left, toward the dining room. Stephanie put her hand on Darren's shoulder.

"You eat, and then get ready for bed. I'll be there to kiss you good night in a minute." She brushed the last of the bread crumbs from her hands to her pants and followed Emily into the dining room, glancing back to watch their eight-year-old brother as he pushed the sandwich around on his plate.

"What?" she said sharply, plopping on a wooden chair.

"Look what I found in Mom's drawer," Emily said, holding out the book like a sacrifice. Stephanie grabbed it from her sister's hand and looked at it, then glanced at Emily and back at the book.

"Is this it?" she asked, her voice pitching high. "*This* is what you had to show me?"

Emily pulled her head back into her shoulders. "You've seen this before?" she asked.

"Yes," Stephanie said, breaking into laughter. "I've read it and tried just about everything in it," she added with a confidence that a fifteen-year-old girl should not have about such matters. "This is Mom's book. Where did you get it?"

Emily stared at her sister, her eyes batting over and over, her mouth gaped open. "I — ah — I can't believe—"

"Believe it, Emily. It's no big deal. It just tells you how to — get — well — you know, without having a guy do you. Mom made me read it a couple of years ago so I wouldn't come home pregnant."

Her lips curved into a sneer. She put her hand on her stomach.

"Didn't work for me, did it?" Stephanie said, rubbing her middle. "I still got pregnant." She eyed Emily. "Maybe Mom was going to make you read it now." A smirk unfolded across her face.

Shaking her head from side to side, Emily choked out, "No! No way! She'd never do that! Never!" Emily threw the book across the room and crawled under the table, pulling her legs to her chest. She'd felt the stirrings between her legs. It frightened her. When she had those feelings, she'd close her eyes and try to chase the thoughts away, but her father's face always came into view. She felt his nearness — smelled him and wanted to vomit. *I cannot escape him.*

"Em." Stephanie's voice was calm and steady as she got on her knees and peered under the table at her sister. "I won't tell. Just put the book back. She doesn't have to know."

Her mother *would* know Emily had read this book. She'd see it on Emily's face and call her the slut that Emily felt she was, just as she'd screamed at her sister just a week earlier when she'd found out Stephanie was pregnant.

Maureen's voice had risen through the wood floor of the house that night. "You no-good tramp! How am I supposed to raise another kid when I can't even afford the ones I have? How could you do this to me?"

Emily heard a hard whack and then soft sobbing.

"Get up to your room. You'll never amount to anything, anyway. Get out of my face. I can't stand the sight of you."

A door slammed, and Stephanie had climbed the creaking oak stairs, her shoulders slumped forward as she passed Emily's open doorway, never looking in. Stephanie's long, walnut-colored hair covered a large red welt on the side of her almond-shaped face. Emily ran to the opening and watched her sister disappear behind a closing door. A wave of pain crossed her heart; she had no way to comfort her sister, no way to help.

Just two days earlier, it had been Darren. He'd been on the porch of the upstairs balcony, his left hand pocketed deep in the front of his pants. Their mother had flung open the door to sweep the porch, and there was Darren — mouth open, horrified.

Maureen stood behind him, her face pulled into a horrific, silent scream. Darren scrambled to pull his hands from his pants, pushing his T-shirt over his open zipper. She began to flail at him, her hands pounding one over the other on his back.

"You sick pervert!" she'd screamed. "You no-good, sick weirdo. You're just like your father."

Darren had ducked, holding his thin arms over his head to shield himself, crying.

She was relentless, whacking him again and again amid the curses. "Get out of here. Get out of my face, you queer." She'd dropped the broom, sobbing into her hands.

Darren had run to his room, the thick red welts on his bare arms and back glowing. He ran past Stephanie and Emily, who stood frozen in the hallway, drawn by their mother's screams. They were silent and afraid. A few minutes later, Maureen emerged from the porch, wiping her nose on her forearm, dragging the broom with her other hand. She glared at the girls, who stood beside the porch door in the hallway as stiff as soldiers. Stephanie had placed her right hand on her stomach.

"You see the heartache you kids cause me?" Maureen said as she pushed passed them. "I can't do this anymore."

The broom thumped behind her down the back staircase, leaving the hallway echoing the emptiness each of them felt.

Chapter 28

Emily
December 1963
Saint John, New Brunswick

THREE WEEKS AFTER STEPHANIE had announced her pregnancy, Maureen was draped over the side of the bed, one arm hanging like a broken tree limb that had not yet been completely severed, the other planted under her backside. Her mouth sagged open, a spittle of drool still clinging to the side of her pure white lips. Her red hair was wrapped with a blue bath towel as though she had just stepped out of the shower.

Although her lids were clamped tight, Emily could see the outline of her mother's eyes darting from side to side in her head. Maureen's breathing was shallow. An empty medicine bottle lay on the floor, just out of the reach of her mother's dangling hand.

Emily screamed, her hands flying to her mouth. She tore at her mother, grabbing her nightgown and shaking her hard.

"Ma! Wake up, Ma! You can't do this! You can't!"

Her mother's body was heavy and limp. Emily shook her again. The room closed in around her, sucking the air from her lungs. A thousand memories began to float into Emily's head. The dank room in the basement. The warmth of the sunshine on her arms when she picked blueberries. The coolness of the river's current as it ran downriver. Dave's drowning. Her dunking in the river. Cain. She pulled away and moved around the bed to stand beside her mother. Leaning in, she brushed her hand across Maureen's forehead and down her cheek, pulling a lock of her mother's red hair from her mouth, where it had lodged as her mother fell into darkness. Her eyes locked for a moment on the tranquil look that covered Maureen's face. It was a look she recognized from her grandfather's face. A look she wanted to carry on her own face. Peace. The telephone was inches away, but Emily did not reach for it. She was cemented in the moment.

Her trance was broken only when she heard the front door creak open.

"Help me! Please, somebody help me!"

Groceries slammed to the wooden floor below as she heard the rush of Stephanie's feet darting up the steps two at a time.

Stephanie stopped at the door, a horrified look crossing her face.

"Nooooo!" Her voice was low and gurgled. She ran to Emily's side and began smacking their mother's face hard, making it roll from side to side. Emily backed away, her skin prickling as she watched her sister try to revive their mother. Her heart seized as she twisted her hands one over the other.

"Call the police," Stephanie directed, swiveling back toward her sister. Emily stood dazed and silent.

"Now!" Stephanie screamed, sending Emily careening toward the blue princess phone that perched on her mother's nightstand. Darren had just arrived home from school and stood silently at the bottom of the stairs holding a book, his face ashen.

Everything began to move in slow motion. An ambulance arrived, red lights and siren echoing a hollow scream. Darren huddled on the bed beside their mother, his hand brushing her forehead. Stephanie continued to shake and strike, yelling into Maureen's limp face. Suddenly, uniformed strangers rushed in, pushing the children aside. Emily heard the rushing of air being pushed into the open mouth of her mother. Another man poked at Maureen's arm with a long needle. In minutes, the strangers hauled Maureen away as her children watched from the upstairs porch — tearful, clinging to each other as Stephanie reassured her siblings that their mother would be fine. Hours later, Stephanie called Aunt Carol. Returning to her mother's room, Emily found the suicide note that had fallen to the floor, kicked under the bed during the commotion.

I can't do this anymore, it read. *These kids are too much. I've got no money, no one to share the responsibility. No one cares about me. I'm sorry. Maureen*

Emily squatted by the bottom of the bed, gripping the note in her lap, trying to make sense of what her mother had done. Not once in the note had Maureen mentioned what might happen to them. Stephanie was not yet sixteen but already pregnant. Emily knew that her sister would never be allowed custody of her and Darren. They'd be split up, Emily was sure of that, and probably relegated to foster homes where who knew what might happen to them? Or worse yet, maybe they'd be given back to their father. She shuddered at the thought, hardening her jaw as she rose, crushing the note in her hands as she moved toward her mother's closet.

Swinging the door open, its hinges creaking, Emily pulled her mother's favorite leopard print dress from the hanger, the triangle swinging empty and listless on the metal rod. She tugged the dress into her face, taking in the scent of Evening in Paris, her tears staining the silken cloth. Her fingers curled toward her palms, her mouth opening into a scream as she ripped the garment to shreds.

Chapter 29

Emily
February 1964
Saint John, New Brunswick

MAUREEN'S RECOVERY TOOK MORE THAN TWO WEEKS, the medicine prescribed by her doctor delaying the comeback of her generally pleasant mood. When she finally returned to her waitressing job, she pulled Stephanie out of school, citing health reasons when the school asked for an explanation. Although Stephanie's form had already begun to expand, loose-fitting clothes had disguised her shame to that point. When she was no longer able to contain her belly, their mother insisted that Stephanie remain in the house, cleaning and babysitting Darren until her time came.

"Who's the father?" Maureen asked one night when the liquor began to talk. Emily's eyes darted between her mother and her sister.

"It doesn't matter," Stephanie said, her head sagging on her neck.

"Tell me, Stephanie! He should take care of this," her mother screamed, raising her hand at her sister while Darren and Emily stood like stone soldiers. "I shouldn't have to pay for his child!"

"Go ahead, Ma," her sister said. "Hit me. It's what you do, isn't it? Like Dad? I don't care! I'm not telling you anything!" Stephanie stormed from the room, leaving their mother sagging into the kitchen chair, stoop-shouldered and crying. Emily never told, either, even though she remembered the boy from the garage.

On the eve of the birth of her mother's first grandchild, Emily watched as Maureen readied Stephanie for the drive to a hospital seventy-five miles away, over the border into Maine. Maureen had been fearful that a birth announcement connecting her to scandal might jeopardize her job or her relationship with Cain. And that they'd be the gossip of the town, maybe ruin any chances for Stephanie to succeed in anything.

"You kids are never to speak of this, you hear me?" Maureen whispered at Emily and Darren, her eyes angry and swollen as she pushed Stephanie at the door. "No one can ever know."

"Yes, Ma," they chorused back.

"I'll be back in a few hours. Now get to bed." The door slammed behind her.

Emily watched from the living room window, the agony on her sister's face evident as the two made their way to the car. She clenched her jaw, tightening her hands into fists and pulled them to her face. Stephanie paused every other step and clutched at her stomach, her mouth frozen wide. A cry, deep and agonizing, emerged as she hunched into a ball, her painful wail jutting into the night sky. Maureen glanced from side to side, hoping the neighbors weren't peering from behind their checkered curtains and hearing the pain of her daughter's telling confession. Emily dropped her hands and tapped her fingers against the living room window, catching her sister's attention as she settled into the car. Stephanie nodded her head and gave Emily a weak smile before the car disappeared. Emily kept her hands pressed against the window, the nearness of her breath making a circle on the glass as she wished the moment away.

The next morning, when the door creaked open, Maureen slipped into the old house — alone. "It's dead. Stillborn." The flatness of her voice, so void of emotion, left a haunting picture. "We'll never speak of it again."

Days later, Maureen disappeared again, returning with a sullen-eyed Stephanie, whose endless silence suffocated the house for two weeks. Then she was silently gone, abruptly, as though her place in Emily's life had been only a dream. She appeared outside Emily's school one sunny afternoon.

"Steph, are you all right? Ma's going crazy trying to find you."

"She's not going to find me, Em. I've been at a friend's house Ma doesn't know about. Says his uncle owns a store in Moncton and that I can work there. I'm hitchhiking there today. I'll be fine."

"But what about me and Darren?"

"As soon as I get some money put back, I'll figure something out. You stay put. It won't be long." She put her arms around Emily and held on. "OK? I promise."

Emily nodded her head yes, though she knew no one ever kept their promises.

"You can't tell Ma anything," Stephanie added.

Emily bobbed her head again.

"Why don't you go to Plaster Rock? Stay with Gram and Gramp. They'd want you there, Steph."

"No." Her voice was quick to clamp off the thought. "I just couldn't lie to them. I'd have to tell them about the baby—" Her voice choked in her throat. "You know what they'd think of me, Em. I just couldn't embarrass them that way."

Emily looked at the ground and kicked at the sidewalk.

"Grampy always said that we're forgiven, Steph, that we're loved no matter what."

"That's a fairy tale, Em. No one really forgives anything, or if they do, they never forget. Don't worry. I'll be OK. I'll see you soon, Sis."

Emily knew her sister was right. She'd never forget, either. They hugged, her sister's hair folding over Emily's arm. She stood in the schoolyard and watched her sister walk away. She hated Stephanie for leaving them behind yet loved her for the courage she knew it took to do it. It would be well over a year before she'd see her sister again.

Chapter 30

Emily
April 1965
Saint John, New Brunswick

"HAPPY FIFTEENTH BIRTHDAY, EM!" Ann, her best friend, yelled from across the smoke-filled room.

"Yeah, Ann," Emily yelled back, "it's a real big deal, huh?" She poured another drink of Canadian Club.

Birthdays meant nothing to her, none of them ever worth celebrating. What did she have to celebrate? By now she was a teenage drunk, hovering over a trash can at a place the kids at school called "The Barn." The remodeled shack sat at the edge of Saint John, owned by the parents of one of her friends.

Mismatched sofas lined the edges of the room, their worn seats telegraphing heavy use. Dimly lit bulbs cast eerie shadows on the painted, black walls. A stereo blasted the latest Rolling Stones record as people danced wildly in the middle of the floor. One or two couples made out in the corners of the room while others lit cigarettes and puffed smoke circles into the air. You could go to The Barn if you knew someone or if they wanted to know you.

Emily was like a sister to most of the guys on the high school football team. She was dull, like a wool sweater. Not pretty, just pretty ordinary. Her long blonde hair was stringy and unkempt. Her legs had turned into pillars, bridging up the thin body of a young woman who didn't yet know she was blossoming. She was the girl the boys bounced their problems off of. A secret-keeper. A message-bearer. A somebody. Most other girls who got invited were there for the reasons boys generally invited girls. Necking. Sex. Smoking dope.

But for Emily and Ann, The Barn became a retreat, a safe zone where they could drink all they wanted, the liquid supplied by the unknowing parents of their friends. Emily watched everything that went on, never participating, protected by the big guys who had taken the girls in for a reason she and Ann never fully understood. Maybe it was the girls who protected them, giving the guys an excuse if they wanted out of the place.

"Hey, I'd stay, but I promised to take Emily and Ann home by eleven," one would say.

"My parents sent them along to make sure I didn't get into any trouble," another said once, motioning to Emily. She'd pointed two fingers at her eyes and then back at him, a stern warning. Whatever reason they had for using her, she liked that she mattered to someone.

She was at The Barn one Friday night when Stephanie walked in on the arm of the school's formidable linebacker. Emily recognized the familiar frame from across the room and squinted to focus on the too-thin face of the brown-haired girl. Emily grabbed at Ann, clutching tightly until she turned to see why Emily was interrupting the conversation between her and the potential new beau.

"What?" Ann asked, her eyebrows kneading in disgust.

Emily lifted her chin toward the newcomer.

"Is that Steph?" Her eyes were unable to focus, the mixture of liquor and weed slowing her senses.

Ann yelled, "Steph! Over here!"

Stephanie caught sight of Ann's flailing arm, her mouth dropping open in surprise as she came running. Emily wobbled to her feet and hugged her sister until she felt no longer able to breathe.

"What are you doing here?" Stephanie asked, knowing full well why people came.

"Just hanging out with my friends," Emily said defiantly, motioning her hand to one of the guys, who lifted his shirt to show a muscled torso — as though she'd signaled a command to do so.

Stephanie wrinkled her nose and turned back to stare her sister in the face. "Come on, Em. Let's talk."

They retreated to a corner of The Barn, dragging the bottle of Jack Daniel's that Stephanie had concealed in her purse, leaving Ann to entertain the boy Stephanie had arrived with. They sat cross-legged, oblivious to the loud music and dancing surrounding them, and waved off anyone's attempt to join them. They passed the liquor back and forth, taking turns from the amber bottle as they shared the events of the missing year, talking until their voices gave in.

"Ma's dating some black guy named James," Emily said, rolling her head to her right shoulder. "That was quite a surprise, coming down the stairs at midnight for a glass of water, seeing him pumping her like an oil rig." She rolled her eyes and dropped her head.

"You've got to be kidding!" Stephanie said, pinching her eyes at her sister. "After what she'd said to us about Emma?"

"They're not in our social class — not near good enough to be, either." Emily lifted her nose in the air, mimicking her mother's two-faced chide — a rebuke brought about when a neighbor had told her mother that Emily had been seen at the mall with a black girl named Emma.

Stephanie's face flushed. "I can't believe her!" she said, tipping her head back and letting the burning liquor soothe her anger.

"Forget about her, Steph," Emily said, the flush of the liquor washing over her. "Where have you been? I waited, you know — for you to call."

Emily listened as Stephanie told how she'd married a boy she hardly knew just days after running away from home. She'd hitchhiked to Moncton, a city an hour or so northeast of Saint John. She found a job as a bartender, telling the owner she was twenty-one. He knew better, but he hired her because he needed the help. For the first couple of nights, she'd slept at the homeless shelter downtown and hitchhiked out to the bar, catching a ride home with anyone leaving at closing time.

"I was feeling pretty low, wondering what I was going to do, when some guy walked in and told me how beautiful I was," Stephanie said, her eyes lowering to the floor. "Nobody had ever said that to me before, Em. I — I know it was nuts, but I slept with him that night. We got drunk the next morning and went to the courthouse and got married. After we had—" Her voice trailed off. "Well, he left for cigarettes. Haven't seen him since."

Emily noticed that her sister seemed so much older than her seventeen years. But then again, had either of them ever enjoyed innocence? Emily reached for her sister's hands, resting them in the warmth of her own.

"Are you OK, Steph?" Emily's voice was barely audible.

"I never knew, you know," Stephanie said, her eyes tearing up. "When you were begging me to stay, I didn't know Dad was hurting you. I left because when he was drinking, he'd hit me, like he did Mom." Stephanie looked down. "I didn't know until after the divorce."

"It's a long time ago, Steph. It's over." Emily pulled the nearly empty bottle from Stephanie's hands and took another drink before handing it back. Stephanie wouldn't look at her.

"We've had some good times, too, Steph," Emily continued, not allowing her sister to notice the tears forming in the corners of her eyes. "Remember how Grampy always had us pick berries in the field behind the woodshed?"

Stephanie looked up and smiled. Emily closed her eyes.

~ ~ ~ ~ ~

"You girls grab those little tin buckets from the woodshed, and don't you come back until the buckets are full for supper, OK?" Their grandfather had shooshed them from the house, his smile wide and wise. Stephanie had been barely eight but motherly toward her younger sister. With buckets in hand, Stephanie wrapped her hand in Emily's, and they clanked toward the field, pails slapping against their tanned legs. The fields were wide and wild, full of green blooming bushes, buttercups, and black-eyed Susans. The girls took turns hiding among the tall, swaying grass, plucking berries and eating them until their lips echoed the blue of the fruit, the sweetness of the berry mixing with the joy of the moment. Minutes turned to hours, and before long, the warmth of the sun gave way to the evening's coming chill.

~ ~ ~ ~ ~

"Did we ever take a berry home for supper?" Emily asked. Stephanie managed a weak grin.

"How are you, Steph? Really?" Emily's voice was gentle; her eyes, though blurred from the sudden flush of the whiskey, were intent on her sister's face.

"Empty," Stephanie said, her face puckering. "They took my baby, Emily, like I wasn't even there."

Emily stared. "The baby didn't die?" Her heart thumped.

Stephanie shook her head.

"It was wiggling in my arms. She had them tug the baby from me while the doctor injected me with a sedative." Stephanie dropped her head and began to sob. "When I woke up, they told me it was dead. I didn't even know whether it was a boy or a girl."

"Who did that, Stephanie?" Emily asked, leaning in and pulling her sister's face upward with both hands. "Who would have done that?"

"Ma," Stephanie said, her voice flat.

Emily's eyes were secured on her sister, a wave of understanding settling on her like a silk scarf. She reached for the Jack Daniel's bottle, pulling it from Stephanie's hands, and lifted it to her lips, emptying the contents into her open mouth. She finished the last swallow and held it back from her face, studying the way the room's soft lighting sent an amber beam through the empty bottle. Emily stiffened, holding back tears that would lead to more questions, more heartache. Stephanie had problems of her own. Hardening her hand around the glass container, Emily pulled back and flung it across the room with all her might. The bottle smashed against the makeshift bar and shattered into a thousand sparkling shards across the now-silent room.

"I've got to get out, Steph."

"I'll see what I can do, Em," Stephanie said, looking straight ahead. "I'll get a ride back over here in a couple of weeks, and we'll talk some more, OK?"

Emily recognized the lie.

Chapter 31

Emily
March 1966
Saint John, New Brunswick

ALMOST ANOTHER YEAR WOULD PASS before Emily and Darren would walk down to the port and wait for Stephanie's arrival. She had a lot of excuses. A broken-down car. No money. No place big enough for all of them to live. For over an hour, the three of them made plans to reunite.

"It'll take a while," Stephanie said.

"How much longer, Steph?" Emily asked.

"I don't know. We've got to get some money, a place where we can all live. You guys have got to finish school."

"Now that I'm almost sixteen, I can quit school and get a job," Emily said. "I promise I'll save every dime."

"Can't you get ahold of Dad?" ten-year-old Darren asked. "Maybe he could give us some money or let us live with him for a while." His face pleaded with his sisters.

"Don't you get it, Darren?" Emily shot back. "We don't want to get ahold of him. We hate him! And trust me, someday you'll understand that he hates us, too."

"Stop it, both of you!" Stephanie yelled. "We'll work this out. For now, we've got to keep you in school," she said, turning to face Emily, "and get Ma to let you come visit me. I'll be back next week. We'll work something out."

The surprised look on Emily's face when Stephanie arrived the following Saturday took her sister aback. Maureen stood watching from the kitchen window as Stephanie and Emily talked on the sidewalk. Emily hugged her sister and then turned to face Maureen, who motioned the girls inside. They sat in the living room, stiff as statues, making small talk as mother and daughters hammered their way through the conversation.

"I'm doing well, Ma," Stephanie said. "I met a nice man. His name is Tim Kendall. We got married last Sunday."

Emily's mouth dropped open and then snapped shut before her mother saw her bewildered look. Stephanie's eyes drilled her sister into silence.

"He has a good job and adores me," Stephanie said in a trilling voice that made Emily wonder who Stephanie was trying to convince.

"I'm happy for you, Stephanie," Maureen said, her face pulled as tight as a rubber band. "I hope you know what you're doing." She kissed her politely on the cheek as she excused herself for her Saturday night date.

Emily walked her sister to the car, leaving Darren sobbing on the front porch steps.

"You got married again, Steph?" Emily said.

"I met him right after I left The Barn last year, Em. We've been dating since then. He helped me pay for the annulment and then popped the question a couple of weeks ago. We couldn't wait any longer." She rubbed her stomach lovingly. "He's so good to me — us, Em. He really loves me."

Emily touched her sister's stomach, wondering how, after all they'd been through, her sister could ever want to bring another child into the world.

"Don't tell Ma yet," Stephanie said. "Promise?"

Emily nodded her head. At least Stephanie wasn't drinking anymore and was overjoyed at the thought of being a mother. She hadn't mentioned again to Emily or to their mother the child she'd lost.

It took months before Maureen and Stephanie became amicable, Maureen finally satisfied that Stephanie had straightened her life out. Maureen liked Tim — and plus, this male addition to the family meant she had someone new to fix little things around the house. While Maureen had Tim doing a chore, she'd pull Stephanie aside and nag at her to dress better or praise Tim more, causing Stephanie to bristle.

"I know, Ma; there's always someone else out there who will be glad to take him off my hands if I don't take better care of him,"

Stephanie retorted, storming from the house. She hated the pushing, the interference. Yet Stephanie, like their mother, often gave Emily unwanted advice, too.

"Have you been drinking again, Em?" Stephanie asked one day as they walked along the Saint John pier.

"No!" Emily had become adept at lying.

"Don't go there, Em," she said. "You see where it got me."

"What? You mean — happy? Safe? Out of here?" Emily flung her hands into the air.

Her sister's voice softened. "Just watch yourself, Em." She turned toward Emily and touched her sister's shoulder. "I've been there. So many people will take advantage of you if you're drunk. Don't be like her — or me."

Emily put her hands on her face, her shoulders tightening, tears working their way down her cheeks. "I promise I won't be like her, Steph," Emily said, wiping her eyes with the back of her hand. She wondered if she could really believe that. "I've learned one special thing from Ma. You can't trust anyone, especially men. I won't fall for their lies. Not ever."

"They're not all like that," Stephanie said, touching her fingers to her sister's cheek. "Think of Grampy and his faithfulness to Gram. They had something special."

Emily nodded her head up and down, choking back tears. *She was right. Grampy wasn't like other men.*

Chapter 32

Emily
September 1966
Plaster Rock, New Brunswick

THEIR GRANDMOTHER, ELLEN, PASSED AWAY in early March with complications from breast cancer. John spent his remaining life rocking in the oak chair near the front window of their crumbling home, his tattered Bible open on his lap, awaiting the summer visit of his grandchildren. It never came. He got word from Carol that Maureen had up and quit her job. There'd be no money for a visit that summer. Emily and Darren were devastated when they found out they'd be destined to suffer through the first summer of their lives away from Plaster Rock.

Their ten-year-old cousin, Peter, found their grandfather one morning in early September, slumped in his rocking chair, still clutching his Bible. The doctor said he'd died of a broken heart. Emily knew what the doctor meant, her own heart bleeding as they laid her grandfather in the ground.

The earth had already stiffened with the first frost. Arrangements were quickly made, and the funeral attendees marched behind the long, black hearse to the knoll that stood high above the Tobique. The service took place at the Freewill Baptist Church, but the interment was at the only graveyard in town — the Catholic cemetery.

Emily recalled that when someone would die, her grandfather always asked the Lord to forgive the fact that they had to be buried in the Catholic cemetery. Heathens. All that pomp and circumstance. Up and down every service like a pump organ. Then he would smile, and she'd realize he'd been teasing.

"No one is right or wrong but God," he'd said. "The only truth is right here in His Word, Emily. Find it for yourself."

The day of the burial was cool, the ground gravelly under their feet as they snaked to her grandfather's open grave. Sixteen-year-old Emily stood behind her mother, grasping Darren with her left hand, her grandfather's Bible with her right. Stephanie, round with the fullness of the baby due any day, stood stoically behind, clasping hands with her husband. Maureen hadn't said three words the whole day, standing in silence next to Aunt Carol, their hands touching, heads pressed toward the dying grass. As the crowd gathered around the grave, Reverend Park, stoop-shouldered and aged, mumbled in a low voice.

Emily watched her mother — the way she dabbed at her eyes, though her hankie remained dry. Carol sobbed out of control, sucking air, tearing hankie after hankie from her purse. It seemed funny to Emily how people reacted to death, their failures more evident as they witnessed their own inevitable destination. Her mother stood erect, as though she might never reach that day — proud, determined, right, unflappable. Aunt Carol sobbed, seemingly recognizing her every shortcoming and regret with each shovel of dirt that covered her father's coffin.

Cousin Peter suddenly slipped in beside Emily. "Emily!" His voice was urgent. "Look who came!"

She spun around to see the familiar frame of a man in a dated blue suit approaching the rear of the crowd. His hands were jammed deep in his pockets, fidgeting, as though he'd lost his keys. The hair rose on her arms. He was out of jail. A few years seemed little punishment for what he'd done to her.

Emily felt a rage building inside herself, a choking resentment. "He has no right to be here!" Her voice rose, causing Mrs. Belcamp to "shussshhhh" her. Emily glared at Stephanie, who'd put her hand on her sister's arm to stop her from forcing her way toward their father.

"Don't bother, Em," Stephanie said, her eyes sending daggers in his direction. "He's not worth it."

"Dad's here?" Eleven-year-old Darren spun around, searching the crowd with a hopeful face.

Emily jerked away from her sister, dropping her grandfather's Bible to the ground. She pushed through the mourners.

"You have no right to be here," she hissed. "Get out!"

A wry smile slit into his weathered face.

"Why, hello, Emily."

Before the words had completely left his mouth, Emily hurled herself at him, catching him off guard and sending him reeling backward to the hard ground. She clawed at his face. Mr. Cook was the first to reach them, grabbing at Emily's arm as they rolled across the graves. He caught the hood of her coat and pulled her off her father, who lay dazed in a pile of newly discarded leaves. The crowd turned to watch the commotion, mouths gaping at the spectacle. Darren started to cry.

Emily continued to swing wildly, trying to close the space between herself and her father as he tried to rise to his feet. Her hair had blown into a funnel around her head, her eyes fierce at the thought of this man entering the only sanctuary she'd ever known.

"I think you should go, Denny," Maureen said, pushing past Mr. Cook and standing between her daughter and her ex-husband. The dark circles surrounding her blue eyes were threatening. Denny took a step toward Maureen, brushing the dirt and leaves from his coat.

"Maureen, I just—" he started.

"Get out, Denny." Maureen's voice was low and hard. Mr. Cook and Reverend Park strode in behind her. Denny's eyes darted from man to man.

He spun around, paused at the open door of his truck, took a deep breath, and climbed inside. He glared at the crowd, whose collective eyes had burrowed into his back. He fixed his glance on Emily. She was still sucking in tiny spurts of air, reeling from the attack. His lips curled into a smile, his hard eyes never leaving her. He reached for a silver thermos that lay on the vinyl seat beside him and stole a long pull from it. A shocked breath overtook Emily, and everything but the face of her father disappeared.

Chapter 33

Emily
June 1967
Munich, Germany

EMILY GRADUATED FROM HIGH SCHOOL the following summer, leaving home for good six days later. She'd been steadily employed at the local drive-up but hadn't been able to contain her anger toward what she considered idiot customers. Her boss fired her when she yelled at a man for not leaving a tip.

She'd already made enough money to buy a round-trip ticket to Scotland. From there, she figured she'd have enough cash to hitchhike across Europe. Maureen hadn't bothered to show up for her graduation, and Emily didn't tell her good-bye, packing her clothes and staying at her friend Ann's house the night before they left. She kissed Darren and Stephanie good-bye when they dropped her off at the Saint John airport.

"Be careful, Sis," twelve-year-old Darren said.

"Sure," she'd said. "I'll be fine. Don't worry, OK?"

By the time seventeen-year-old Emily boarded the flight bound for Glasgow, Scotland, she was nearly drunk, sneaking sips of whiskey from a Mason jar she'd hidden in her purse. Later, looking back at the three months that followed, she would remember little more than drunken spurts and nights spent in youth hostels and strangers' homes as she drank her way across Europe, trying to escape the haunting memories of her father's face. She saw him everywhere, when the sun created shadows, when sharp movements woke her with a start. *She had to fight this. Fight him with all she had.*

A week before she was set to return home, she'd settled in her mind that her last night's celebration would be held at the Haufbrau House in Munich, Germany, a famous tourist beer hall that students from the youth hostel had suggested she and Ann visit. By the time she arrived, drunks were spilling into the plaza each time the big wooden door swung wide, their voices sending curses and revelry into the air.

"Canadian girls!" a soldier shouted, recognizing the red maple leaf pin on Emily's sweater. A group of eleven soldiers clad in fatigues aimed their call in the two girls' direction just moments after they stepped inside. One of the soldiers, a young man named William, jumped up on the long wooden table, swinging a half-empty beer stein, liquid sloshing over its rim to the table below, signaling for the girls to join them. They'd found everyone they met along the way to be more than hospitable, and Emily was anxious to talk to people from her homeland.

"I promise," she yelled, holding her index finger into the air and shouting over the noisy crowd. "We've just got to run to the ladies room. We'll be right back."

The girls giggled their way to the back of the bar hall while the soldiers elbowed each other and laughed at their good fortune. Just before reaching the restroom, Emily stopped and gasped as she pointed at the backside of a soldier who'd bent to retrieve a pack of cigarettes from a vending machine.

"Look at that guy's butt," Emily said, pressing her hand on her girlfriend's arm but never taking her eyes from the soldier. "Now, *that's* the man I'm going to marry." She shot her hand to her mouth when she realized she'd spoken out loud.

The soldier swung around to face her, a smile etching his face. Electricity shot through Emily as their eyes met, his the softest blue she'd ever seen. The feeling was irrational, real, and complete. Later that night, the soldier, Aaron Evans, walked Emily back to the youth hostel. His hesitant kiss was gentle, as though he sensed her vulnerability. He never moved to touch her inappropriately, a surprise to Emily; the boys she'd always taken up with had enough hands to be considered an octopus. Aaron just held her, brushing his hand across her face as though he somehow knew and understood her. On the second night, beneath a moon that shimmered like the waters of the Tobique, the stars so close she thought he might pluck one from the sky, Aaron proposed.

"Marry you?" she sputtered. "Really?"

"I mean it, Emily," he said. "I know it's crazy, but I mean it."

"Yes, Aaron. I will marry you."

"I'll be out of the army in a few months. I'll come to Saint John, and we'll be married there, OK?" he'd said.

She marveled that he would move from Calgary just to be near her. No one had ever sacrificed anything for her before.

The next few days were a blur. She remembered little more than the warmth of his kisses and his promise to love and protect her for the rest of her life. Inside, Emily struggled between believing him and remembering the lies of the others who had promised to love her and hadn't. She promised herself she'd give this man a chance to prove she could believe again.

Chapter 34

Emily Douay Evans
May 1968
Saint John, New Brunswick

SHE WAS JUST EIGHTEEN when she found herself sitting on a toilet seat in the basement of the Nazarene Church, her gown hiked up around her waist. It was May 13, her wedding day. Ann pounded on the stall.

"Emily! The pastor has been down here three times. Are you OK?" Ann's voice was high-pitched and restless.

"I'll — I'll be just a minute. My stomach..." Emily's voice trailed off. "Is he here? Is he up there?" Her voice cracked. *Why would he be? I'm trash. My father used me for years. What do I have to offer Aaron? More lies?*

"Of course he is, you idiot. Get out here." Ann's voice tensed, her knock insistent. "Your mother is already seated. You should see her. She's acting like she's really somebody," Ann chuckled, "and she's with another loser."

Emily's knees buckled as she tried to stand. Her gown billowed around her like an ivory cloud. She couldn't bring herself to wear white, though her mother had tried desperately to make her do so. Something about white ate at her. Too pure. Too innocent.

Emily heard her grandfather's voice in her head, encouraging her with his deep, searching eyes as he told her to believe in the Lord, to trust and be saved. *Saved from what?* she wondered. *The mistake she was about to make? Or from herself?* They were just words her grandfather believed. But he was long dead, and the words didn't ring true for Emily. She didn't believe or trust in anyone. Emily realized she didn't even really trust Aaron.

"Give me another drink, and then go on up, Ann," Emily said, placing her hands above her head on the stall entryway. "Tell them, please, five minutes." She pressed her forehead on the cool metal door and closed her eyes.

"Do you really need another drink, Em?"

"Don't start on me."

"Well, don't make it much longer," Ann retorted, passing the silver flask into the stall. "I'd better not have put this ugly dress on for nothing."

The door slammed behind her as she pounded out of the room. Emily unlatched the door and strode to face her reflection in the full-length mirror, her hand wrapped around the flask, her head cocked to one side. Her veil poked from under the sequined cap that covered her long, blonde hair. She looked at herself, her eyebrows pulled taut, wondering if Aaron realized he was marrying a slut. She'd covered it well enough; her virginal moves with him the first time he reached to caress her wouldn't have given her away. Even after their brief engagement, when he'd tried to be intimate, she'd recoiled, furthering the lie. Last night, just hours before they were to become man and wife, she'd allowed him to make love to her, the first time she'd given herself freely to a man. Afterward, she'd found herself unable to control her tears. *Did he know? Could he tell? Did he perceive that the tears were not for giving in, but for giving up? It was all I knew how to do.* Emily sucked in a long swallow of whiskey and then hid the flask inside her garment bag.

She climbed the fourteen steps to the vestibule as though she were headed to the guillotine. Darren, now thirteen, waited like an old man, raising his arm to capture Emily's as she entered the landing to the entrance of the church. His smile was warm, tender, the way she'd imagined a father's face should be. The walnut doors were pulled open. Emily squeezed back the tears, searching for Aaron's face. *Is he here? Did he know I lied?*

Entering the sanctuary, she caught his eyes. They were fixed on her. His smile was wide, his blond, curly hair disheveled, the way it had looked the night before as they'd lain as one. She saw him pull in a deep breath, his chest puffing. Emily's legs shook, unsteady with each step. Darren cupped his arm under hers as if he knew her secret thoughts, steadying her, holding her, calming her.

"Don't do this if you're not ready, Sis," he whispered.

Emily's eyes were locked on Aaron's. His stare comforted her.

"I love him, Darren. I — I just didn't tell him—"

Darren cut her sentence off. "Don't." Darren's voice was clipped, angry. "Dad said it was a lie, anyway. He wanted to be here, Em — to tell you, walk you down the aisle."

Emily turned to look at him, her eyes begging for an explanation. She'd told him the truth over a year ago. Now he believed their father? Darren's mouth was taut. He wouldn't look back.

"He what?" Her mouthed dropped open.

"I called Dad a few months ago. Mom's never home. She doesn't know. I need to get out, too, Em. I had to." Darren stared straight ahead, a silent, serious young man.

Emily stiffened and tried to pull her arm away. The organ began to blare the wedding march as Darren tugged her forward. Each step was rigid, but Darren held tightly to her arm. They reached the front of the church. The pastor asked, "Who gives this woman?"

Darren turned to Emily, his eyes watering. "The people who love her. The people who matter."

He leaned in to raise her veil, kissed her on the cheek, and paused to whisper, "The only truth that matters starts today, Emily." She pulled back, her eyes signaling understanding of his words. They were old souls united by pain. Darren retreated to his seat next to Stephanie. Maureen sat beside a new beau, glancing around the room, looking for someone to notice her, not seeming to really see Emily. She would never understand any of her children, nor did her children believe she really wanted to.

Aaron reached for Emily's hand, his face radiant with expectation. He was there — willing, ready to commit his life to her. For a moment, she allowed the evil in her past to retreat and experienced complete and total acceptance. The pastor pronounced them man and wife, and for that moment, Emily let herself believe in happily ever after, secretly hoping her demons wouldn't consume every part of their marriage.

Chapter 35

Emily
October 1970
Saint John, New Brunswick

"YOU HAVEN'T HEARD FROM YOUR FAMILY for a while, Em," Aaron said one night. "Everything OK with them?"

"It's none of your business, Aaron," she retorted, a flare of anger rising in her.

"I was just asking, honey," he said, throwing his hands into the air. "Why are you always so defensive?"

"I'm not defensive," she screamed, storming toward the bedroom. "I'm just sick of you nagging me about my family. Don't you have anything better to do?"

A few months later, Emily wondered if maybe Aaron did have something better to do. He was absent more often, his excuse being the highway construction project he'd been working on, rushed with the coming winter weather and commanding overtime, leaving Emily alone to wallow in doubt and anger. She noticed his absence even more on rainy days, remembering how he used to rush home so that they could while away the hours locked in each other's arms. The divide had come slowly as Emily's anger increased, but she'd never considered her part in his retreat.

"He's never home anymore, Steph," she'd told her sister.

"Do you blame him, Emily?" Stephanie sounded incredulous. "Every time I see you two together, you're accusing him of something he swears he'd never do. Has he ever given you reason to think otherwise?"

Emily thought about the day she'd walked the short distance to the post office to return kitchen curtains she'd ordered from the Sears catalog. Aaron had found a good job as foreman of a road construction company, allowing Emily to concentrate on decorating their new home. As she passed Linton's Café, she glanced through the window and saw Aaron having lunch at the counter with a woman he worked with. They were laughing. Comfortable. Emily's back arched in anger, her blood beginning a slow boil that moved through her like a wave. She couldn't contain the rage that filled her, and she stormed into the restaurant.

"So you don't have time to come home for lunch, but you've got time for her?" Emily whispered. She could feel the heat crawling up her neck into her face, her breath driving from her mouth in small bursts. The woman pulled her napkin from her lap and began to coil it around her finger, her eyes darting between Aaron and Emily.

"Honey, this is Liz, our new administrative assistant." Aaron stood up and held out his hand in the direction of the woman. "We just happened to be here at the same time—"

Before the words had completely fallen from her husband's mouth, Emily lunged. Her right hand came down hard across the face of the young brunette. The woman tumbled backward from the stool, her body crashing to the floor, the napkin floating in the air like a distraught cloud. Aaron latched onto Emily's arm and shoved her at the door.

"Get out of here, Emily! I'll call you later."

She stood outside the building, her hands shaking, her chest heaving up and down — the fact that Aaron had returned to the young woman and not to her cut her heart. But had she expected any less? Hours later, Aaron stormed into the house, the door slamming behind him.

"What in the hell were you thinking, Emily?"

Her face felt like a stone, hard and unmovable. *Let him explain. Not that I'll ever believe him.*

"It was lunch. An accidental meeting. In public. I wasn't trying to hide anything. We work together, for Pete's sake."

Emily watched his face change from rage to pleading, a look she'd seen on her guilty father's face so many times when he begged her mother's forgiveness after his indiscretions. "Come on, Em. When are you ever going to believe me?"

Never. She let him hold her, told him she was sorry, but the current of suspicion and anger remained inside, flowing over every conversation.

* * *

The phone rang shortly after seven. "Em?" Darren's voice was unsure.

"Darren?" she said.

"I thought I might have the wrong number. I miss you, Sis."

"I miss you, too. What have you been up to?"

"Uh — joined the army."

"You what? You just turned sixteen. How can you do that?"

"Lied. They don't check anything when they need you. I just finished basic training. I'm being shipped to Vietnam shortly. Just wanted to see you and Steph before I go."

"You can't—"

"I'm going, Em. I'm not going back home. Not with her. She acts like I don't exist. I called Dad. He sent me some money. Helped me out."

Emily's face flushed, a slow burn rising in her chest.

"Now he's gonna step up and be a father?"

"Em, don't go there. Dad's the only one I told when I left — the only one who knew how I felt. We've been in touch for three years. You knew that. I told you at your wedding. I knew how you felt. I didn't want to hurt you. But we don't know everything that went on between Mom and Dad."

"I wasn't talking about them, Darren. Did you forget what he did to me?"

"Are you sure, Emily? Dad said that never happened. He said you were a little girl, and Mom put it in your mind."

"That son of a—"

"No more, Em!" Darren shouted into the phone. "He was the only one there for me when you guys took off and left me with her. The night I left Ma, I called him. She was working and didn't even know I was gone. He drove hours to pick me up. He took me to the recruiter's and let me stay with him until I shipped out to basic. He does care! He does!" Darren breathed heavily into the phone. "It doesn't matter anymore. I was too little to remember anything, Emily. Knowing how manipulative Ma is, maybe—"

"Maybe what, Darren? Maybe *I* don't remember him raping me? Maybe it was all in *my* head?" Her face flared red. "I'm happy that you and your father have connected again, Darren. But that ain't never gonna happen with me in my lifetime."

"I'm sorry, Em. I — I've got to run. I love you."

The line went dead.

"Darren? Darren?" Her eyes clouded with tears. *Why did I say that? Now he's gone, maybe forever.*

"Honey? Is everything all right?" Aaron asked, entering the kitchen.

Emily rubbed her eyes with the back of her hand. She hated to let him see her vulnerable. "It was Darren. He's joined the army and is headed overseas." She straightened her back and punched her hands into the cold dishwater.

Aaron pressed. "What do you mean? The kid's only sixteen, isn't he? We can go down there and stop this, you know. We could tell your mother."

"Why in the hell do you always have to try and fix things, Aaron? Let him do what he wants. He's miserable with Ma. We were all miserable with Ma. You'd think by now you'd know how manipulative she is, how much Darren needs to be out of there! Just stay out of his life, will you?"

Emily flung her hands up, water wisping into the air and all over the counter, and then pounded out of the room, leaving Aaron standing slack-jawed in the kitchen, wondering what he'd said this time to set her off.

Chapter 36

Emily
January 1972
Plaster Rock, New Brunswick

THE FIRST OF HER MOTHER'S life-threatening episodes happened when Emily was twenty-one. It was January and cold enough to freeze beef in the living room. Her Aunt Carol's call came in the middle of the day. Maureen was in intensive care in Plaster Rock, her chest torn open and a new pacemaker being woven into her heart. She had been visiting her sister when the attack came.

Maureen had asked Carol to call her children so she could say good-bye. Stephanie and Darren had been notified earlier, she told Emily. Carol hung up, leaving Emily terrified, with bits and pieces of information she didn't understand. She paced back and forth, her mind racing, and then dialed Aaron.

"He's out of the office, Ms. Evans," the secretary mumbled. "Can I take a message and have him call you when he returns?"

Emily slammed the phone to the wall. With her not working, they had no savings, no vehicle safe enough for her to travel the distance she needed to go. She dialed his office again. No answer. *Where is he?* Emily let her mind wander in the accusing direction that usually had the couple fighting before the day was over. At times, Emily purposely prodded her gentle husband to the point that he'd leave the house, slamming the front door with such force that the wall plaque hanging next to the opening would rattle to the floor.

Throwing a few things into a torn suitcase, she picked up the telephone and then hung up again, deciding to run next door to her best friend's house. "Jane, I would never ask you this if I weren't desperate, but I have to get to Ma before she dies. I need some money," Emily paused, "and your car." Emily's eyes were red and swollen. Jane never hesitated, disappearing into her bedroom, exiting with a handful of cash and a key ring.

"Here's three hundred dollars. Is that enough?"

Emily hugged her friend. "Find Aaron and tell him I had to go. I'll call him when I get there."

An hour later, Emily was driving into the dark, snowy night, the flakes of a winter storm howling across her car. She took a wrong turn at Fredericton and ended up in Perth, the long way to Plaster Rock. She inched into town, crossing the icy bridge near the Tobique Narrows in short bursts. Hunched at the steering wheel, she maneuvered the car out of town with little vision of the winding road. The warning signs "No railings" and "Steep drop-offs" choked Emily's throat, the feeling in her fingers lost in her fearful grip on the wheel.

A deer darted from a small opening in a stand of pines, its legs giving way to the ice. Emily slammed her foot at the brake, and the car careened across the narrow roadway on a film of black ice. The front of the car pulled like taffy, wrenching the vehicle across the glossy pavement. She had no sense of where she was headed, but she knew the last minute of her life would be spent in terror. She saw flashes of herself reeling from the roadway into the nearly frozen Tobique River, her car sinking in slow motion, the river sucking her to the same watery death that had befallen Dave Cook so many years earlier. She'd be swallowed by the waters that, years ago, had promised her grace. She gripped the wheel, her mouth open, releasing the scream of a child lost, languishing alone, abandoned in the last moments of life. "Oh, God! Help me!"

The car thumped to a halt, the back wheel catching a piece of bare pavement and slamming the vehicle to a stop. Emily was less than two feet from hitting a stand of pines head-on. Her purse had toppled to the floor, the contents spreading across the car. She couldn't breathe, her air coming in short gasps, and she laid her head on the steering wheel and wept. *What has my life come to?*

Two hours later, just before dawn, Emily arrived at the hospital, still shaking from the accident. She rushed through the hospital doors to the reception desk, frantic to find her mother, though she didn't understand why she'd felt such panic.

Maureen had distanced herself from the girls, never calling, not seeming to care when one or the other had tried to share some tiny success. Stephanie seemed settled with her new husband and baby in Moncton. Darren had left for the service, leaving Maureen — finally free — to seek the life she'd always thought she wanted. Emily and Aaron had stayed in Saint John, fighting to keep their marriage solvent, Emily's boredom turning to anger with any new success her husband seemed to be enjoying. But Maureen didn't have to know that. For now, Emily had to focus on her mother, who was lying in a hospital with a bad heart at the age of only forty-one.

The hospital attendant was slow, too kind for Emily's patience.

"What room is Maureen Douay in?" she asked, her voice near a scream.

"Well, dear — let me look." The woman had blue hair kinked into wild ringlets and Coke-bottle glasses she kept taking off. She licked her finger as she began to turn the pages of the admittance log.

"I'm in a hurry—" Emily said, drumming her fingers on the desk.

Carol emerged from a room down a narrow hallway, a long black scarf wound around her pale neck.

"Never mind," Emily said, racing toward her aunt. Carol stopped, looking at Emily with slight guilt etched on her face.

"Emily," she began hesitantly, "you came!" She paused, twisting a small corner of the scarf. Emily could see the blood rush up her aunt's neck and color her face. "I told you I'd call if she worsened. They'd told me it was serious, but I found out that this procedure is common nowadays. Your mother wanted you guys to know — just in case." Carol's face puckered, her eyes narrowing and filling with tears. "I'm — I'm so sorry to make you come so far when she's going to be fine. She — she wanted me to."

Emily's mind flashed back to the bits of information she hadn't understood, her aunt's strange tone at the end of the conversation, the pause before she'd added, "I'll call you if her situation gets any worse…"

"You mean she's going to be OK?" Emily's mouth dropped open, her head tilting to one side. "You made it sound like she was going to die tonight! Like I needed to be here, Aunt Carol!" She could feel her face flush, the fingernails on her left hand biting into her palm. "I had to borrow money we can't pay back and drive through a blizzard! I was almost killed, and Aaron doesn't even know where I am!" Emily's voice pitched high, accusing.

Carol's eyes were disturbed, guilty. Her gaze stayed fixed on the corner of the scarf she still twisted. "She's my sister... Maureen told me to call."

"I can't believe this." Emily turned away, red-faced, and stormed toward her mother's room, her feet pounding the yellow tile as though they were hammers on ice. She stopped short of the door, turning her body to watch her aunt disappear out the wide hospital door and into the cold.

Emily called Aaron from a pay phone, reversing the charges when he answered.

"I was so scared not hearing from you, Emily," Aaron said. "I'm borrowing a buddy's truck, and I'll be on my way."

Emily wondered how her husband still managed a civil conversation with her after the tongue-lashing she'd given him a day earlier just before he'd left for work. He'd been working overtime to help pay off their bills, but Emily was bored all day alone and nagged at his ambition.

"Why don't you look for a part-time job to keep you busy, Em?" he'd suggested, sending her into a tirade.

"Why can't you just make a decent living so I don't have to?!" she'd screamed back at him, storming into their bedroom until he left for work.

Now he was willing to drive the snow-covered roads just to be there for her. *I don't deserve him.*

Emily told Aaron she'd call him when she knew more but that, for now, there was no need for him to be here. She heard the hurt in his voice when she hung up, but she didn't need him to see the scene she believed her mother had concocted to get her children's attention.

Darren and Stephanie arrived a few hours later, Stephanie's face swollen from crying. Aunt Carol returned with their cousin, Peter — still troubled but resolute. They assembled in the waiting room and chatted for several hours before the nurse entered and announced that Maureen was awake.

Maureen was facing the door as they arrived. Her eyes fluttered and she acted stunned, as though she'd not set up the entire scene. *Always the martyr.*

"I didn't mean for *you* kids to come all this way," she said, her voice a whimper. "I... I just wanted Carol to tell you that I loved you — you know -- in case I didn't make it."

Maureen turned toward Stephanie and said, "I didn't think I'd ever see *you* again."

Her voice emphasized "you." She lifted her left arm toward Stephanie, their hands clasping. Stephanie looked at Darren and Emily, her eyes wide with surprise. Maureen's other children were in the room, but she'd seemed to see only one. Darren and Emily were left hanging like empty socks at Christmastime. Within minutes, the room filled with their mother's voice; she was again the center of attention.

"Don't forget, girls, when I die, I want you to wear—"

Emily cut her mother off. "Ma, give me a break," she said, her voice stiff and terse. "I'm not wearing a hat with a veil."

"I'm asking you to do that for me. Is that too much for you?" her mother retorted. Maureen coughed and clutched at her chest. Carol's expression begged at Emily, who rolled her eyes at her aunt.

"We'll see, Ma."

"I'll haunt you until the day you die, then." Maureen winked at Darren and gave a weak grin. "By the way, who's taking me home?"

Emily was silent and looked away. Stephanie stood and walked to the window. Darren stared at the floor.

"You know, I'd take you home with me, but you couldn't live with our thirteen cats," Peter finally said, eyeing his cousins. His kind demeanor irritated Emily. He was the lucky one, with parents who cared so deeply for him. He'd grown into a good person, influenced by the grandparents he lived so close to. It was something Emily envied. She wished she could be the kind of person Peter had become.

Maureen's nose scrunched as her hands sprang into the familiar claws they all remembered from their youth. She retold the story of why she hated cats, a story they all knew by heart. Emily couldn't keep her lips from curling upward. Maureen pushed herself into a sitting position, her complexion now a soft blanch that matched the rose color she'd dyed her thinning hair.

Carol hovered in the corner of the room on a straight-backed chair, the silent accomplice, grinning like a guilty child. For a split second, Emily wondered what Carol saw in Maureen. The need for attention, the manipulative behavior, the self-centeredness — did Carol fear her? Perhaps she saw an insecurity, a need for love. Emily brushed off the thought, resentful; she saw through her mother's act. Sitting in silence, she rocked back and forth while Stephanie, Peter, Darren, and Carol chatted with her mother. She drew in a slow, angry breath, releasing it through clenched teeth, her cheeks quivering in rage. Her mother would outlive them all.

Emily left the next day, citing Aaron's insistence on her coming home. Darren and Stephanie stayed for another day, well aware that Maureen was recovering faster than she wanted any of them to believe. Arriving home, Emily didn't reveal to Aaron the reason she believed her mother had lured them to Plaster Rock: to get attention, to be the center of their lives — though they'd never been the center of hers. Aaron held her and offered support as well as suggestions — advice Emily didn't need or want from anyone.

Chapter 37

Aaron Evans
June 1974
Saint John, New Brunswick

EMILY'S EYES FLASHED as Aaron explained why he was late. Her eyes accused him again of something he'd never had any intention of doing. He'd stopped to have a beer with his buddy Phil Reneaux. Work had been especially tough on the Mackay Highway project that week, the new Saint John throughway extension that would connect the suburbs of Rothesay and Quispamis. The land had been formally owned by the prominent Mackay family; accordingly, the extension was named after them.

Aaron had already lost two days of work that week due to the heavy rains that had moved through Saint John from the south. The water caused equipment delays and an accident that had injured one of his best men. Aaron needed a break.

"Who were you with?" Emily demanded, slamming her bottle of Moosehead beer to the kitchen counter. Aaron could see from the empty bottles heaped in the trash bin that it was at least her third.

"Phil," he replied. "We were just having a couple of beers. I told you this morning we were going to stop after work, remember?" Aaron closed the door behind him and walked over to kiss her, a sheepish grin cutting into his handsome face. "Come on, let it go, Em. Have some fun with me." He reached to kiss her; the look was meant to suggest something more.

She pushed him away. "Figures you'd think that's all I'm good for."

"Aw, Em. I'm joking! I just thought—"

"Where'd you go?" Emily's face exploded again with anger.

"Sully's—" he said, his face scrunching into a puzzle.

"Liar! I called there, and they said you hadn't been in all night. Who were you really with?" Emily was toe-to-toe with him, her growing rage accusing him the way it always did when some ugly memory surfaced. She didn't seem to be able to stop herself.

He slammed his fist to the counter. He was fed up.

"What is it this time, Emily? Your mother? Father? What?" Aaron exclaimed.

"Don't!" She pushed her finger deep into her husband's chest, moving him backward. "Don't try to put this on them — now who is she?"

"You're nuts!" Aaron shoved past her and opened the refrigerator, pulling out a beer, opening the top with the bottle opener. The foam rose out of the opening, dripping to the floor.

"I won't stand you running around on me, Aaron." She knocked the beer from his hand, the bottle making a hollow sound as it hit the floor, the liquid mushrooming across the linoleum. He stood in disbelief, his mouth open. At times she made him feel helpless, that no matter what he did, it would never be the right thing for her. He'd taken her angry rants repeatedly, even when he didn't deserve them. Like tonight.

Emily swung at him. Aaron caught her forearm and squeezed it tightly.

"Don't push me," he said, shaking her arm. "I was at Sully's. They have a new bartender who probably doesn't know me yet. Why don't you ever believe me?"

"Liar!" she screamed, punching her hands deep into his chest. "Liar!"

He pushed Emily back — hard — and then raised his arm as though he might hit her. Get her to finally back off from accusing him. Scare her. Keep her from hitting *him*. They stood toe-to-toe, his 6'2" frame hovering above her. Something in Emily flared, a look crossing her face just as Aaron raised his arm. It was a look he didn't recognize. Something he feared. He stopped short, dropping his arm to encircle her. He pulled her close and apologized again and again. *Did she want me to do that?*

"I was with Phil — honest, Em." Aaron was shaking. "There's never been anyone but you. I'm so sorry. I'd never hit you. I promise."

Emily was uncontrollable, an eruption rumbling within her that he was just beginning to understand. *She would have killed me. I saw it in her face.* He held her so close that she had to pull away. He apologized a hundred times, but he knew the words echoed hollow in her.

He finally calmed her enough to realize that she'd wanted him home to share her news. She'd found a job in the customer service department of J. D. Irving, a foresting outfit in Saint John that was impressed with her knowledge of the New Brunswick woods. Aaron was glad it would get her out of the house and into a social world he knew she needed. He alone wasn't enough to keep her mind off of whatever still tore at her from the past. Maybe no one would be enough for her, but he still hoped. He suggested she drive to Moncton the next day to spend the weekend with Stephanie. It would give her time to cool off. They both needed space.

Chapter 38

Emily
June 1974
Moncton, New Brunswick

HER SISTER WAS SITTING on the couch when Emily arrived. Tim was cuddled next to Stephanie, their eight-year-old son, Brian, playing with the new Legos his father had bought in Maine. *The perfect family.* Emily rolled her eyes at the scene when she stepped inside. She offered them a drink from the whiskey bottle she'd brought along, but neither took her up on the offer. Tim smiled and then left the room with Brian when the talk became girlish.

A pang went through Emily. Aaron had hinted more than once that he'd like to start a family, but she had no intention of bringing a child into this world. She'd gone on the pill without his knowledge, just to make sure of that. She wondered why she'd even bothered to do that; they hadn't been intimate in months. Aaron often reached for her in the dark, but Emily felt herself tense and roll away at his sudden touch, her fear unexplained, leaving her husband confused. The feel of his back against hers made her feel alone in the room. She'd never told Aaron what her father had done, just bits and pieces of who he was. She shook herself from the thought.

"I got a letter from Darren. He sounds so old," Emily said, pulling the envelope from her purse. She unfolded the penciled letter, the wrapped and unwrapped creases making his words hard to read. "Says he made it home safely from overseas. He met a girl named Betsy. She's the sister of the chaplain in his unit. Evidently, he'd spent a lot of time with him." Emily turned her head sideways and lifted her eyebrows. The thought of their nineteen-year-old brother in a relationship unsettled her.

"He said he and Betsy wrote back and forth for a while. She met him at the airport when he got back. They're getting married!"

Stephanie's face lit up, and she bounced up and down on the sofa. "When?"

"He'll let us know when the plans are made. Oh, and one more thing." Emily paused and locked eyes with her sister. "He suggests I get back to church." Emily threw her head back and laughed. Stephanie choked on her Pepsi, spewing the brown liquid across the room.

"I'd told him I've been working on you," Stephanie said. "Or I should say, I've been praying for you." She smiled and reached over to touch her sister's hand.

Emily knew that Tim had been making Stephanie go to church with him since Brian was born. She seemed changed, but Emily knew her sister, knew she didn't believe the lies of faith any more than Emily did.

"It's not so bad, Emily," Stephanie said settling back into the couch. "I actually like going again. There's something special about being there that I haven't quite put my finger on yet."

"Yeah, yeah." Emily pulled her hand away, pretending to read the letter again. "Anyway, he'll be home in two weeks. He'll call as soon as he gets here."

Emily felt a twinge of excitement; she'd not seen or talked to Darren in two years, since the night he'd hung up on her. She'd gotten one letter shortly after their fight, but it was only recently that he'd been sending more messages, sharing with her his new church-going ways.

"Must be that new love in his life," Stephanie said. "We all know what that does for you." They both laughed.

"Yeah, look where's it's gotten me," Emily said, holding her arms out to her sides, sighing heavily.

"You don't get it, do you, Emily?" Stephanie's face morphed to anger.

"What?"

"You are so lucky. Aaron is a great guy. He's handsome, he's fun, and he really loves you."

Emily swigged another drink from the whiskey bottle. "You don't live with him. You have no idea—"

"No, I don't, but I can see that you have someone who loves you and that you seem blind to it. Watch it, Em, or some other woman will be happy to take him off your hands."

Just what she needed. Something more to worry about. He'd almost hit her, so she already knew she couldn't trust him. What was next?

Chapter 39

Emily
October 1974
Saint John, New Brunswick

EMILY STOOD ON THE PORCH of their little green house, their collie, Thor, pressed to her leg. Aaron put the suitcase in the truck and turned to face her, the snow fluttering around him as though he were encased in glass.

"I've only wanted you, Em. She didn't mean anything to me. It — it just happened. I love you. It doesn't have to end this way."

"Yeah, right," she said, pursing her lips. "I'd never be enough for you. I knew you were seeing someone all along, Aaron, so get on with it."

"Let's just give it a little time, OK? I'll call you."

She pulled the dog inside and slammed the door. Aaron stood looking at the house for a long time, his face slick with tears. Emily watched through the curtain as he shook his head from side to side and climbed into the truck. Although she'd accused him many times, he'd never failed her until now. But she'd known it was coming all along. She also knew she'd never be able to believe in him again. Hadn't her mother warned her that men were all alike? But even as she condemned him in her mind, she knew she'd been tempted herself since taking the new job.

He told her he'd been a fool, tempted by someone who flattered him during one of the times Emily had been away. He was lonesome, he said, felt vulnerable. And she'd pursued him. A pastor's wife, no less. Emily could've figured — so much for the faithful. When he'd finally confessed, he swore it wasn't anything she'd done, but Emily knew he blamed her parents for crippling her this way. She guessed he was right.

When Aaron drove away, she heard his final words ringing in her ears. "Maybe you'll finally be free when they're out of your life for good, Emily," he'd said. "Then maybe you'll be able to forgive me." Emily could only hope, but she wondered if even being free of her parents would give her the peace that seemed so fleeting. Her grandfather had said some choices followed a person to the grave if you let them.

Chapter 40

Emily
December 1974
Plaster Rock, New Brunswick

WHEN EMILY FIRST LEARNED that Maureen was battling an aggressive form of cancer, an urgency to see her mother again overcame her. It didn't soften the memory of her mother's manipulation or move Emily to pity. Any emotion Emily had been born with had disappeared years ago in the darkness of her bedroom. She wanted to go to her mother's side not to say good-bye but rather to see if she would reveal some of her past so that Emily might make sense of her own.

Maureen was slumped over the kitchen table in her cramped apartment wearing an oversized cotton print dress that draped her forty-two-year-old frame like a feed sack. The cancer had withered her body, making it look ancient, though she'd only recently been diagnosed.

Her head, once rich with brilliant red hair, now looked as though only a few thin radishes had taken root. Her ankles were swollen over her matted pink slippers. The veins on her legs stood out sharply, and her usual spark had drained from her face, withered and swallowed by the disease.

"Look, Emily. This is when I was a freshman in high school," Maureen said with a thin smile, shaking a sepia-colored picture of a young woman at her daughter.

"That's when I was young and good-looking. Could have had any man I wanted."

She peered at Emily, her sad eyes conveying loss, her thin hand patting her pocket for a tissue.

"*Did* have any man I wanted." Maureen shook her head back and forth and dropped the photo to the table.

"Back in high school, everybody loved me. I was the life of the party." Her mother's voice quavered. "I just had to get out of that little town. Mum and Dad were smothering me. I would've done anything to get out of there. I just wanted to *be* somebody. That's why I married that boy at fifteen and then left him for your father a few weeks later when Brian went off to war."

Emily ran some water in the sink, closing her eyes. She'd heard her mother's haunting memories many times before when she drank too much. Emily had taken a few days off work to be here...

"I was pregnant with your sister when I met Denny. I didn't know it for sure until after we were married. I never told him she wasn't his, but somehow he knew. He threw it in my face over and over when he found out for sure."

The thunk of a plastic glass in the kitchen sink caused Maureen to pause long enough to take in the look of surprise on Emily's face. She'd forgotten about hearing that in the courtroom so long ago.

"Who's Stephanie's father?" Emily asked, her arms elbow-deep in the soapy dishwater.

"Brian Pelletier. The boy I just told you about. He was headed overseas. We slipped away and got married, telling no one. Dad found us in the barn that afternoon. I embarrassed my parents so much." Maureen dropped her head. "I never told Dad we'd gotten married. Never told anyone. Brian was supposed to come home after a few weeks. Then I got a letter saying he wasn't sure when they'd let him come home. Dad had grounded me, but I couldn't stand it. I snuck out one night a few weeks later. That's when I met your father at the Legion dance. I knew I loved him right away." Her voice softened as she continued.

"When Brian left, I had no one to help me, nowhere to turn. Then I found out I was pregnant. I couldn't tell my parents. I'd done enough to hurt them." She stared at Emily, her eyes cold and certain. "I talked Denny into marrying me. I knew I'd made a mistake with Brian. I told Denny it was his baby. I didn't think anyone would ever find out. I'd written and told Brian I'd filed for an annulment. He never wrote back. I never filed. Thought since nobody knew, it wouldn't matter." Maureen wiped her eyes. "Brian never knew he had a child."

"Does Stephanie know, Mom?" Emily asked, wiping her hands and dropping into a wobbling chair next to her mother. The cracked seat was scarred, hard, like her mother. She searched her mother's frail face.

"I just couldn't tell her." Maureen reached for her last hankie and dabbed at her eyes. "I thought when I divorced your father, that day in court — you remember." She pinched her eyebrows together and stared at Emily. "I thought you'd tell Stephanie the minute we got back."

"Ma, I was a little girl. I didn't understand—" Emily leaned in at her mother, clasping her withered hands in her own. "You've got to tell her, Ma. You have to — before..." Emily's voice trailed off.

She rose, strode to the kitchen, and fixed a plate of food for Maureen, the silence deadening between them. She knew her mother was watching her. Analyzing her, maybe looking for a weakness to manipulate. Emily dropped the plate in front of Maureen: peas, grilled chicken, mashed potatoes. Maureen's hands shook when she picked up the loaded fork, sending the peas scattering around the table and to the floor. She grunted, lifted her arm, and threw her fork across the room. Emily turned to see her mother drop her head forward. She was still so young, but the disease had crushed her spine, hunching her body into a curve.

"I knew a lot of things, Emily," she screwed her body around to face Emily, "but not everything. I was helpless against him." Her eyes pleaded.

Emily's chest heaved up and down, her breath quickening as she wrapped the dripping dishcloth around her fingers, the water soaking the floor.

"Why didn't you stop him?" Emily turned to face her mother straight on, her voice strengthening. She pulled open the kitchen drawer, pulled another fork from the holder, and pushed it into her mother's hand.

"You kids never saw him beat me... sometimes until I couldn't walk."

A picture flashed in Emily's mind: the young housekeeper, her arms full of bloody towels, pushing Stephanie and Emily away from their mother's bedroom door. Their mother was sick, she'd tell them, so she'd be staying to help for a while.

"Why didn't you leave, then? Why didn't you help me?"

"Back then we never talked about such things to anyone. It wasn't done. Besides where would I have gone, Emily? Back to the parents I'd embarrassed and made fools of? The husband I'd run out on? Who, Emily?"

"Then what made the difference, Ma?" Emily's skin prickled with anger. "Why'd you finally decide to leave when you did? Some other man? Some friend you'd do anything for?" Emily's fists were pulled tight against her thighs. Maureen lowered her head again, tears dripping on her robe.

"When I saw for myself what he was doing to you," she whispered.

Emily clutched her hand to her mouth, the bile boiling into her throat.

Maureen held out her left hand, her right still clutching the fork. Emily recoiled. She turned around and heaved into the sink, clasping the cool porcelain with both hands to steady herself.

"I'm so sorry, Emily." Her mother's voice cracked. "I should've taken you to Mum and Dad's sooner. They loved us. They would've helped. I — I was so busy trying to do it on my own, wanted to protect myself; I didn't realize the extent of his abuse of you. It's taken me a long time to talk about what happened to you kids. But Emily, I can now." She straightened. "Talk to me, Emily."

Emily's back pricked against her mother's words. *She* could talk now. What difference did that make? It was always about what *she* could do. Maureen curled toward the table and placed her fork on the hardly touched platter, pushing it to the center of the table.

"I've helped a lot of people since then. I tried to make things better for you kids. You'll never understand what I went through." She arched her neck around to watch Emily, her daughter's form still hunched over the soapy basin.

"You remember that Thanksgiving when we didn't have a dime, when we first moved to Saint John?"

Emily did. A local church had brought food, more food than they'd see all year. Maureen had Stephanie and Emily start cooking while she ran to the local bars to invite total strangers to eat with them. They'd shared the food with people who had no other place to go. Emily smiled at the memory. The good times they had... they'd escaped her thoughts and focus somehow in the bleakness of the painful ones.

"They were good to us, Ma, those strangers." She wiped her mouth with a kitchen towel, then shed her cardigan and brushed the sweat from her forehead. She pulled open the cupboard door, retrieving a mug for Maureen's coffee.

"Not that cup!" her mother shouted, her voice sharp, her thin finger wiggling at the cupboard. "The blue one, the blue one!"

Emily replaced the mug and pulled the blue cup from the cupboard, banging it harder on the counter than she'd meant to. Her self-centered mother would never change.

"I used to love to dance." The sparkle returned to Maureen's voice, her faint eyebrows lifting. "Your father and I danced a lot, years ago. After I left him, you kids would get so mad when I wanted to go out with my friends. You never understood that I was always working, always trying to keep you kids fed. It was just too much. I needed time for myself."

Yeah, Emily thought, *time for yourself. Like the time you had Steph get up at two in the morning to walk you home from the bar because you were too drunk to find your way? Or the time I woke up to see some guy screwing you on the couch? Or maybe it was the time you forgot to tell us you'd moved when we went away to church camp, and we came back not knowing where we lived anymore?* Emily covered Maureen's lap with a quilt. A current of anger flowed through her.

"Have you heard from your brother or sister?" Maureen asked, not waiting for an answer. "They never call. They send money and whatever I need, but they never come to visit." She smoothed the quilt over her thin legs.

"Your sister came to visit one time with that kid of hers. It was into everrrrryyything." Maureen drawled out the sentence with disdain.

Emily walked back to the kitchen and rubbed at the counter, her hand pushing the dishcloth over and over the same spot, her eyes blinded and angry.

"I could take you kids anywhere," Maureen said. "If I pointed to a chair and told you to go sit down, you'd kill each other to get there." Her mother smiled and tipped her head forward, commending herself. "Stephanie's boy doesn't have any discipline at all. He runs all over her. You kids knew better."

Emily continued rubbing at the surface, her hand burning with the speed of the circle. *Maybe because Dad beat us, Ma, and you never stopped him. Maybe because we were afraid.*

Emily whirled and stepped toward her mother, stopping just behind her.

"What really happened to Steph's baby, Ma?" Emily's voice strained with the question.

Maureen's shoulders dropped. The slow tick of the clock counted twelve before the low sob came out, heavy, sad.

Emily's chest tightened. "She has a right to know, Ma. She heard it cry. She knew it was alive."

Silence cloaked the room.

"She has a right, Ma!"

"I couldn't keep you kids fed." Maureen's voice was just above a whisper. "There was an attorney and his wife — Keating, I think their name was — she couldn't have kids." She turned to face Emily. "I was trying to protect her — us. I just couldn't have your sister end up the way I had. I just couldn't." She dropped her face into her hands and cried, her cancer-riddled frame heaving up and down. Emily padded to the kitchen and retrieved the hankie her mother had left on the counter. She held it out, the tiny blue forget-me-nots embroidered on its edges faded with use.

"She has another child now," Maureen gasped, pulling the hankie from Emily's hand. "Someday she'll understand."

Emily stared at her mother, incredulous. Did she really believe one child could make her forget the loss of another? She cleared the table, dumping the dishes on the counter. Refilling the basin with clean water, she scrubbed the dishes with fury, sending the dishwater splashing down the front of the pine cabinets.

"We're all busy with our own lives now. Stephanie's married, and Darren can't just up and leave the service whenever he wants. We come when we can—" Emily bit her tongue and ran more hot water in the sink.

"Promise me I won't have to go to a nursing home if I get any sicker," Maureen pleaded. "I can't stand the thought of dying there alone." She paused, jerked the hankie from her pocket, and blew hard. Grunting in pain, she pushed herself from the kitchen table and rose. She clung to her walker and edged herself to her blue recliner, where she fell back, groaning. She started to hum an old song, one Emily recognized from one of the revivals she'd attended so long ago. Emily moved in beside her mother and brushed back her thin hair, leaning to kiss her on a pale cheek. She wondered how things had come to this... playacting to her dying mother.

"I'm not a bad person, Emily." Maureen's eyes pleaded with her. "Neither was Denny. We were married so young. We never had a chance to live. He had a hateful father who did unspeakable things to him. I didn't know for years how it haunted him, what it did to him."

Emily pulled away from her mother.

"So that makes what he did to me OK?"

"He was sick, Emily. He didn't mean—"

"Didn't mean to — what? Rape me, Ma?" Emily stepped back, her head swinging back and forth. In one swift movement, she swept her arm across the table, scattering everything on it across the kitchen floor.

"Emily!"

"I've got to go, Ma," she said, gasping in fury. "I'll come back later and clean up."

Grabbing her purse and jacket, she made her way to the door, hesitated in the doorway, and looked back over her shoulder at her failing mother.

"You'll always have a home to go to, Mom. I promise. We'll see to that." *It just won't be mine.*

A phone call from her Aunt Carol, eight months later, beckoned Emily back to Plaster Rock.

"I can't do any more to help her, Emily. I need you kids to take turns staying here until she goes. You can stay at her place because it's empty now. She's back at the hospital. It won't be long now."

Maureen had moved back to be near Carol shortly after Christmas. The disease was closing in on her. She'd rented a small apartment near her sister, where Emily spent the night when she went to help. One bedroom, spic and span.

Aaron had let Emily take his truck so she'd have something decent to drive. Having taken her car to the garage one too many times, he was worried she might get stuck far from home. He promised he'd join her by the weekend. Although Emily was glad he was back in her life for the moment, she wondered why he hadn't given up on her months ago, or she on him. She was sure he knew she'd never forget, even though she'd been trying to put their past behind them, to make it work this time. Aaron had been trying, too. He'd even taken to going to church again — something they'd both abandoned long ago. And he'd been right about a job being good for her. She'd been given many opportunities at the forestry company and had been promised another promotion in the coming year. Her work kept her busy enough to forget, most days.

She pushed open the door of her mother's apartment. Directly in front of the open door was a cherry table, round, highly polished, as though her mother had just dusted. Emily smiled when she saw her mother's face in the only frame. She knew that if Maureen had known Emily would be staying there, she'd have hastily replaced her own photo with one of her daughter's. It was what she did when her children came by.

She touched the pictures on the wall above the stand, all of her mother. Maureen as a child. Maureen in high school. Maureen at twenty, thirty, forty. Only Maureen, always alone. A woman of little emotion and mixed memories. And suddenly, Emily saw her mother for the first time. An unfinished game. Self-centered and regretful. No one but herself to rely on. Pulling in a deep breath, Emily realized that what her mother had done with her life, with her children, was all that she knew how to do. Keep them fed. Keep them clothed. Keep them together the best you can. Love had little to do with it. This was the bed she had made, and now she had to lie in it. It was her obligation.

Emily pulled her suitcase in the door and stopped to look around. An elegant cluster of fake roses hovered above a glass coffee table. The blinds were all drawn, as if peeping Toms lined the window outside. The rose-colored chairs ached to be rocked. A half-played game of dominos sat idle on the maple dining room set. Emily walked toward the tiny, tangerine-colored kitchen. She could still smell the paint of her youth as she closed her eyes and remembered her mother smearing on the brilliant shade.

"You've got to have color," Maureen had said. Her face always broke into a smile when she painted, as though she were covering her past.

Emily moved to her mother's bedroom a bit hesitantly, as though Maureen were hiding somewhere, waiting to see if she would touch something. A small doll with a china head lay on her mother's mattress. Foam rubber pillows were neatly stacked at the headboard, along with a fancy, ruffled bedspread. Next to that lay a pink, furry rug where her mother's fuzzy slippers cushioned her feet each morning. The lovely maple dresser stood off to one side, inviting Emily to explore.

She gently pulled open a drawer, unsure whether she was an intruder or welcome friend. Emily's eyes were drawn to a small notebook, which she pulled out and cradled in her hands. The pages were laced with questions about Maureen's past. *A Mother's Memories.* It had been given to her by Darren, inscribed on the inside cover.

Maureen had written in the pages, Emily supposed, shortly after her diagnosis. As Emily perused the pages, she envisioned her mother writing answers to the silly questions. *Who was your best friend? What was your favorite class in school?* Emily knew her mother well enough to know that she would write things according to the way she wanted people to view her, not necessarily what was true. *Protect them.* But Emily didn't know the woman in these pages. She heaved a sigh. Her mother would leave no real trace of her personal struggles behind. Just secrets. One last page turned. *What is one lesson you learned from your parents that you'd like to pass on to your children?* Emily's nose burned, her eyes watered as she choked back tears.

To forgive, both others and themselves.

Chapter 41

Emily
August 1975
Plaster Rock, New Brunswick

WHEN EMILY ARRIVED AT THE NURSING HOME the next morning, her mother was lying on a small twin bed that was positioned awkwardly in the tiny room. The foot of the bed was toe-to-toe with a second twin bed that awaited another dying patient.

The room was painted an off-brand of pale green, like an unripe lemon. A battered movable closet, three feet wide and six feet tall, was where Maureen housed the few possessions she was allowed to bring with her.

"I'm not staying here long," Maureen told her daughter as soon as Emily entered the room. "These nurses are not clean at all. I've heard they steal everything you have, too."

Darren and Stephanie were perched on folding chairs near Maureen's bedside, rolling their eyes.

"Mom, what are they going to steal?" Emily asked as she removed her coat and embraced her siblings.

"My things!" Maureen said, her voice incredulous. It was as though the closet held items that should've been kept at Fort Knox.

Emily jerked at the cabinet door. A polyester leopard top and a sagging white cotton sweater hung there. On the floor of the closet lay two pairs of tattered slippers, one a pale pink, the other a faded shade of blue. There were two rolls of toilet paper, three Kleenex boxes, and a black comb that looked as though it'd been used to groom a cat. She reached to touch the wild animal print top, its silky feel irritating her again.

When she'd been younger, she'd wished she could put her mother away in a place like this, where crumpled old women spent the rest of their selfish lives wasting away alone. She'd seen the slumped bodies in the hallways of the nursing home when she'd visited Plaster Rock the year her grandmother died.

Back then, Emily wished she could've made her mother change places with her grandmother. The thought had woven itself in and out of her head like an unwanted intruder. She'd always believed Maureen looked at her children as intruders.

"You kids get outside and play. You kids are into everything. If it weren't for you kids, I'd be richer, married, better off." You kids.

They were silent troops, assembled at their mother's command. Maureen would disband them, issuing orders for them to get outside "to get the stink blown off you." When they'd visit Maureen's friends, they'd be marched to the car, fit together like a puzzle in the backseat, and allowed to play quietly until they arrived. Maureen liked solitude when she didn't have an audience. Once at their destination, the children were herded like chickens into a small living room where Maureen's barking voice directed like a drill sergeant. "You kids get over there and sit down," she'd say, wiggling her finger in the direction of the chair.

There was usually one straight-backed chair in the corner of the modest room — and three obedient soldiers. Without hesitation, the children would reposition themselves in one big clump, their mother's eyes pinpointed on them. Stephanie always seemed to reach the chair first, perching her rear end on the only cushioned seat. Darren and Emily would drop in around their sister like a collapsing tent. Sometimes they'd cling to the side of the chair for more than an hour, silent, looking like begging orphans.

Maureen entertained, her pale white arms flying wildly into the air as her animated stories grew from half-truths to outright lies. Her newly permed hair, jiggling and bobbing around her head, made her look as though she were a Shirley Temple bobblehead. Her curls cast a red glow, like an ember just before it bursts into flames. Shoulder-length earrings flailed around her head as she jumped from her seat and rose to her tiptoes to imitate Mrs. Rabitisch, a neighbor known to be high-minded. She would pull her arms close to her sides, her palms pushed flat, perpendicular to the floor, and then she would sashay side to side across the wooden planking, screwing up her face and lifting her nose into the air as if she were a *somebody*. Then she'd pinch her lips into a taut red circle and raise one of her unmatched eyebrows in a questioning glare. Her friends would roar. Their mouths gaped open, their heads flying back, the vigorous laughter driving them to the bathroom to release the half gallon of tea they consumed.

"People love having me around," Mother would say, beaming, as they drove away. Emily knew her mother craved being the center of attention. Maureen made everyone laugh. Except her children. Her mother's friends didn't mind the children being along because they were so well behaved — as though they had an option. Maureen had little time for misbehaved children. In fact, she had little time for children, period. Even her own.

For a short time after their parents' divorce, Emily had seen her mother become that free-spirited woman the children had come to recognize when she performed for her friends. But it didn't last long. Maureen became frustrated and frazzled, her head always down poring over a pile of bills, giving excuses to someone over a telephone. When she was in a hurry — and she was always in a hurry — her tongue would wag, her face redden. Her eyes would pinch together, and her fists would clench, like a jaw. She'd bark out a command, expecting no hesitation.

Maureen had told them she loved them. A lot. But the words had only echoed off the hollow walls of the heart of a little girl who couldn't bring herself to believe she meant it. Studying her mother's face, Emily knew she wanted to mean it. But looking into those blue, blue eyes, Emily still saw only regret.

It was Stephanie's turn to stay with Maureen, the girls dividing the week until Darren could get leave. Emily would leave shortly before Stephanie arrived. She had a project meeting to attend later that evening, and the drive would take her a few hours. Aaron had called and offered to stay with Maureen, but Emily wasn't ready to face him just yet; their last parting had been ugly.

Maureen was sitting in a wheelchair that was too small and had no footrests. Her thin hair flew around her head like baby chicken down. Soft and feathery. A halo on a devil's head. Her eyes were dull with tears. Pleading.

"Don't go. Please don't go."

Emily busily worked around the room, doing tasks that some nurse would later repeat. She'd dressed Maureen that morning in a new purple-and-black print top that draped on her thin frame like a worn flag. Emily pulled a new pair of knit black pants on her, placed slippers on her feet, and then gently strung long white pearls around her neck, braiding them down her sunken chest. She clipped Maureen's favorite earrings on her lobes, the earrings that moved like a thousand chains down her neck, hitting her shoulders when her head moved. Emily fluffed her mother's thin hair with her fingers, looking in Maureen's eyes, telling her she loved the pale tint of red that was still evident after so many years. Maureen explained that she'd be having it colored in the next few days. Back to her *real* red. Emily thought of radishes.

She glanced around the room that was so void of her mother's personality. Empty, a cavity of bland. Her twin hospital bed was covered with a newly purchased quilt and a fluffy pillow with a pure white satin pillowcase. The pillow Emily had promised to smother her with should she act up with the nurses. She wondered to herself whether she'd been kidding. One brown nightstand stood to the right of the bed. It held a pink water pitcher filled with ice and a small Kleenex box that her mother asked for every two minutes so she could spit into it. There was a pen and paper and a small CD player that relentlessly belted out Andy Griffith songs too loud for them to talk over. Two metal folding chairs, another twin bed, empty until needed, a white trash can, a small yellow clothes hamper, the green rocker Darren had brought from her apartment, a TV, a day lily, and a large potted fake plant with purple blooms that Maureen insisted be watered every day. That completed the decor.

Emily almost wanted to stay and decorate the dismal room. Paint the walls a bright tangerine — but Maureen would call it peach and want a different shade. Put up lacy curtains with tassels. Her mother would want roll-up blinds. Get matching stool covers and floor rugs for the bathroom. They'd have to have a toilet tank cover and thick towels as well. Emily wanted to turn the air conditioning on to cool the room from the 90-degree heat Maureen now needed to stay warm, but she knew that when she left, Maureen would press the call button she kept clamped in her right hand and have the nurse turn it up again.

Emily had thought that seeing her mother this way might change her a bit. She ached to turn back the clock and start over, create a different ending than the one happening now, but she could tell her mother saw nothing that needed changing. And, she guessed, neither did she.

She heard a glass break across the hall and turned to see another patient looking over and smiling at her, his hands splayed to his side at the accident. He motioned to her to join him. Emily glanced at the nurse who rushed into the hallway to retrieve a broom.

"That's Bill," Maureen said. "He's a great guy. Just likes to talk."

Emily strolled across the hallway. Bill was sitting in a green recliner watching the old TV series *M*A*S*H*. He had a well-worn cowboy hat on his bald head. When Emily reached his side, he introduced himself and then weakly pointed to a large photo hanging on the wall above the television.

"That's my ranch," he said with a slight smile. "Three hundred acres. Raise cattle and breed horses."

There was a small photo of four men taped to the larger photo. Emily looked closer. "Your family?" she asked.

"Yup. Me, my two sons, and my grandson. They're working the farm now." His voice softened, and he adjusted his straw cowboy hat to cover his tear-filled eyes. He looked about sixty, but Emily understood that impending death aged people.

"Well, Bill, Mom loves to play dominos, if you're up for it. But keep your eye on her for me, will you? She's still looking for a man to marry, and I don't want you swept away."

They both laughed, a good feeling Emily had all but forgotten. Bill's face softened.

"You're a good daughter," he said. "I believe that God would like that you're a good daughter."

Believe. The word stung. He gripped her hand and nodded his head rapidly. Emily felt a twinge of sorrowful familiarity, as if he knew her, saw through her stone facade. She searched his eyes and wondered if he saw that she *wanted* to be a good daughter, wanted to believe that her mother had changed, that Aaron had changed. Emily had gone through all the motions, but inside there was no feeling but anger left for either of them. She touched Bill on the shoulder, his warmth moving through her, and then walked away. She heard him blowing his nose as she crossed the hallway.

Maureen watched from her room, leaning into the doorway, her head tilted as she tried to hear their conversation. "Now what did you say to him about me?" she asked, her face a ball of curiosity, although her voice was ragged.

"I told him that you were still looking for a man, Ma," Emily said, reaching for her jacket.

"My land. What did he say?" The familiar twinkle had returned, though a gray veil still covered her eyes.

"Said he'd have to keep an eye on you," Emily said flatly, her sullen mood returning.

Maureen leaned forward and weakly smiled at Bill. He gave her a small wave back.

"Mom, I hate to go, but I've got to," she lied.

"I wish you didn't have to," her mother replied, reaching for a tissue as tears suddenly began to tumble from her eyes.

"I wish I didn't either, Mom. Look for me shortly. I'll be back, OK?"

Emily bent over the wheelchair and pulled her mother's frail frame into her own. The touch of skin and bones. Maureen sobbed into her daughter's chest as Emily pushed into her mother's hair. She kissed the top of Maureen's head and cupped her face for the last time. Emily wanted to love her, forgive her, but her own heart was empty.

Honor thy father and thy mother. The words appeared in Emily's head from nowhere. From a summer, years ago. She'd been sitting on her grandfather's lap as he read to her from his Bible. Emily closed her eyes and still felt the way her finger had pressed over that verse of his tattered old Bible as he read to her. *Honor thy father and thy mother.*

"I love you, Emily," Maureen said.

"Love you, Ma." Emily cried inside for the mother she'd always wanted, not for the woman in the wheelchair before her. She resisted the tug she felt in her heart, the tug that would make this relationship right, and moved toward the door.

"I've always loved you kids," Maureen said. "I'm so sorry for not showing you enough. Please forgive me."

"Sure, Ma," Emily said, pulling away, her lie covering the room. She left for home, looking back only once. Maureen's thin hair puffed around her head. Tears streamed down her face, her hand clutching the nurse's call button.

The heat was smothering the day Maureen died, the last of her life flickering and then burning out. The winds did little more than whisk the dust into tiny tornados that cut through the unshaven land like a dull razor. It was late August, an uncommon summer. Steam rose from the cracked sidewalks of Plaster Rock, dizzying those whose eyes fell on them.

Emily was beating an egg for her breakfast when the call came. Sally, the young nurse who cared for Maureen, sobbed the news through the telephone line. Emily hung up the phone and dropped into the sofa. Staring out the window, she watched the cars passing one after the other, as if they really had somewhere to be. She brought her hand to her eyes, feeling for the tears that never came. *I should pray for her.* The thought exploded through Emily like a headache. Instead, she picked up the phone and waited for the voice on the other end.

"She's gone," Emily muttered. Silence.

"What do we do now?" Stephanie asked, her voice steady.

"How about you call Aunt Carol; I'll call Darren," Emily said. "I'll make the arrangements and call you when everything is set. I told them at work I'd be off for about a week when it happened."

"You'll let Aaron know, won't you?" Stephanie insisted.

Aaron and Emily broke up and reunited often. She'd sent him packing again the day she'd read her father's name in her company's newsletter. His carpentry skills had won him the honor of Builder of the Year. She'd come home and slammed the paper on the dining room table and then stormed into the bedroom when Aaron told her she shouldn't be affected by what her father did or didn't receive... that her father had tried to rebuild his life after his mistakes, and she should, too. *What right did he have to decide what should and shouldn't affect her?* He'd been gone this time for two weeks, sending her flowers and leaving pleading calls on the answering machine, confused again about what he had done.

"Sure," Emily told Stephanie, though she had no intention of letting Aaron know.

The phone dropped into its receiver, and she turned off the stove, allowing the egg to sizzle and burn in the pan. She pulled the vacuum from the hall closet and tapped at the switch, the sucking roar deafening the pounding thoughts that shot through her head, sending her back to the previous day, the last time she'd seen her mother.

* * *

Nine-thirty in the morning. The hospital janitor was whirring his way down the corridor, banging his sweeper off alternating walls. Maureen seemed to welcome the intrusion, closing her eyes while Emily talked louder for a few seconds before giving up altogether. They remained quiet as he passed, bobbing his head as if to apologize when he caught Emily glaring at him. Then the vacuum in the hallway turned off, its silence allowing the women a chance at a conversation again.

"I want to be cremated," Maureen said, pushing her hand toward her daughter.

"I thought you wanted to be buried," Emily replied, her voice flat and puzzled. "The black hearse, the big white limousine we all have to crowd into. Us in all black with hats and gloves."

Maureen smiled at her daughter's remembrance.

"That's proper for a funeral, you know," she said, her voice a whisper.

"I know, Ma. I just don't look good in black. Steph and I are wearing red." Emily's voice was taut. She stared out the small window.

"Now, Emily, I'll come back and haunt you. You know I will." The corners of Maureen's mouth were upturned, her eyes fluttering closed. "I just want to die, to get it over with." Tears settled on her chalk-colored cheeks, chasing a path down her face, launching to the hospital bed beneath her.

Emily took a deep breath, trying to wrap her head around the thought of her mother's impending death. She'd been like a cat with nine lives. Emily was still convinced she'd outlive them all, even though Maureen had talked again about her burial wishes days earlier while her children sat around reliving memories. She wanted her girls to look like Jackie Kennedy had looked at her husband's funeral. Elegant. Regal. Proper. Real somebodies. "I want a black hearse and a white limousine, long and clean, with you kids in it."

Maureen had told them the same thing so many years ago, the day of the Kennedy assassination, looking over their heads as though they weren't in the room. "And I want you to mourn for seven days," she'd said. "That's proper."

* * *

Maureen's funeral was over in a couple of days. The girls wore the obligatory black dresses and pillbox hats with small veils that covered their faces, difficult to find in a world filled with denim and long hair. Darren wore his uniform. An old boyfriend of Mother's supplied the car. Aaron stood in the back with Tim and Betsy — notified, Emily supposed, by her untrusting sister. Maureen's children stood tearless at their mother's gravesite. Carol, Peter, and assorted friends and family wept behind them. Carol arranged for her sister's burial plot behind the new Baptist church. A pastor Maureen had met briefly gave parting words. A woman from the nursing home sang a hymn. They watched as their mother was lowered into the ground next to a marker that bore the name Ralph Brennan, an attorney who'd made his fortune in the shipping industry of Saint John.

"She always wanted to be a *somebody*," Darren said, a slight smile carving into his face. "Well, at least she's buried next to a *somebody*."

"She knew, you know," Emily said, not facing either of her siblings, her eyes firmly cast on the lowering casket.

"About the beatings? And what he did to you?" Darren said.

"All of it." She turned to her brother. "She told me the last time I visited her at the apartment in December."

"What else did she say?" Stephanie asked, pushing toward Emily. "Did she tell you about my baby?"

"Baby?" Darren furrowed his eyebrows.

"She said she was sorry but that she had to protect herself. Dad beat her. She didn't know then what he was doing to me, so she took the beatings because she had no place to go, no way to stop him."

Stephanie's eyes furrowed into Emily's. "I know she wanted to make peace with us before she died, but he beat me, too, Em. She knew that and never left."

"If he'd had the chance to say he was sorry, maybe it would have—" Darren started.

"What does it matter now, Darren? Will it take away the years I've had to relive him pressing himself on me? Or Stephanie's beatings? Will it take those memories away?" Emily's face burned.

Darren lowered his head.

"Sometimes I hate them both for what they did to you guys — us." He looked up and stepped toward her, his arms opening. Emily pulled back, twisting away.

"I'm tired of hating," she said. "It's got me nothing but fired from jobs, a drinking problem, and a husband I've chased away, a husband I've never felt good enough for… *wasn't* good enough for, proven by the fact that he had an affair." She kicked at a clump of dirt near the grave. "I'm sick of it all." *There, I've admitted everything.*

Stephanie neared her sister, touching her on the arm.

"What else did she say, Emily?" she asked quietly. Emily looked back at her mother's grave and then at her sister.

"When you ended up pregnant like she had, she panicked. She let some attorney and his wife adopt your baby. It was a boy, Steph. They promised to give him everything. She never told anyone, not even Aunt Carol. She said she had no choice but to protect you from ending up in a life like hers. She thought she was helping you." Emily paused and took her sister's hands. "The attorney lives in Moncton, Steph." Emily's eyes locked on her sister, letting the news settle. "Moncton."

"What baby?" Darren was still openmouthed.

The girls both beaded their eyes on him. He went silent.

"A boy? Why didn't you tell me, Emily?" Stephanie's head cocked to the left.

"I was hoping she would. She was trying to change. I saw that in her, but I can't forgive her for what she did to you."

"Maybe I can find him, Emily!" Stephanie blurted, her voice rising an octave. "Maybe I can make him understand what Ma did, that I didn't give him away, that I still love him, that he has a brother!" Her voice was breathless, her face lighting.

She dove at Emily, her arms wrapping around her sister's neck, her joy spilling into the day. Emily held her close, their tears merging like the waters of the Tobique and Saint John.

"We'll help you find him, Steph," Darren assured his sister. "I promise. We'll start looking tomorrow." Emily knew he must be wondering how much more he didn't know about his sisters' lives.

The smell of pine moved through the air as they joined hands and strode away from their mother's grave, a lonely plot far removed from the graves behind the Catholic church. Emily glanced back only once, wondering if her fate would be the same.

Chapter 42

Emily
October 1976
Moncton, New Brunswick

STEPHANIE TOLD EMILY SHE'D ALWAYS PRAYED for the day when she'd see her child's face again. She'd thought that wouldn't be until she got to heaven. She'd promised God anything. The news that her child was alive and the adoptive parents lived right in Moncton shocked her. She needed her siblings to help; between them all, they were bound to find him. Emily wondered how many times Stephanie might have passed her own son on the street, seen him playing in the park. Seventeen phone calls unearthed the attorney.

"Is this Mrs. Keating?" Emily asked.

"Yes." The voice sounded hesitant.

"Did you adopt a baby boy in 1964?"

Silence.

"Mrs. Keating?"

"Who is this? What do you want from us?" The woman's voice was sharp.

"I'm — I'm Emily Douay, Stephanie Douay's sister. She gave birth to your son." She heard the woman on the other end take a deep breath.

"What do you want?"

"Our mother died a short time ago. She'd always told my sister that her baby was stillborn. Stephanie never knew whether it was a boy or girl. They had sedated her, then took the baby from her, telling her the child had died in birth. She didn't know he was alive until my mother confessed."

Silence. Emily drove on, knowing she had little time to convince the woman.

"She just wants to see him, meet you. Thank you for loving him." A wave of anxiety washed over Emily. "She wants him to know she never abandoned him. Never gave him away! Do you understand?"

She could hear small sobs on the other end of the line.

"Mrs. Keating?"

"I — I understand," she said, her words arriving between gulps. "I'll tell our son and let him decide. Call me tomorrow."

The phone line went dead.

* * *

It was a Sunday morning when Emily and Aaron joined Stephanie and Tim to meet the boy and his parents at Grace Baptist Church in Moncton. The Keatings explained everything to their twelve-year-old son, Kevin, who was anxious to meet the brother he never knew he had. But Stephanie's boy, Brian, stayed overnight at a friend's house for the first meeting, sensing his mother was nervous about seeing the son she'd never known.

Kevin was standing in front of his adoptive parents when they arrived, wearing a soft blue shirt with rolled-up sleeves and a pressed pair of black pants. He was tall, like the boy Emily had seen her sister give in to so many years ago. His hair was dark — his eyes, hers. Emily watched as she warily embraced him, the boy's arms flat at his side. His parents stood near them, wiping tears from each other's faces.

They walked into the church together. Being there made Emily feel uneasy, out of place in church since her grandparents had died. Aaron attended a church just down the street from their house, alone. He'd asked her to go but made no demands when she said no. She'd seen a change in him since the affair. She'd catch him on his knees praying for forgiveness and for the healing of their marriage. He'd become such an easygoing man, always giving in to any demand she'd make of him. *Testing him.* Why couldn't she just tell him everything and then let it all go? Maybe that would be the end of her picking him apart. Maybe then she could be happy.

The pastor explained the Keatings' situation to the congregation during the morning service. They bowed in prayer for the new relationships that were being born. During the service, the pastor spoke of the prodigal son. Emily watched Stephanie stare at her boy, his hands firmly clutching a worn Bible. She'd found him, this miracle son. Emily knew her sister's prayers had been answered, though she herself had never trusted in prayer. Good things never happened to her.

When the pastor made the altar call, Kevin looked over at his mother. She nodded. And then he reached for Stephanie. She bobbed her head, dabbing at her eyes, and they rose together and made their way to the front of the church. A mother and son. Reunited in Christ. Emily felt a tug on her heart to follow them but cupped her hands around the hymnal and looked at the floor, something she'd done every time she'd been in church since Dave Cook's death.

"I'm so happy for you," Emily said a few weeks later when her sister called. Stephanie's voice was excited. Different.

"Em. Please come again with me to church next week. I want you to get to know Kevin and his folks. We're going to try to find his father." Her voice softened. "Just come, will you? Maybe you'll realize it's the peace we've been missing for so long."

"Sure," Emily lied. "I'll call you next week."

She never did, instead allowing jealousy of the newfound happiness Stephanie and Darren seemed to have found in the church to grow in her. *How had they all been duped? Did they really expect that it would last? Nothing lasted. Nothing but lies and anger.*

Her jealousy boiled over a few nights later when she threw Aaron out again. She'd almost beaten up some woman in the restroom of a restaurant. Perhaps the woman was innocent enough — a subtle glance across a crowded restaurant, the stranger's eyes landing on Aaron. Emily happened to look up at the exact moment the woman's face locked on him. Emily's eyes narrowed as the stranger looked away. The woman had looked at her husband, a look that glanced and then lingered, and Emily had seen this look before. Aaron seemed unaware as he perused the menu for the evening meal, whipping the menu open and closed, mumbling something about a steak. Emily glanced at the menu and then turned her head toward the table on the other side of the room. The stranger's head pushed down again when she caught the woman's eye for the second time.

Emily gulped in a slow mouthful of air, the way she always did before an attack, so very protective of her things. A surge went through her, a prickle that climbed her spine, choking off the room around her. The feeling took her back to when she was ten, the first time she'd let the rage boil over in her, shortly after moving to Saint John.

She'd punched a boy in the face for trying to look up her dress. She recalled the feeling of exhilaration as she watched him reel and then fall to the pavement, clutching his face. Her knuckles were swollen and red, but she felt no pain, just release and joy. Her fists had served her well since then. She'd punched a classmate in high school when the girl gave a congratulatory hug to a boy Emily liked. She'd been expelled and the boy quit dating her, but she didn't care. She had control.

A couple of years later, she'd thrown a bottle at some Frenchman from Quebec whose snide remarks were aimed at her as she passed him on Main Street. She'd kicked a man at the airport and was escorted from the building by two security guards, each burst of anger making her feel somehow stronger. Her grandfather's voice would well up in her just before she'd strike, causing her to pause, but it never stopped her intended attack. *Love suffers long and is kind...*

It amazed her that the art of her father's intimidation and cruelty had been passed from his father to him, and then to her... generation to generation... without anyone even recognizing how that was happening. There'd been no forgiveness from him or for him, no chance of redemption for what he'd done to her. *I'll never be like him.* But a flash of a little boy she'd babysat years earlier burst into her mind, her father's uncontrolled anger reflected in the child's eyes, the child who was looking at her.

The little boy had somehow turned on the faucet and then crawled from one sink to the other to avoid the warming water. He'd slipped on a cookie sheet and tumbled to the floor. At first Emily had tried to comfort him, but the boy had wailed on, his little arms and legs flailing, each scream louder and longer.

Finally Emily had grabbed him by his arms, giving him a jiggle. "Enough. You're fine." She felt her fingers dig into his arms, the feeling stoking her annoyance. The boy's face was closed except for his mouth, a black hole with dagger-like screams rising from it.

"Stop it, Kenny!" she'd barked, her hands continuing to tighten on his arms. Emily shook him once, making his head jerk backward. She shook him again, then again, her eyes frozen on his face as though she could not see him. As she watched his head flip forward and back, it was as though she were standing beside him, watching and not holding him. Then the rag doll between her angry hands finally came into focus, his mouth open and quiet, his eyes closed. She'd gasped, clutching him to her chest, realizing he was unconscious.

"I am my father. What have I done?" she'd screamed, her face arched toward the ceiling. "Forgive me, God. Please forgive me!" Wrestling from his fog, the boy had blinked his eyes open and shut before he popped upright in her shaking lap. "I'm sorry," Emily had wailed, hugging him hard as he wiggled to push himself free. "I'm so sorry. I'll never do that again. Never."

* * *

Now at the restaurant with Aaron, Emily saw the woman look up again. She blushed at Emily's stare, pulled her napkin from her lap, and excused herself. Emily watched.

Then, "I've got to run to the bathroom, Aaron." Emily placed her menu on the table and pushed back her chair, eyes on the woman's back. "Order me the fish and scallions."

She moved toward the restroom, her black dress dancing across her legs, feeling excitement at the coming confrontation. She pushed open the bathroom door and planted herself near the mirror, dabbing at her lips with gloss. The woman emerged from the stall, and her eyes widened. She clutched her purse tightly to her thin frame.

"Do you need to take a picture of my husband?" Emily asked, placing herself in the path of the woman. "Or do you know him from somewhere?"

"I — I don't know what you mean." The woman hesitated and stepped back into the stall.

"Listen, honey." Emily stepped forward, her face hardening, her voice a low whisper. She reached toward the woman's throat, pressing her fingers deep into the woman's flesh. "If you look at my husband one more time, I'll be across that room and at your throat like a Doberman. Got it?" Emily's hands were steady, her eyes cutting.

The woman nodded her head rapidly, her face white with fear.

"Now, go have yourself a nice little dinner." Emily pulled her hands back to her sides, pausing long enough to brush away nonexistent dandruff from the woman's shoulder. Then she spun around and strode out the door, back to Aaron, who had poured the evening's first glass of wine. Emily studied her husband. *Was Aaron watching the woman? Maybe they did know each other. Another lover?*

Cupping the wineglass in her hands, Emily watched the woman gather her jacket and leave the restaurant, followed closely by her dumbfounded date. *Maybe it had all been innocent.* Emily felt a twinge of regret.

She placed the wine on the table as their dinners arrived, vowing once more to detour from the road of rage and jealousy she'd been on. As they fawned over dessert, she jokingly told Aaron of her bathroom confrontation.

"You did what?" Aaron asked, a flash of disgust crossing his face.

"Well, she couldn't take her eyes off you," Emily said, hurt that he was defending some supposed stranger.

"Em, don't you understand that you just can't keep wondering whether every woman is after me, or I them? I made my mistake. But I'm different now; don't you see that?"

"So I'm just supposed to let them come after you?"

"They're not after me! It's you, Em! It's something in you that I can't fix. Nobody can! You have to let the past go — forgive your old man, forgive me — or at least put it out of your mind. Whatever happened was a long time ago. It doesn't have to hold you prisoner forever. Don't you get that?" He put his napkin on the table and waved for the waiter. "Let's go. I should've known better than to think we'd be able to have a nice time. We never do anymore."

Inside, Emily died a little as she recognized the prison she'd been holding Aaron in. He'd been the only one to ever believe in her, though she'd never given him reason to. In return, she'd given him only bitter disappointment. She couldn't do that to him anymore. Maybe she couldn't save herself, but she could let him go. She made a plan that would drive him from her for good and realized she'd be better off alone, anyway — or dead.

PART THREE

Chapter 43

Denny
May 17, 1977
6:18 a.m.
Perth, New Brunswick

DENNY'S FARMHOUSE WAS WHITE, shuttered with peeling black-painted pine. A red Ford, its sheen polished to an apple shine, was parked near the door to the barn. Every day before dawn, he rose, filled his thermos with a copper liquid, made a cup of strong coffee, and stood at the kitchen window watching the dawn emerge. It always made him think of Emily. He used to watch her from the kitchen window while Maureen was working and Stephanie was at Carol's for the weekend, babysitting Peter.

He let out a small huff of air and crimped his face into a smile. Carol never had the guts to say anything about Stephanie's bruises. The girl deserved them, mouthing back to him like that. He'd taught her some good lessons over the years, ones she'd never forgotten. Stephanie had been so different from Emily. Prissy. Cocky. Undisciplined. Like her mother. Denny hadn't really been surprised to find out that Stephanie wasn't his child.

His boy, Darren, had always been too quiet for Denny's taste. Like he was watching. Like he would tell. Too much like Stephanie, Denny thought. Darren was only five when they'd all left. That wasn't enough time to make him into a real man. Now it was too late. He liked that he still remembered Emily had been so much like him. She used to poke away at the dirt outside, not concerned that she'd get dirty. She'd pound with the little hammer he'd bought her, building some imaginary horse from wood. He'd always wanted to run out and hold her. Protect her. Tell her he was sorry for what he'd done when he drank. She'd be grown now, around twenty-seven, he guessed. He'd been sure she wouldn't remember anything from that time, though the way she attacked him at her grandfather's funeral made him rethink that. He'd hoped someday he could make it up to her. But Maureen had taken his children away the night she'd attacked him, seeing to it that he'd never have that chance. *Someday, maybe.*

He shook himself from the past and gathered his lunch pail from the refrigerator, edging out of the house before his second wife, Trudy, expected something out of him. He knew she'd heard him leave, knew the slamming door signaled that his obsessive ways were out of her life for the day.

Denny hated people calling his work habits obsessive. Sure, he had a certain routine of time and place, of job and pattern. He liked to work alone if he could, preferring to do things his way, not wanting to put up with the cheerful cajoling of the fools he usually worked with. He never understood what they had to laugh about. Most of them were like him, barely able to squeak by — with nagging wives, overdue bills, and kids poisoned by ex-wives.

His old man had been like them — jovial to everyone in Perth... everyone but his own family. For them he was a drunkard, unable to control his temper or his lust. Denny felt a brief flash of guilt as he recognized a bit of his father in himself. *But I'm not that kind of man anymore, am I?* Taking a swig from his thermos, Denny squeezed his eyes closed and tried again to put away the memory.

The sun was less than an hour from rising when Denny arrived at the job. The faint sound of him pulling his toolbox from the back of his truck pricked the ears of a cluster of rabbits. Hearing the hollow slam of the tailgate, they scurried away, each choosing a different path. He kicked at them, sending a small ball of dirt into the air. He counted seventeen steps from the truck to the front door.

Just inside, he dropped the box, the clinking sound of his tools reverberating throughout the structure. He hit the light switch, sending a beam of brightness across the kitchen. His eyes flinched. He looked up, determined to finish the second story before nightfall. He pulled his thermos from his toolbox and took a long swig.

He was sure the flashes of abuse that slipped in and out of his mind, with the fearful face of his daughter lying beneath him, were just dreams that came and went when Jim Beam muddled his mind.

She had been a child. His child. He would've never done that. Not like his father had done to him. The truth still ate at his soul, but someday he'd ask her to forgive him.

Stepping over the loose lumber, Denny inched his way into the center of the incomplete house. A metal ladder leaned against a half-finished set of stairs, the hardwood meant for the step risers scattered in heaps amid a small pool of water that had leaked in from the unfinished chimney. He tinkered in the living room, dragging pieces of lumber into the kitchen. He stacked the wood and then inched along the studded wall below the second floor, pointing the flashlight just above him.

Looking up, he saw an electric screw gun teetering on the lip of the landing just above the ladder, its cord frayed and tattered, a small pile of thin wire circling its handle. His eyebrows pulled together. He'd never left his tools out before. He laid the flashlight on the floor and picked up his thermos with his right hand, taking another swig of whiskey. Standing to the side of the ladder, he reached up, catching his left hand in the tangle of wire that dangled from the screw gun. He tried to shake it off as though it were a spiderweb, but it would not free itself.

Grasping the eye-level rung with his wire-entwined hand, he stepped forward, his steel-toe boot slapping the puddle of water. Fffftttt. A long spark arced from the electric screw gun down the wire, through the ladder, and into him. *Someday.* His body jerked and tossed with the current as though he were on a timer. His face turned ashen. His hair stood out around his head like fine chicken down. *Someday.*

His body arched backward, held in place by the electric current flashing through his body. His mouth opened in a silent scream, his eyes bulged wide, his body wrenched at the foot of the ladder. *Someday.* The lights went out. He collapsed to the floor. A black line burned its way up his arm to his face. His right hand still clutched the silver thermos, its contents forming a bronze puddle under his ashen face.

Chapter 44

Emily
May 20, 1977
10:30 a.m.
Plaster Rock, New Brunswick

IT WAS ONLY AN HOUR AGO that Emily had punched her dead father in the face. She'd thought it would feel good to get it out, express her hatred, show herself she could give him the disrespect he deserved. But it didn't, really. She just felt numb. Hollow. As the sign approached for Plaster Rock, she could feel her fingers tightening on the steering wheel, her fingers whitening. The bits and pieces of her memories and conversations with her mother about her father and their lives together began to make sense. Just months earlier and only days before her death, Maureen had owned up to a myriad of paralyzing mistakes about her own choices, things Emily wished she'd been told earlier. Maybe knowing that her mother realized she wasn't always right — and that she cared — could have helped Emily accept herself, too. Instead, the series of secrets had crippled her and compounded the hatred Emily harbored for her father.

The Corvette rumbled into the outskirts of Plaster Rock as she made her way to her grandparents' abandoned home. Emily drove the long way through town, turning left at the post office and slowing down at the Legion hall before continuing on past the indoor ice hockey rink and Dave Cook's house. By the time she reached her grandparents' house, she could feel the warmth of their love surrounding her.

The house had been reclaimed by tall grass and weeds, still stiff from the cool hand of the day. The Adirondack chair colors had faded and were barely visible through the vines that choked them from a visitor's view. The porch roof hunched as though the winter's snow had not yet melted and disappeared well below the late spring's soil.

Emily pulled a string of vines from in front of the door that led to the woodshed and found the key to the kitchen entry that her grandmother had hidden beneath a flyswatter when Emily was a child. Unlocking the kitchen door, she slipped inside, the screen door slamming behind her as she remembered it doing in her youth. The squeak of the unoiled hinges evoked the same response as they had in her past — a turning head to see whether she was being followed by one of her siblings. Slapping cobwebs from her path, her soft-soled shoes made no noise on the linoleum floor as she crossed the kitchen, straining to see in the darkness. The house stood sturdy, untouched inside by wind and weather — much as Emily remembered, though seemingly smaller.

Pale, pasty paint, a mint color too long in the sun, still covered the cracked walls in the kitchen. Emily ran her hand across them, feeling the grainy texture her grandfather could never smooth. Eyeing the windowsill above the sink, she caught a glimpse of the round clock that had entertained her as a child — round and green, decorated with a surly robin whose mouth tugged at a worm. The face of the clock had faded, but the saying, "The early bird gets the worm!" was still visible. Emily picked it up, cradling the antique, turning it over and winding it as she had done in her youth. To her delight, the bird began to move, pulling and tugging at the little red worm as he had done for her so many years earlier. She covered her mouth with her hand, willing the tears not to come.

Emily swung around to face her grandfather's oak rocking chair that sat hopelessly empty in front of the window. It had never moved since her last visit, the arms worn by the touch of his gnarled hands. She closed her eyes and saw him there, rocking steadily, his large-print Bible lying open on his lap. In her mind, she could hear her grandmother removing fresh bread from the old oven, the scraping of the metal pan as it was pulled from the woodstove. Her mouth watered at the memory of the warm dough dripping in bright yellow butter.

The button box still perched precariously on the ledge of the oak Hoosier cabinet, its presence another reminder of why she had come here. Peace. She took a deep breath, walking from room to room;

touching everything; breathing in the heavy, dusty air; searching for why the pain of her past disappeared whenever she entered this place. It was a peace she had never been able to take with her.

A sliver of light cut through the darkness of her grandparents' bedroom, landing on the small, hand-painted plaque that hung next to their bed. Emily ran her fingers over the saying — *As for me and my house, we will serve the Lord* — and shook her head as she headed back to the exit. As the door closed behind her, she understood why Carol had held onto the house, though no one had lived here for years. So many wonderful memories here. So many more to yet be made.

A few minutes later, Emily made her way to the Catholic cemetery, parking the car at the footpath that led upward to the graveyard. A late spring wind, warmed by summer's arrival, whistled through the stand of white birch that surrounded the graveyard. She started her search, her hands shoved deep into the pockets of her jeans, her shoulders hunched.

Strolling around the perimeter of the cemetery, Emily was careful not to tread on graves, although wayward sticks crunched beneath her feet. The place was flowerless, waiting for Victoria Day. Then the faithful would migrate here, their arms filled with bright plastic flowers or cement benches that embellished loved ones' graves until fall. The names on the tombstones she passed were familiar. Reverend and Mrs. Park, Mary Belcamp, Aunt Amy, Dave Cook, Ronnie Dowd.

Emily's grandparents lay buried in the back of the cemetery, lonely plots destined to house Baptists or other wayward denominations of Plaster Rock. With a new cemetery in town, the one Aunt Carol had told her about a few years back, she wished she could pull them up and replant them near her mother, where Baptists rested among friends of like faith.

Emily found and knelt before the simple gray marker identifying John and Ellen Polk. Just a few steps away rested Aunt Amy — stink eye at the ready, she supposed — the memory causing her to smile. Squatting to touch the cool marble, she wiped her fingers over the carefully chosen scripture engraved there. *Believe on the Lord Jesus Christ and thou shalt be saved. Acts 16:31.*

The words rang in her ears. How many times her grandparents had repeated those words to her, though Emily never understood what difference believing them would make. She believed in God. Didn't everyone? Jesus was another story. He was a carpenter like her father, a man who'd said he loved her. But her father had lied. Her mother had lied. What made this Jesus any different? Emily couldn't believe in him now, could she?

Believe on the Lord Jesus Christ and thou shalt be saved. The words stabbed her. The memories of her self-centered mother circled in Emily's head. *Words, just words,* she thought, though the change she'd seen in her mother before she died — the concern to explain, to convey that she did know and care, and that she was sorry — made Emily wonder if her mother had finally felt forgiven.

The wind fanned a discreet hint of spring, whipping Emily's hair up and into her mouth. She pulled a deep, cool breath into her lungs. White sheets billowed on a clothesline just below the church's hill, hovering almost straight out and snapping hard like the revival tents of long ago. Emily imagined she could hear Reverend Park's deep voice as he hollered his plea of repentance, his big hands pounding on the portable pulpit, his eyes searching the crowd for any lost soul who would respond to the words of the Bible.

"We are all sinners," he'd cry, "doomed to an eternal death if we do not accept Jesus Christ as our personal Savior."

Emily closed her eyes. She could still smell the sweat beneath the white tents of those long August nights, see him pull his wrinkled white hankie from his pocket and wipe his glistening bald head while he waved the tattered Bible high in the air.

"Come unto me, all ye that labor and are heavy laden," he would cry, *"and I will give you rest."*

Women fanned themselves with paper programs; men shuffled their feet beneath their chairs — most, Emily was sure, wishing they were someplace else.

No sin here, she'd thought as a child, twisting her head to look around the room, watching for anyone willing to confess their sins in front of such a crowd. Now she wondered if she'd been guilty as well, sitting stoically in her seat when God's tug on her heart had been so real. Now she was empty inside, and nothing she'd tried on her own all these years seemed to lessen her pain. Those words couldn't be still meant for her, could they?

Believe on the Lord Jesus Christ and thou shalt be saved. Emily struck her hands to her ears. The words flooded over her. Even with her eyes squeezed shut, she could hear the prayers of her grandfather kneeling at the foot of the old iron bed. Behind Emily, the sharp whistle still sounded a make-believe lunchtime at Fraser's Mill. Her eyes flashed open. She twirled to absorb the panoramic scene that was once so familiar, its beauty returning her to another time. *Believe.*

The water fluttered, its skin mirroring ghostly vehicles that rumbled across an old wooden bridge, now gone, that had taken Emily and her grandfather to Wapske Creek, where they'd fished a whole day away. Emily imagined Dave, Ronnie, Rene, and Kent clasping hands and jumping from the old wooden bridge into the cooling waters of the Tobique.

The fragrance of blooming flowers and the promise of life budded everywhere. The landscape was reassuring, calm, something she'd taken for granted as a child but whose memory now flooded her with peace. The mill had long since sent its wooden gold downriver, the bodies of the trees tapping the shorelines and barriers until somewhere they were grasped and hauled from the water to become lumber in some city west of Quebec. The last of the timber had floated the Tobique in 1969, the plant harboring paper pulp rather than the harvest of trees. Then the stream of horses and logging wagons were replaced with modern pickups that snaked down the hillside toward waiting homes or semis making their way to Highway 108. The Tobique, too, appeared changed, its waters emptied of the shaven logs that once bumped, lurched, and latched into diving pools for the adventurous children of Plaster Rock. Its flow shifted easily now, unfettered and unhurried by the long-gone surging timber.

Groups of dandelion puffs floated above the water, bobbing across the tributary like parachutes… touching, rising, and then sinking into the face of the slow-moving current. The gliding seeds united with drifting debris in shallow pools along the shoreline. The tiny clouds of white reminded Emily of Reverend Park's mushroom clusters of saved souls. She cocked her head, trying to recall the strains and steady beat of the clapping hands of those who stood on the riverbanks to sing hymns of praise as sinners were washed clean in the river.

A fish jumped, then splashed a sphere of reentrance, the movement sending a circle of water rippling toward shore. Emily closed her eyes and felt the many summers of joy spent wading there, polliwogs flitting between her toes, tiny fish along the river's murky edge. The wind was gentle, the memories warm.

~ ~ ~ ~ ~

In summer, he always took her fishing. Trout. Downriver, Emily and her grandfather donned tall, green rubber boots and waded into a shallow cutting of the river. The morning was crisp, the water cool through the rubber, chilling her feet like the water bottle her grandmother used to bring down a fever.

They'd stop to pull goodies from the green clumps lazing along the banks of the Tobique, the scroll-like ferns punching from the soil. Emily filled her tiny bucket with the fiddleheads that went so well with fresh fish and then followed her grandfather to the edge of the river.

John tugged the handmade canoe to a felled log, securing it in the shade for seven-year-old Emily to play in while he fished. He rubbed his callused hand across the top of her head, shaking it back and forth as he cautioned her about respecting the river. He shared stories of his own mistakes on the river and of his baptism beneath the watery skin. He settled her in the boat and prepared his lure before pushing into the quick-moving current.

She loved the way the canoe bucked forward and back with the rippling water. Breaking twigs from the branches overhead, she fashioned them into tiny boats and then watched them float away. She hung over the side of the canoe, dangling her fingers in and out of the water as she tried to catch the tiny fish beneath her.

She giggled at the frogs and turtles that sunned themselves just out of her reach. When she tired, she leaned on the green metal cooler and watched her grandfather fish until the warm blanket of sun covered her and pulled her into a gentle sleep.

A patient man, her grandfather stood in the ever-shifting current, fashioning a brightly colored feather to a silver J-hook that was looped with a sparkling gold bead. Once it was attached to the line, he held it up for inspection, the blue of the sky framing his creation. He waded to the center of the river, the water rising around his thighs, separating and shooting between his legs as though they were bridge trestles. He began to hum a familiar hymn.

Clutching the thin pole in his right hand, the invisible line in his left, he positioned himself sideways to the river. He tugged the slender pole backward, its shape rounding into a horseshoe with the force of the pull. He launched it forward, its form stretched and extended, simultaneously releasing the unseen line he clutched in his left hand. The thrust accelerated the bejeweled lure upriver, its flight a slow-motion surge of fly connected to an invisible, wiggling line whose journey ended when it kaplunked yards away into the swift flow of water.

Without allowing the fly to sink, her grandfather tugged the line, the fly skipping backward across the skin of the water. When the length of the cord had been retrieved once more, he snapped the pole forward again; then he tugged it back, the fly tickling the surface of the Tobique over and over, awaiting the silver-bellied trout that hovered just beneath the surface.

The river was silent except for the tapping of the water and the occasional jumping trout whose slap on the flow sent flutters of skimming bugs skittering. The water's coolness, the warmth of the sun, the fish's elusiveness, and the continual pumping of the arm satisfied the fisherman's thirst for peace and Emily's wish for unconditional love.

~ ~ ~ ~ ~

So much of her childhood, she'd seen nothing to grab hold of, nothing good. But love had been there all along, Emily knew now. God's love, like Grampy said, and like he'd showed her.

Believe. Dropping to her knees on her grandfather's grave, Emily let her eyes scan the town, the moist earth soaking her pants and rising into her bones. Even at the top of the hill, Emily could hear the children's squealing voices rising from the school playground just downhill from her grandparents' empty home. She saw women stop to gossip in front of the post office, heads thrown back in laughter, babies clapped like newly picked watermelons under their arms. Teens ambled arm in arm toward the Squeeze Inn, joining screechy-voiced friends for lunch and gossip. The town was still alive, vibrant, and moving, though the mill had choked most jobs from its inhabitants when logging shut down. Three-fourths of Plaster Rock's employees had been laid off, Carol had told her, but few residents had left, choosing instead to support and share with those in need.

Along Main Street, Emily could see the roof of Aunt Amy's house sporting fresh shingles installed by its new owners. Uphill, barely visible through the unkempt maples, she caught a glimpse of her grandfather's white clapboard home. She felt a flutter in her chest, the sweet smell of life all around her. This place was as strong as the poplar trees her grandfather once harvested from the rich forests of this tiny Canadian town. *Believe.*

Emily was a *somebody* here at one time. When the world had forgotten her, her grandparents had not, choosing to water the seeds of faith that had been planted in her so long ago. *Believe.* Seeds of faith Emily suddenly understood.

I will never leave you nor forsake you. The words of the Bible were familiar, powerful... believable for the first time. Emily couldn't help but feel renewed by the beauty of the river before her, the strength and faithfulness of the people here beneath her. Over her lifetime, these people had given her the words and examples she needed to change her life. She'd just never heard them fully until now. Tears burned a trail down her face. She'd spent her life in hatred, its weight saddling her with insecurity and the uncertainty of whether she'd ever be good enough for anyone to really love her.

She thought of Aaron, the jobs, the people she loved, all lost to her bitterness. She'd even been jealous when Stephanie started getting to know her recently found son and his adoptive parents. Watching her sister's joy return had further revealed to Emily how far from contentment she really was.

Though Emily had feigned happiness when Darren was promoted to captain and then announced his forthcoming marriage to his girlfriend from Vancouver, Emily had been angry that his station would be so far from her and Stephanie, angry at the change in him. *Why did he now seem so satisfied? Nothing about their past had changed, had it?* At his wedding, Emily noticed that Darren's face was as radiant as their grandfather's had been. He said he'd been saved. *Saved from what? Me? Nothing had changed.* He seemed sweeter, gentler, and kinder. She wanted that joy.

Ambling toward the car, her shoes plucking tufts of grass from the moist ground, Emily stopped to take one last look at the river that had been such a part of her life. *Believe.* Pulling in a deep breath, she realized what she needed to do. Pushing herself behind the wheel of the idling Corvette, she gunned the engine and pointed the car downhill. Arriving at the side of the Anglican church, Emily jumped from the vehicle, leaving the car door open. There was urgency about her movements. She ran behind the church — breathless, searching — then stumbled down the steep, overgrown path to the river's edge.

Today was unlike the day she'd lost her best friend to the river. It was a cool May, the new leaves hatched and fluttering. Discarded buds covered the pathways like a chocolate blanket. Violet bouquets poked from the clay, decorating the shadowy banks of the Tobique as though a wedding might take place at any moment. Her grandfather's voice continued to echo in her ears: *Jesus will never leave you, Emily. You can bet on that. You just have to believe.*

Thoughts of her mother tut-tutting the first time Emily had sought her way to the altar clouded her mind. She'd been very young, a few days past seven, but the tug on her heart had been real. Two years later, Maureen had pushed Emily into a baptism when so many of the young people of the church went forward. By then Emily was angry, unclean. The ensuing dunking in the Tobique never really seemed to take, the loving God everyone spoke of having already abandoned both Emily and Dave Cook the day he'd lost his life — just when Emily was supposed to have found hers.

Her eyes scanned the river. *What am I seeking here? Can anybody even hear me? Does anybody care?* The tears streamed. She hadn't cried at her mother's funeral months earlier, still angry at her mother's confessions. And just a couple of hours ago, she'd punched her dead father in the face. *What am I doing here?*

At the edge of the Tobique, smells of sweet pine and fish mingled. Emily envisioned her grandmother standing near her, the woman's gentle voice singing a favorite hymn, lifting a soulful prayer to God. Dave Cook was running behind the old Pontiac, desperate to catch his best friend. Reverend Park was still herding the lost down the pathway and into the water, a circle of blooming white mushrooms at the edge of the red clay shore. Miss Cogswell's angelic face beamed at Emily from the clouds, her kindness still offering Emily comfort. So many people had shared Christ with her in one way or another over the years, appearing and then disappearing like ghosts when their work was done. *Was God beckoning to her once again? Or was it just the Tobique offering her a final peace?*

Emily touched her foot to the water, allowing the coolness of the river to permeate her leather moccasin. She closed her eyes and waited to sense the wariness that had come over her the day Dave Cook had drowned. She stood anchored by nothing more than scriptures and memories. Though the river had sliced a wider swath through the land, it seemed shallower than Emily remembered. Small islands sprouted in the center of the river, the water surging sometimes around but often over the tiny land masses, producing pockets of water ripples over them. The leafy twigs shooting from the soil trembled in the breeze. She opened her eyes and let them sweep the river. *Could she ever believe?* Taking a final, deep breath, she waded in.

Her legs pushed against the cool current that fought her decision. *I can't go on like this.* She was no good to anyone, even herself. The water sucked and swirled between Emily's legs, rising around her hips as she lunged forward. Her arms swung wildly. She was unable to choke back the tears, the cold permeating her body, the stream on her face mixing with the river's current. The water reached chest high before Emily gave herself over to its surge, pulling her head underwater, then rising and crying, "Dead to sin, Risen with Christ."

The water accepted her as she dunked again, this time her escaping breath bubbling to the surface as she let the river pull her deeper into the current, her arms and legs floating listlessly away from her body, her eyes squeezing the light from the sky as she let the river suck her in. *Run, River Currents. Run away with me.* The words pushed through Emily as she floated ever downward, pulled by the Tobique's current. And then the words she'd heard so long ago suddenly became real: *I will never leave you — just believe.*

Emily popped her eyes open and flailed toward the surface. She felt for footing; she'd floated into a pocket of deep water. Her feet searched for a solid object, her arms thrashing frantically for the sky. *Believe.* In one final, frenzied grasp for life, she broke through the water and pulled small gasps of air into her burning lungs. She swung her head like a newly bathed dog, sending pebbles of water cascading across the skin of the river. Her arms beat the current toward shore. She scrambled to find her footing near the banks of the river, her feet sinking into the red clay, her arms thrashing to free her body from the grasp of the river.

"Forgive me," Emily gasped at the sky as she collapsed to the ground. "God, please forgive me. I *do* believe!"

She lay on the ground sucking in air, her tearful cries releasing her pain, her life. She felt the rigid blackness melt away, really knew for the first time that God had understood all along, had carried her pain and darkness. Loved her unconditionally. His Son, Jesus, had paid the price with His life just to prove it. *And she believed.* Peace covered her like the last of the day's sun, and there was no more room for the anger Emily had always known.

Chapter 45

Emily
May 20, 1977
5:39 p.m.
Perth, New Brunswick

EMILY CREPT HER WAY ALONG the gravel driveway and parked next to her brother's Buick, its frame casting a long, gray shadow that bumped to the porch. Aaron's beat-up Ford slumped shamefully near the barn. *Of course he'd be here. He's always been there for me, even when I drove him away.* She eyed herself in the rearview mirror and glided some lipstick over her mouth. Pulling her damp hair into a ponytail, she pressed down on her wrinkled shirt and jeans, newly tugged from her yet-unpacked suitcase to replace the soaking clothes she'd left hanging in the woodshed at her grandfather's house. Emily hoped Darren wouldn't question her change of clothes. She stepped from the car, fluffed her nearly dry hair with her fingers, and made her way to the old house, her gait easy, unfettered.

Through the window, Emily watched her family gather at her father's long wooden table, her stepmother heaving a large ham onto the sideboard, her sister and aunt following from the kitchen with beans and potatoes. Though Emily hardly knew their stepmother, Trudy seemed to be enjoying the gathering of this brood. *So much we have missed.*

Stephanie dropped the heaping bowl of mashed potatoes to the table and then stood behind her two sons, young men now, her hands on their shoulders as she kissed them in turn on the head. Peter slipped a bone to Trudy's new dog, its tail whacking at Peter's leg under the table. Darren and Betsy stood across the room wrapped in each other's arms. Emily marveled at the man Darren had become. So assured, so loving. *Forgiven*, she thought. *He was right all along.*

Uncle George banged on the iron skillet, calling the family to prayer, their hands weaving one into another as they gathered at the table and bowed their heads. Emily closed her eyes, the corners of her mouth curling into a smile, her mind resting in the newness of grace. This odd and dysfunctional family had finally blended, their lives renewed like spring rains mixing with the river, their joy complete.

Waiting, listening to the sound of food being piled onto plates, the forks clinking against china, Emily put her hand on the doorknob and pushed the door open. Stepping inside, she swung her eyes between her brother and sister, toward her Aunt Carol, and then to Aaron, who sat at a corner of the table near the kitchen door. Her smile lit the room.

"Emily!" Aunt Carol pushed back her chair, wood scraping wood, and rushed toward her niece. Carol's hair hung to her waist, the curls framing her thin face. She was dressed like a Picasso painting — wildly colored, vividly floral — a far cry from the dowdy Aunt Carol of their youth.

Darren stepped between the women and pulled his sister's cheek close to his. "I thought you'd left," he said, whispering in Emily's ear. "You look great — happy. I'm sorry for whatever happened, Em. I love you. Steph loves you. Aaron loves you. God loves you. We all love you! Do you understand?" He searched her face, his voice sincere and tender as he pushed away, his eyes secured on hers.

Emily nodded her head in little bobs, eyeing Aaron over Darren's shoulder, her smile tentative when she caught his eye. *I can forgive him.* The closeness of her family felt different. Complete. Her brother's scent, earthy and warm, lingered on her. It was no longer a reminder of her father's sins.

"Darren, Betsy, the boys, and I are staying with Aunt Carol for a couple of days," Stephanie said. She laughed and patted a seat beside her. "You want to stay with us, or do you have something more pressing?" Her eyes danced with mischief as she glanced at Aaron.

"You are such a drama queen, Stephanie," Carol blurted, her teacup teetering between two skinny fingers, a King Cole tea bag bobbing up and down in the steaming liquid.

"You're a jer—" Stephanie shot back with a big grin.

"Hey!" Darren cut in. "Enough, you two. Now promise me we'll do this more often. Get together, I mean."

"It's a promise, Darren," Aaron spoke up. He motioned at the chair next to his as his wife worked her way across the room. Darren looked around, satisfaction reflected on his face.

"Good," Darren continued, "because I don't want our new baby not knowing this family when we move back here next month." The room buzzed with excitement as everyone formed a circle around Darren and his newly pregnant wife.

Spring had erupted inside and out, the trees and flowers releasing a fragrance that seemed to freshen the whole house. The plates and silverware clinked throughout dinner, adding an orchestra of sound to the laughter and conversation. Emily joined the women as they stacked and carried the half-empty and dirty plates into the kitchen. When the dishes were done, Aaron excused himself from the gathering of men in the living room and grabbed at Emily's arm, pulling her out the back door and onto the porch, the door closing and then popping open. Inside, Emily could hear her family engrossed in a conversation that filled the house with laughter. Her lips wrinkled with a grin as she pulled the door behind them closed. She walked to the edge of the porch. Aaron stood next to her, staring toward the river.

"How did you know?" Emily asked.

"Darren called me at work. No one knew you were in Toronto until they called me." Aaron looked down. "They didn't know we were separated, either."

"Why did you come?" She turned to face him and narrowed her eyes.

"I wanted to be here to support the family — you," he said, his shoe scuffing at a leaf that had drifted onto the porch.

Emily knew how close she'd come to losing everything good in her life. She reached to touch his face. "Aaron, I was angry at what my father had done to me. I've never told you the whole truth about what happened, what he did, how I struggled. And then when you had the affair—" She dropped her hand and turned away. Aaron touched her shoulder. She leaned her head to touch his hand, a stirring moving through her. "Something happened today. I can't explain it, but the anger is gone. I feel new inside. Forgiven." She turned to look at him again.

Aaron's eyes searched her face. She knew he saw something different about her, just as she'd seen the difference in him.

"I'll tell you everything if you'll let me — give me another chance. I promise." Her tone was soft. "Come home, will you? For good this time."

"Em," he said, as he cupped her arms in his hands and lowered his voice, his eyes welling with tears. "I'm the one who needs another chance. I never wanted to leave. I've struggled all these years trying to figure out what I could do to make things better for you. I tried — honestly, I tried. I know I failed you just like everyone else did, but I'm different now. I need you to forgive me, but I don't know if you can. You have to know I'd never hurt you like that again." He hung his head. Emily looked away.

A small silence filled the air. "We can try," Aaron said, not looking up. "You're the woman I've always wanted. You just wouldn't believe it." He kicked at the slatted floor. "I'll be waiting when you decide to come home."

Emily stepped in front of Aaron and pushed into his arms, closing her eyes and touching her head to his chest, letting her tears fall unfettered against him. *Thank you, Lord.* He pulled her close, his head drifting into her hair. *How long had she sought the peace that filled this night? Her grandfather was right. She was not alone, and she never had been.* Wrapping her arms around Aaron's waist, she looked up and then turned to let her eyes sweep the Tobique. Its waters raged through the Narrows, plummeting into the Saint John with a fury that settled into a gentle flow a few hundred feet downriver. Emily watched silently, her arms threaded through Aaron's, her understanding of the river's lesson complete.

Around her, the land smelled of fresh-furrowed soil, the wooden barrels of seed potatoes standing ready for burial beneath the trough of earth. The pines beyond her father's land echoed with chain saws, the ache of the trees that slammed to the forest floor resonating in her ears.

Just beyond the dam, the ceaseless waters of the Tobique shifted downstream, the river bumping the banks, rippling the surface. Beneath its skin, the anger of the water tore away at intruders until many surrendered, slammed and churned in a torrent of rage. Yet in that river, some would learn its deepest lessons, struggle against its power... until they, like she, learned to ride the current to peace.

~ ~ ~ ~ ~

MORE GREAT READS FROM BOOKTROPE

Tulip Season by Bharti Kirchner (Mystery) A missing domestic-violence counselor. A wealthy and callous husband. A dangerous romance. Set in the US and India, an exotic, compelling tale.

Always and Forever by Karla Nellenbach (Young Adult), a story of tenderness in tragedy. A doomed teenager, facing a terrible illness, wants to take back control and end her own life – until love intervenes.

Jailbird by Heather Huffman (Romantic Suspense) A woman running from the law makes a new life. Sometimes love, friendship and family bloom against all odds…especially if you make a tasty dandelion jam.

Deception Creek, by Terry Persun (Coming of Age Novel) Secrets from the past overtake a man who never knew his father. Will old wrongs destroy him or will he rebuild his life?

Riversong by Tess Hardwick (Contemporary Romance) Sometimes we must face our deepest fears to find hope again. A redemptive story of forgiveness and friendship.

Throwaway by Heather Huffman (Romantic Suspense) A prostitute and a police detective fall in love, proving it's never too late to change your destiny and seek happiness. Of course, the mob might have different ideas.

… and many more!

Sample our books at:
www.booktrope.com

Learn more about our new approach to publishing at:
www.booktropepublishing.com